The massive mound of dirt and the low tin roof
serve to hide f   at the
true purpose   who
pass by know   It is,
quite simply,   e eye
of death, when   they
find salvation   coming

Follow all the action . . .
from the qualifying lap
to the checkered flag!

Rolling Thunder!

Forthcoming from Tor:

Rolling Thunder

STOCK CAR RACING

ROAD TO DAYTONA

Kent Wright
& Don Keith

TOR®

A TOM DOHERTY ASSOCIATES BOOK
NEW YORK

This book is a work of fiction. All the characters and events portrayed in this book are either products of the author's imagination or are used fictitiously.

ROLLING THUNDER #2: ROAD TO DAYTONA

Copyright © 1999 by Kent Wright & Don Keith

A Tor Book
Published by Tom Doherty Associates, Inc.
175 Fifth Avenue
New York, NY 10010

Tor Books on the World Wide Web:
http://www.tor.com

Tor® is a registered trademark of Tom Doherty Associates, Inc.

ISBN: 0-812-57507-5

First edition: April 1999

Printed in the United States of America

0 9 8 7 6 5 4 3 2 1

For man, maximum excitement is the confrontation of death and the skillful defiance of it by watching others fed to it as he survives transfixed with rapture.

—Ernest Becker (1924–74),
U.S. psychologist, cultural anthropologist

I took the dictionary and I found me the page where they defined the word "second" and I ripped it right out of the book. Far as I'm concerned, there's no such word in the English language.

—Jodell Bob Lee, stock car driver

The sun rises up slowly, sluggishly, as if he, too, is hesitant to actually get this sultry day underway. A thick morning fog holds on for dear life, but already it has pulled back to the lowest ground, to the swamps and creek bottoms.

Highway 151 snakes its way lazily around the mossy bogs and the mostly stagnant streams and what passes for hills down here in the coastal plain. Then the road suddenly stretches itself out, as if it's some reptile sunning itself, and extends past a strange, high mound of dirt, a preponderance that seems foreign to the surrounding clumps of live oaks and top-heavy pines and tall, spindly sweet gum trees and the monotonous, deflated land.

At first, the ridge might appear to be Indian in origin, maybe a burial mound, something of sacred proportions. But then, a huge, shiny, corrugated tin roof can be seen, an odd temple that runs alongside the highway for a couple hundred more yards.

The massive mound of dirt and the long tin roof serve to hide from the unknowing passerby what the true purpose of this place might be. But most who pass by know quite well what goes on there. It is, quite simply, a province where men spit in the eye of death, where they worship speed, and where they find salvation in winning. It is a place where coming in second is precisely the same thing as losing; where only one person can claim victory and where all the rest of them are simply "back there," somewhere among the lost.

But let's say that the tourist is among the uninitiated, casually driving into the rising sun from the west on Highway 151 toward the little town of Darlington, South Carolina. There might well be some serious curiosity about what could be happening on the other side of that dirt mound and in front of the strange structure. What could possibly be attracting all these people so early in the morning? Revival? All-night gospel singing?

But the uninformed passerby could hardly imagine it if he doesn't stop to see it for himself.

The sights.

On the far side of the mound he could see the orbit of heat-rippled asphalt, furrowed by the weight of a herd of heavy, relentless, circling machines. The dusting of black tire rubber, scraped away by incessant speed and the force of the turns, drifting like a black sandstorm, settling on those who watch the spectacle from beneath the tin roof.

The smells.

The intoxicating incense of gasoline fumes and blue-burning oil smoke and way-too-hot metal tantalizingly mingled with onions and frying burgers and something smoking over an open pit.

The sounds.

The agonizing squealing and hellish screeching of the tires as they struggle mightily to maintain contact with earth in defiance of all the laws of physics and common sense. The accumulated captured thunder of three dozen or more primed and pushing racing engines competing with the perpetual roar of the crowd beneath the tin roof. And then, ultimately, the sound of metal against metal, car hurtling into car or slamming into the steel guardrails as somebody else, some other machine, inevitably meets its match in this life-and-death battle between driven men and their automobiles.

Maybe the passerby would be able to overcome his curiosity, squint into the sun, and hurriedly drive on past this mysterious place, eager to get to a family reunion down the way or to Myrtle Beach and the ocean. The lazy Pee Dee River, the stream that gives the region its name, manages to do just that. It wanders past, too, but somehow it keeps on going in its own relentless search for salt water.

Maybe not though. Maybe inquisitiveness wins out after all. The ocean and the beach will still be there tonight. Family, down here anyway, will understand tardiness on a race day.

The wanderer pulls to a stop with the rest of the multitude, learns the way into the lot where thousands of others have already parked, pays his tithe at the gate, and then goes inside the place to see what manner of activity it might be that has attracted so many to come, to sit, to worship so devotedly in the harsh, blazing sun.

And if he is like so many others who might have curiously lifted the flap of the revival tent and crept inside, he, too, finds the religion. It seizes him, fills him up.

He will never be able to drive by such a place again. Nor will he be able to dial past a race on the radio, nor on the television set when the races one day become commonplace there. He may not be able to tell you why, but he probably knows it's the combination of all that is racing. It's the danger, yes, but it's also much more. It's also the competition, the rare confluence of man and machine, of both physical and mental toughness. It's the combination of lightning-quick, instantaneous moves and full race endurance that go together to help determine the one who wins and all the others who lose.

Ultimately, that's what makes it so addictive. After all the carburetor adjusting, tire cambering, gasoline hoarding, paint swapping, steering wheel sawing, and the thousands of other factors that get fused together to make it a race, it all comes down to one thing: there can only be one winner.

There's no such word as "second."

HIGH BANKS

The old dark-colored Ford and its tow sailed down Highway 151, heading straight into the rising sun. Its passengers, eyes sore from a dearth of sleep, squinted ahead intently, looking for anything that even vaguely resembled a racetrack here in what was, to them, the next best thing to a foreign country. Finally, they realized that all they had to do was follow the growing stream of cars heading the same way they were traveling. Clearly, they were all destined for the same place.

Then, in the misty distance, they saw a towering mound of dirt that seemed to have grown up out of the flat fields of corn and tobacco like something volcanic. That was promising. They were, after all, travelers from the mountainous country to the west. Any kind of hill looked good to them about then.

A mite farther along and the tin roof over the grandstands came into view, the sun glinting off the metal like sharp flashes of lightning. Finally, up ahead, they could see the track entrance where the spectators were already lining up, even though it was still early in the morning and several full days before the actual race they had come to be a part of was to be run.

One of the old Ford's passengers spied the drivers' gate off to one side. They cut out of the line of traffic, and the guard waved them to a stop there.

"Y'all 'spectin' to drive in the race?"

"Yessir," they all three confirmed, in perfect unison.

The guard spat a wad of tobacco into the dust, eyed them for a moment, and then directed them over to the small stand that served as the track's registration office. Soon as they had pulled to a halt there, one of the young men, the one driving, climbed from the Ford, stretched his tallness out full-length, and ran a hand through a mane of dark hair. He looked to be in his early twenties, handsome, athletic, maybe a bit cocksure. Someone passed by and handed him a registration form. He studied it for a bit and then placed it on the hood of the Ford, bent over it, and began filling it out with a stub of a pencil he had pulled from his jeans pocket.

Another tall young man, almost a twin of the first one, climbed out of the back from the passenger side of the car. He, too, stretched and yawned and squinted at all the folks milling about, then idly scratched his belly through his T-shirt. Someone else handed him a slip of paper, telling him it was a waiver form, to read it and sign it. He didn't actually take the time to read all the words on the page, but instead, snatched the pencil from the first man's hand while he was studiously contemplating one of the blanks on the registration form. The second man signed his waiver, handed the form back to whoever had given it to him, and stuck the pencil back between the other man's fingers.

A third man rolled out of the Ford's passenger seat and then had to do his best to maintain his balance. He appeared to be drunk but he wasn't. As soon as he got his wobbly legs beneath his huge body, he was steady, stretching the kinks out of his muscles from the long ride. He was much bigger than the other two, a mountain of a man, with a crew cut, red face, and arms the size of truck axles. He, too, signed a waiver without reading it, also borrowing the first man's pencil as he studied yet another one of his form's questions.

"Jodell, what's a waiver?" the big man asked as soon as he had handed his slip of paper back to the official who had given it to him.

"I don't know, Bubba," the second one, the one named Jodell, answered, surveying some of the other race cars that had already pulled in beside their own. "Joe, what's a waiver?"

The young man bent over the hood of the car was just then signing his name on his own piece of paper.

"Heck if I know. But you gotta sign it to get a pass to the motor pits, so that's it."

"My grandma uses vanilla 'waivers' in her 'nanner puddin'," the big one was saying. "I'd sure like to have me a slug of some of that right about now."

Both look-alikes good-naturedly shoved the big man into the driver's side of the Ford. Joe slid into the front next to Bubba while Jodell stretched out across the back seat. Their paperwork now dutifully completed, they were issued their passes and directed to follow the dirt road around behind the track to the third-turn tunnel. The big man, Bubba Baxter, drove, guiding the old Ford sedan through the tunnel, beneath the race track and toward the infield.

In the backseat, Jodell Bob Lee already had his eyes closed. He was still half-asleep from the all-night drive they had just made over the mountains, through tobacco country, and then on across the breast of the Carolinas.

Jodell's first cousin, Joe Banker, fought sleep too, but there was too much to see, too much activity going on all around them for him to doze now. Besides, he had to try to make some sense from the printed set of rules the registration folks had given him while guiding Bubba in the right direction through the maze of folks and cars. The big man was prone to distractions. As he drove, he kept raising his nose in the air, sniffing like a coon dog, catching the scent of grilling food drifting on the breeze, looking about wildly for the source of such delicious aromas.

Behind them, hooked up with a logging chain and a tow bar, following along obediently, was a still-gleaming-new 1958 Ford automobile.

A guard was waiting for them when they emerged into the brilliant sunlight on the other side of the tunnel. He checked their passes then waved for them to stay to the right and told them to follow the hand-lettered signs. Neither of them was ready for the sight that presented itself to them when their eyes finally grew accustomed once again to the bright sunlight.

The place was massive and it seemed to surround, to engulf them. The gleaming belt of deep black asphalt circled all the way around where they had parked. A narrow metal guardrail framed the pavement. Down the front straightaway, the towering grandstands stretched all along the highway side of the track, its inhabitants protected from the sun by the corrugated roof they had seen from the highway. The large infield was already filling with race cars, a fine dust from their tow cars' tires hanging in the still morning air like a fog that could be tasted, its grit felt between their teeth. The spacious pit area was fenced off from the rest of the infield.

For country boys from way up the other side of the Smoky Mountains, the sight was more than they could have ever imagined, its sheer size hard to take in with a quick gaze out a bug-specked windshield. They had never even seen a race track bigger than a half-mile circle of loose dirt, or grandstands that held more than a few hundred people at a time. They were more accustomed to rough tracks scraped out of cornfields, with maybe a few rickety bleachers, or with most of the spectators scattered among the cow pies and anthills, watching from their seats on the ground amid the Johnson grass and bitter weed on some pasture hillside.

Joe Banker reached over the back of the seat to shake Jodell, to make sure he was awake. He was certainly not going to let him sleep through all this.

"Jodell Bob!" he shouted. "You got to see this place, cuz! The newspaper pictures and newsreel film in the movie theater don't do it no justice a'tall!"

"Ungh," Jodell groaned. "I reckon I'm awake if you'd quit pokin' me in the ribs." The bright sunlight stabbed him in the eyes when he opened them. He moaned again as he shaded his face with his hand, pulled himself upright to a sitting position, and looked around. His cousin was right. The sight of this place was nothing short of dazzling. "Man! I believe I have done died and gone to heaven!"

"Get a load of that grandstand over there. It looks like it could be a mile or more long. It's gotta hold a million folks!" Joe shouted. He had lost all concept of distance and space in his awe of the racetrack. "Where in the world could they ever hope to find enough people to fill all those seats?"

"It'll be full directly and then some," Jodell offered.

Jodell Lee had heard races from Darlington many times before as they were being broadcast on the radio. He would usually take his favorite place there on the floor of his grandmother's parlor back home in Chandler Cove, Tennessee. The signal came in clearly from the station in Kingsport, twenty miles up the road. Jodell preferred resting with his back against her big upright Zenith, the volume cranked up so he could actually feel the roar of the cars' engines through the radio's big speakers as they dropped the green flag to begin the race. He'd close his eyes and imagine that the announcer would be saying his name when he ran down the list of starting drivers, as he described the action out there on the track, as he declared the winner of that day's wild and woolly race. Now, here he was, actually inside that mystical place, about to drive a race car out onto its storied track as if he actually belonged there.

"Look at them banks in the turns, Jodell," Joe exclaimed, still wide-eyed. "Man, them things sure are steep. I don't see how a car could stay up there without just rolling right on over, bottom over top."

Jodell had seen banking on some of the dirt tracks they had raced, but not inclines that were almost three stories high. Hell, he had hardly ever seen any buildings that tall, much less a racetrack!

Bubba Baxter, still steering along following the slow line of traffic, was speechless himself. He had even quit sniffing the air for hints of cooking food and forgotten how badly he needed to go to the bathroom. This was all far more than he could absorb for the moment.

Joe Banker squirmed in the front seat like an eager kid trying to spot Santa Claus. There were people everywhere and he had already picked out several women he might have to double back for and give the opportunity to meet him.

Jodell Lee's head was on a swivel, staring out one window then another, from rear window to windshield, trying to take it all in before it came to an end as the races he had heard on the radio always seemed to do. He had forgotten how much his head hurt and how bone-weary tired he had been.

They were there! They had been delivered into the promised land.

TWISTING MOUNTAIN ROAD

It had, indeed, been a twisting mountain road that had brought Jodell, Joe, and Bubba to this place in the heart of the Pee Dee. And it had been a curving, bucking byway, literally as well as figuratively.

Only six months had raced by since Jodell Lee had driven in his first real competition. Joe and Bubba had worked nights and weekends, stealing time from Joe's own farm chores and Bubba's day job to help Jodell get his late grandfather's whiskey-running car ready for that race. The race had been run on a cornfield track at the Meyer farm not far from Chandler Cove. Never mind that they had avoided telling Grandpa Lee what they planned to do with his car before that race.

Plenty had happened to them since the race bug had bitten so hard. The three of them had run competitions everywhere they could find a place and someone to duel until, a couple of months back, they had completely destroyed a car while winning a sportsman race at Hickory, North Carolina. But the important things were that Jodell had not been hurt in the process and, amazingly, they had won the race. And, in so doing, they had beaten some of the best North Carolina drivers, men who were already making names for themselves for something besides delivering moonshine whiskey, scatting past lurking revenue agents on dark, foggy mountain roads.

But the harsh reality was that the finish-line calamity had destroyed the only real race car they had to drive and promptly put them out of competition. And to make it worse, the car they had demolished had once belonged to Jodell's father before he had died in the Second World War. It was one of the few things he had left behind for his son, and now it was no more than a scorched pile of bent and twisted metal, reverently laid to rest in a back corner of his grandmother's barn.

Jodell had been able to pick up a few rides here and there as he continued to hone his skills on the racetrack. His driving abilities had caught the eyes of several car owners who wanted to put their vehicles out front. But they paid little money, even when Jodell finished near the front of the pack. And the cars that were put under him were more often than not junkers, not fit to be on the track in the first place and long shots at best. Jodell had overachieved to simply finish in the money in some of those mutt cars, but it ate at him to not be first every time he went out there, to not be the leader when the checkered flag fell.

The three of them knew that they had to own a car to race if they intended to make a serious go of it. That was the only way to have control over how it was put together, how well prepared it was for earnest competition. They finally used the money they had won in the high-water mark of their racing careers so far, the Hickory race, then tossed in the payoff for one last whiskey run, and were able to sweeten the pot with a loan from a most unusual source in order to be able to buy the gleaming new race car they had towed all the way from upper east Tennessee to Darlington, South Carolina.

The three of them had spent every spare moment of the last week on their backs beneath the car or up to their waists under the hood, trying to get it into shape for this initial run at the big time. There was no way yet to actually know if the car would be competitive, if it could hold its own with the other cars that would be running there. No way to tell but to put it out there and see how it matched up, head to head, hubcap to hubcap.

Jodell Lee's own driving abilities had been honed the same way as had many of the others he would face at Darlington: running moonshine whiskey from corn-liquor stills scattered through the backwoods and hollows of Tennessee, Georgia, and the Carolinas, delivering the clear brew to bootleggers and their perpetually thirsty customers. For Lee, it had certainly been a family tradition. Jodell's father had hauled whiskey for his own daddy, Jodell's grandfather, in the very car that had been so seriously maimed at Hickory. Then, when his father had been lost in a submarine somewhere in the Pacific, and as soon as he was old enough to see over the steering wheel, never mind get a license, Jodell had climbed into the driver's-side seats of his grandfather's old Fords.

And he had learned to handle an automobile so well it might as well have been an extension of his own body. He had no choice if he wanted to stay ahead of federal revenue agents, the dogged men who were usually better equipped and would always have him outnumbered. But they were no match for Jodell Lee's deftness behind the wheel of a car on a familiar, moonlit road. When he had finally given up 'shine running, he was undefeated, uncaught.

Now he was more confident than ever that he could run with the best of them in legitimate stock car racing. He had proved it on mountain cutbacks as well as dusty dirt racetracks. And now, finally, he was eager to try his hand at racing against the best there was, on the best track there was.

They couldn't get the car parked in the pits fast enough for Jodell Bob Lee. His gas foot was already itching.

Joe Banker, his cousin, brought the mechanical aptitude it took to make the car go fast while still sticking to the track. He had learned his skills working on farm equipment for his father and grandfather, keeping their machinery wired together enough of the time so that they could eke out a living on the rocky hillsides of upper east Tennessee. And keeping the fleet of old cars and trucks running well enough so Jodell could deliver their Grandpa Lee's famous recipe. He was a self-taught technician who could sense a slightly sour engine by sound and instinct and who could coax more RPMs from a reluctant motor with a caress or a wink.

Bubba Baxter was the muscle in the trio, though he, too, knew his way around an internal combustion engine. Bubba also seemed to have a sixth sense for the intricate spring and front-end setup it took to make a car grip the track as if it was a roller coaster on rails. He had opened holes in the offensive line for Jodell and Joe when they had been quarterback and halfback, respectively, for the Chandler County Consolidated High football team. He still took great pride in playing whatever role it took to help them win the tough ones.

The three of them had made a good team so far. The true test was just ahead of them, though.

The scene in the Darlington pits was unlike anything else they had encountered so far in their brief racing careers. There were people and cars everywhere. Certainly, they had never seen so many race cars in one place anywhere, and amazingly, there were more coming through the tunnel all the time. Even the spacious pit area seemed to be filling up already and the sun was hardly knee-high yet. They hurried to mark off their territory with the toolboxes while there was still a stretch of dusty grass available and set to work to get the car unhooked and ready for the track.

All across the vast expanse of the infield, Confederate flags snapped in the brisk breeze. With the temperature coming up quickly in the bright sunshine, that wind would be more than welcomed by the time practice started.

"Joe, what day is it anyhow?" Bubba asked, studying the swelling crowd in the grandstand.

Joe surveyed the sun, used his thumb to site the horizon, going through an elaborate ritual that made it appear he was trying to discern the precise day by observing the heavens.

"I'd say it's Friday. Yessir. Friday. Seems we left home on Thursday if I recollect correctly," Joe said, trying to keep a straight face.

Bubba scowled at him.

"Shoot, man! I'm just all out of kilter from ridin' all night. And look at all them people come out here to watch us practice. Lord. How many they gonna be here on Monday for the race itself if all these folks come to watch us practice on Friday?"

Sure enough, spectators were filling the stands even though it was three days before the Labor Day race. There were people milling about everywhere in the infield, too, many looking as if they might be homesteading there for the duration.

The three of them spent the next hour feverishly getting their assigned pit area set up to their liking. Bubba went to work taking the headlights out of the race car. It had been Joe's idea to leave them in and hooked up for the drive down for a very practical reason. There was a too-real chance the old tow car might overheat and they would have needed to use the race car to tow it on in instead of the other way around. That would have given a rather ignominious beginning to their big-time racing debut but they would have been there, at least.

Joe was arranging the tools like a surgeon laying out his instruments. He needed to know instantly where to lay his hands on a Stilson wrench or a ball-peen hammer if he needed one or the other in a big hurry for some procedure he might be performing.

Jodell was already working through a mental checklist for the car. It was a ritual that he had developed for himself over the last few months and it had not failed him yet. He believed strongly that preparation was often the difference between winning and not winning, and that was such a powerful distinction to Jodell Bob Lee that he would not tolerate leaving anything to chance.

A track official worked his way through the pits, telling the crews that the first inspection would begin at 9:00 A.M. sharp. Then, once the cars had cleared the detailed inspection, they could take to the track for their first chance to practice on the high banks. There was to be a mandatory drivers' meeting thirty minutes before inspection, so Jodell had to reluctantly hustle off while the other two men finished getting the car ready for the official once-over.

"Joe, while I'm gone, be sure y'all crawl under the front end and take a look at that—" he called back over his shoulder, but his cousin interrupted him with mock irritation.

"Hush! Hear me? Just hush! I done seen a race car before this morning, Jodell. You go on to your little old drivers' meeting and let me and Bubba work in peace now."

And with that, he blew Jodell a sweet kiss. Several crew members in the pits around them laughed out loud and gave Joe a thumbs-up. They doubtless wished they could talk to their own drivers that way.

Jodell walked quickly over to the area around Victory Lane where the drivers' meeting was to be held. He was anxious to get this over with, to hustle back to get the car ready, to wheel her out there on that black snake of a track and see how she felt beneath him when he gave her the gas and hit those high-banked corners at speed for the first time. But right now, this meeting was in his way and he was more than ready to push it aside.

As he showed his driver's pass and walked into the roped-off area, he was stunned by some of the faces he saw there. They were all the greats he'd heard about, read about, heard interviewed over the radio, seen pictures of in the newspaper clippings he kept in the scrapbook on the top shelf in his bedroom closet. Standing around in small clumps like gossiping old women at a quilting party were Lee Petty, Junior Johnson, Buck Baker, the Flock brothers, Fireball Roberts, Curtis Turner, Little Joe Weatherly, Speedy Thompson, and many others whose names were as familiar to him as were those of his own relatives. Jodell could only stand there meekly, quietly, reverently.

And that's when the enormity of what he was trying to do hit him square in the gut like a pool-hall sucker punch.

Here he stood, in the hot sun in the infield of the celebrated racetrack at Darlington, South Carolina, hundreds of miles from the foothills of the Smoky Mountains and a million miles from the cornfield track at Meyer's farm. And furthermore, he was standing there, shifting nervously from one foot to the other, among the best of the best in Strictly Stock, or, as it was officially called, Grand National racing. Jodell was the interloper. He was in their environment, not his. They already knew this track like their own driveways, knew how to get around it with their eyes closed, navigating by feel and guile. Jodell realized with a sinking feeling in his stomach just how far he was now from the small, bumpy dirt tracks he'd circled around to this point in his racing career.

How in the world could he hope to measure up to these guys? Could he even run with them at all? Would his dreams get lapped and sent to the pits by these legends and this slithering length of menacing black asphalt? Those were questions that were about to be answered, one way or the other.

He only prayed he could live with those answers.

But as he stood there and watched the others talk like long lost kinfolk, Jodell Lee found new determination, set his jaw, squinted into the sun, and decided one more time that he was here for one thing only. He was here to win. That instinct was as deeply ingrained in him as was survival or mating. The poor so-and-so in second place still lost the race. A race car driver either wins and receives all the accolades that come with it, or he finishes somewhere else back there, his nostrils full of the dust and exhaust smoke of the one guy who gets to savor the victory when the day is done.

For Jodell Lee, the reason for racing was winning. He was not out there simply running around in a circle for the thrills. It wasn't even the money. That was primarily the means to the ultimate end, a way to get better equipment, to travel farther to find new tracks and even better competition to conquer.

He simply had to beat everybody. Had to.

And even as he stood there among the familiar faces and bigger-than-life names, a trickle of sweat tickling him as it ran slowly down the length of his spine, Jodell knew in his heart that he had what it took to win, even when thrown up against these accomplished drivers. And he was more determined than ever that he would settle for nothing less.

Then, amazingly, it was Junior Johnson who was waving him over to where he and several of the other drivers were talking.

"Lee! Bob Lee!" Johnson called. That had been the name that had been scripted in white shoe polish over Jodell's race car door the few times so far he had driven against Johnson. Jodell had not wanted his grandparents to know he was doing such a silly, dangerous thing as stock car racing. And that was especially the case when he had driven his grandfather's whiskey car without him knowing about it. "Com'ere and meet some of the boys. This is Bob Lee, y'all. He ain't a half-bad race car driver. I watched him burn up a car winnin' a race over at Hickory while me and ol' Lee Petty was doing a little talking among ourselves about the weather or somethin'."

Petty and Johnson had tangled mightily in that race, ultimately wrecking, leaving the way clear for Jodell to scoot past them and win it.

Jodell grinned and he could feel his face flush at such high praise from someone who was already a legend in the sport. He shook hands all around but five minutes later could not have told anyone else a single word he had said to the men nor what they might have said to him.

The drivers' meeting was primarily for those who were racing the Darlington track for the first time. The officials explained how to enter and exit the pits and the road that led from the track into the pit area. They emphatically cautioned those rookies to take it easy before they pushed their cars full bore and tried out the steeply banked turns at high speed.

"Learn the track first," they cautioned. "Get a feel for it before you try to beat it. And that especially goes for the turns. We don't want none of y'all to get hurt out there and knock down any of our pretty guardrail. Stay down real low until you get used to it!"

They explained that the track could bite a driver fast and hard, like a cur dog, seeming so docile and easygoing and then chomping down without any warning at all. A sudden trip to the guardrail and the car was more than likely finished and the driver himself in no small amount of jeopardy. The steel in that rail seemed to have a way of devouring a car and its pilot, then spitting them out again, usually in a lot of much smaller pieces.

A bit after ten that morning, with little more than three or four hours real sleep in the last twenty-four, and with a hot dog and a warm, fizzy grape soda for breakfast, Jodell was finally strapping himself into the car, ready to crank up and roll out for the morning practice. The inspection line had proved way more thorough than they could have ever anticipated. The grim-faced officials had gone over the car with almost surgical precision, making sure everything on the vehicle was legal, just the way the rule book said it should be. There was a mandatory roll bar and seat belt system check. It was a sacrosanct rule that if the car looked in any way different from one you could find on a showroom floor, then it could not be raced. And that was that. One of the reasons that stock car racing was flourishing was because the cars on the tracks were the same and looked the same, basically, as the ones the spectators had driven to the event that day. There was even a good chance that some of the race cars would be driven to the track as well as get raced on it.

As Jodell, Joe, and Bubba looked on, the track officials had crawled around inside their car, slid underneath, climbed beneath the hood, and dived into the trunk, all the time prodding, checking, measuring, referring to grease-stained sheets on their clipboards, eyeing what seemed to be every single tiny, insignificant part of the car. The three of them had held their collective breaths the entire time. While they had followed the rule book religiously, they had tweaked the car in a few places to help it run the distance. They'd mirrored the rule book the best they knew how, but never really thought about the ramifications if they failed the inspection. Failing and not being able to fix it would leave them no choice but to pack right back up and double back toward Tennessee, and they would have to listen to this race that was so important to them on Grandma's big Zenith radio.

But finally, the head inspector had slapped a sticker on the front windshield and waved them through the end of the line. They all three grinned and quickly moved the car out of the way before the inspectors changed their minds or thought of some other thingamajig they had forgotten to pinch or probe or put a caliper to.

Twenty minutes later in the stand down the front straightaway, the flag man was vigorously waving the green banner signaling the start of the first practice session. Jodell sat there in the driver's seat of the Ford, sweating, impatiently tapping the steering wheel with his fingers, keeping the beat to some unheard Elvis Presley song. The car had no radio. It didn't need one, of course, and that had saved them fifteen dollars.

The other cars that had been through inspection already sat lined up behind and in front of him on the pit road. This was, he had quickly ascertained, the worst part of it all. The few minutes in the car, confined as surely as he might have been in a coffin, hellishly hot, with nothing to do but ponder what was about to happen and how fast it would occur. That's the only time he ever encountered anything even closely akin to fear. Once out there circling with the others he never had any thoughts about the risks.

The danger faded, left behind in the dust and tire soot. And it was a good thing, too. There was no room for hesitancy, no place for skittishness. Either one could get a driver in a deadly fix and would certainly keep him from the winner's circle.

Finally, gratefully, with the waving of the green flag, they were guided out onto the track by the officials standing there. They seemed as anxious as the drivers to get things started, to have something to do, to have the passing cars kick up some kind of breeze as they grumbled past irritably like thoroughbreds straining at the reins as they danced in the starting gate.

The engines rumbled to life and as one, the people in the crowd stood and cheered this first sign of serious activity out there in front of them. Shifters were pushed up into low gear. The cars moved slowly at first, then eased on down the pit road and spilled out onto the track. As Jodell lifted his foot off the clutch and the car surged forward, he felt a rush that was indescribable. And as he sensed the slight bump beneath him as the car rolled onto the track proper, he tingled all over, as if he were about to be struck by lightning.

He was there! He was on the track at Darlington! He could occasionally catch a snatch of the running commentary from the tinny track PA and it might as well have been the radio broadcast on the Zenith back home. Once, he thought he heard his name and Number 34 mentioned and he grinned broadly beneath his goggles.

As he slowly, patiently drove off down into the first turn, as he ran the car up through the gears, it was hard for him to comprehend that he was actually driving a race car on this giant track, in this sacred place. He glanced in the rearview mirror as he came up off the second turn and then roared down the back stretch. It seemed as if he drove for a mile down that straightaway, as if the distant third turn up ahead might well be in another county. It was certainly nothing like the little "bull rings" he'd been racing in so far, places where it was turn, straight, turn, straight, turn, straight, finish, all in such quick order it was hard to keep track of laps.

The car rolled easily through the narrower turns, three and four. Jodell listened to the engine, the sound the tires made as they ate up the track, the slight roar of the axles and all the car's parts meshing together harmoniously. He wanted to hear or feel anything that might sound amiss, out of tune, off-rhythm, so they could pry it apart and put it back together correctly before it led to disaster.

So far, it was a symphony.

Then, as he steered out of the fourth turn, Jodell floored the Ford's accelerator. He felt the smooth power as the V8 engine responded to his emphatic command and as it obediently pulled the car easily down the front straight. The vehicle sang. He smiled to himself and enjoyed for a moment the throbbing of the steering wheel in his hands, the pulsing of the accelerator against his right foot, the feel of raw power that the car's body transmitted all the way into the deepest marrow of his bones.

His father must have felt the same thrill as he steered his whiskey-running car through the mountains back home years before Jodell had even been born; must have exulted in the same visceral thrill that a well-honed machine and finely tuned parts and millions of precisely controlled little explosions in the guts of the engine out there in front of him sent

coursing through his body the same as lifeblood. Jodell Lee never felt closer to his father than he did
when he was behind the wheel of a speeding car, be
it on a hairpin cutback above the cove on a moonless
night or on a racetrack somewhere.

Jodell eased off on the accelerator a bit going into
turn one, once again allowing the car's momentum
to carry it through the corner. He did the same for
the next several laps, getting a feel for the track and
its characteristics, as well as for how the new car felt
beneath him. He had tried it out on the mountain
roads back home, doing all he could to simulate the
turns he knew to expect at Darlington in the sharp
switchbacks and one-eighty curves, but there had
been no way he could get the exact feel there. Not
until he was actually out here, doing it for real.

He noticed that most of the other rookies were
running much slower than he was, with some of
them actually avoiding the high banks completely,
cautiously keeping their cars down on the apron of
the track as they navigated the turns. Coming up off
the second turn after his seventh or eighth trip
around the track, Jodell knew he had reconnoitered
all he needed to. He had assayed the track to his
satisfaction and knew the only way to learn more
was to test it at speed. And test his mount and himself at the same time.

He grinned broadly, tapped the dash, and talked
to the car, the way he always did.

"Okay, sweet little Susie. Let's see what you can
really do."

And with that, he let out a quick yelp, danced once
more on the accelerator, and he was off as if he and
the Ford had accidentally trod on dynamite.

Joe and Bubba stood along the inside guardrail,

dead even with the start/finish line. Joe held the stop-watch while Bubba strained to watch the car all the way around the track. That was another difference between this place and the smaller tracks they had grown used to running. It was difficult keeping up with the car when it was so far away, and that had always been Bubba's job. He needed to see how her body leaned in the depth of the turns, how she held her line into and out of the corners, all to better know how to effectively set her up for actual racing. But Bubba found he would lose sight of the car as it went down the back stretch, only to pick it up again as the car drifted up the banking in the turns. And besides the distance, with many of the cars painted dark blue or black, it was hard to pick their car out in the far reaches of the turns when they all looked as if they had been poured from the same bottle.

Meanwhile, out on the track, Jodell had jammed his foot down even more fervently on the accelerator as the car came up off the second turn. He had a clear track in front of him as he roared down the back stretch at over a hundred miles an hour. The air that rushed in his window was cooling on Jodell's face. It felt almost as good as did the sheer sensation of speed, the surge of power, the rush of adrenaline.

Going as fast as he was by then, the third turn came at him very quickly, sooner than he had antic-ipated. He got out of the gas entering the corner, but it tightened up on him dramatically as he hit the middle of the turn. The car wobbled once, then twice. For an instant, Jodell thought he might be los-ing her, with the rear end about to slide up and to-ward the dreaded car-eating, driver-maiming rail. But he held on tenaciously, like a rider holding the reins through his horse's stumble, and was able to gather her back up as she rolled out of the fourth turn.

Then he pushed her hard again, the motor screaming as he flew down the front straight, running much deeper into the corner than he had planned. Once again, the car wobbled slightly, but once more she claimed a firm grip on the asphalt, dug in, and he was able to power up off the turn, building momentum and speed for the straightaway.

The run down the back straight was lightning-quick again. Jodell Lee drove as deeply as he dared into the narrow and tight third and fourth turns. Then, before he knew it, the rail in the center of the turns had rushed up at him and he had to jerk the wheel violently at the last instant to try to keep from smacking it hard.

The guardrails seemed to reach out, to be grabbing for him as he roared up into the center of the turns. For an instant, if felt as they were trying to suck him in toward their unforgiving metal clutches. But then the car's rear end caught traction just as the right rear fender kissed the rail slightly. Surprisingly, the car held her own preferred line, never scrubbing off any speed.

"Girl!" he said to the car. "That was unbelievable!" he screamed, still not able to believe he had not planted the car firmly into the metal of the guardrail, that she had smooched the rail and danced away with no loss of momentum.

Jodell noted the line and made certain that he repeated the identical route on his next trip through three and four. And again, the rear fender gave the briefest of caresses to the railing in the center of the turns. This time, though, Jodell bravely, maybe even foolishly, held the wheel steady as he flew through the corner. But she came through famously, and never lost speed.

After trying several more lines around the track and again coming ever so close to the ragged edge of wrecking the car in the center of turns three and four, he took the line right up to the railing as he entered the corners one more time. As he zoomed safely out of the fourth turn this time, Jodell had a broad grin on his face. He took one hand off the wheel to pat the car's dashboard and then pumped his fist in the air in sheer triumph.

He had just found what had to be the fastest way around Darlington!

Bubba stood on the inside guardrail, more than somewhat worried, still desperately trying to follow Jodell and the new Ford all the way around the track. He could see his driver picking up speed going down the back stretch toward the third turn when all logic told him Jodell should be backing off the throttle, shearing off speed to keep the centrifugal force from sending him skidding up and into the murderous outside rail.

What's he think he's doing? Bubba asked himself. No way was he going to make it through the turns going that fast! It was a basic law of physics, after all. Plain old natural law was going to assert itself any minute now, and with a vengeance toward he who so foolishly defied it. It was going to try to sling the car outward if it was going too fast to stick to the track. Sure enough, he could see the new car they had scraped together enough money to buy, that they had worked so hard to get ready, that they depended on completely for the race, begin to drift up high enough to smack the outside guardrail hard in the center of the corner.

"Dadgummit! Aw, look, Joe!" Bubba groaned, pointing toward the corner with a shaky finger. "Jodell Bob just run all over that outside rail."

"What? What are you talking about?"

"He just hit the rail hard. I seen it!"

But then, Jodell whipped out of the corner and soon flashed by, directly in front of where they stood. Joe looked hard at his stopwatch, at where the watch's hands had crossed the numbers. Could that be right? The time was a half second better than any lap they'd run so far.

Joe kept the watch on Jodell as he made his next lap. Bubba strained even harder, eyes narrowed, trying to follow the car all the way around the track. He only wished he could see the right side of the car. It had to be a mess.

"Joe, look! Look!" Bubba screamed, hopping up and down like a galloping horse. It might have been a hilarious sight but neither man felt very comical at that particular moment. "Danged if he didn't hit it again! Same place."

It seemed most of the people in the grandstands were keeping their eyes directed toward those turns as they watched the better cars and more experienced drivers run right up there high, touching the guardrail, on the verge of wrecking every time. These fans knew what to watch for and they were already enjoying the show, practice or not, and showed their appreciation with continual cheers.

"You sure?" Joe asked, keeping his eyes on the stopwatch. "This looks like it's going to be an awfully quick lap!"

"He hit it again, hard. I know he did. I seen it clear as day. Just tore up that side of the car. I just know it." Bubba had to scream over the noise of the dozens of roaring race cars as they passed, including, soon, their own.

"I don't see how he could have hit it and still be going that fast. He had to have just come close to it, that's all."

They both peered intently, looking for dangling, mangled sheet metal, as the car circled the track once more, still flying. Jodell was clearly steering the car low through the first and second turns, then racing off down the backstretch before driving hard, much too hard, into the third turn. The car sailed high through the turn once more, heading straight for the center of the turn and the outside guardrail. Joe watched as persistently as Bubba did this time as the car grazed the wall but kept right on going, never slowing a whit, actually getting faster coming out of the turns and down the front stretch. It was as if Jodell wasn't even aware at all that he had come so damned close to total metal-rending disaster.

"Well, I'll be. He did hit it!" Joe acknowledged, hollering to be heard over the tornadic roar of the other cars. Already he was running through a mental list of over a dozen different things that would be broken on the car, that he would have to scrounge for parts for and try to make them fit in a hurry.

"I told you!" Bubba screamed right back. "We got to get him back in here quick and fix the danged thing before he tears the whole side plumb off of it."

They both waved wildly at Jodell when he came past them, sailing along down the front straight as if all was perfect with the world. The car screamed right on by as it headed back into the first turn, again at well above a hundred miles per hour.

Inside the race car, Jodell Lee was still grinning, singing to himself, talking to the car. In the wake of the excitement over his discovery, the driver was oblivious to everything around him. Nothing existed but his car and the racetrack.

Jodell Lee had reached that point that was already becoming so familiar to him. With his hands tightly gripping the steering wheel, his right foot glued to the accelerator pedal, it felt for all the world as if the car had become a living, breathing part of himself. He could feel every bump and ripple of the tire rubber on the track, too, sensing how tight or loose their grip was, when they were on the raw edge of letting go of their traction. Now, he could actually sense his way around the track as much as drive it.

And he felt another familiar sensation, too. The assurance that he was born to do exactly what he was doing now. He was born to race.

THE WIDEST HIGHWAY AROUND

Jodell Lee peeled off another couple of quick laps while Joe and Bubba continued to frantically signal for him to come in and get the car fixed before it disintegrated into a million whirling, hot pieces.

"What the Sam Hill is he doing?" Bubba screeched, scratching his crew cut.

"He's lost his ever-lovin' mind is all I can figure," Joe guessed. He looked at his watch again, his eyes squinted. "But he's gettin' faster every lap."

Sure enough, on each of the laps, Jodell again gently nudged the wall at almost the exact spot through the third and fourth turn. And on each lap, he continued to pick up speed. There were now only a few cars out on the speedway and that left Jodell plenty of clear track to run on. That was precisely what he needed. He wanted to spend what time was left learning the track until he knew it as well as he did the main road through Chandler Cove or the spiraling blacktop over Goodner Mountain that had led to some of his grandfather's best 'shine customers. He would learn how to deal with traffic on the racetrack later on in other practices.

Finally, Jodell slowed going into the third turn, the engine growling in protest as he braked and geared down, as if the car wanted to keep circling Darlington and never come in to roost. This time, he stayed low all the way through the sweeping corners. He pulled down into the pit lane and rolled to a stop where Joe and Bubba stood, just now catching their breaths after watching their driver pound the outside rail over and over.

Jodell shut the engine off and scrambled through the open driver's-side window to sit on the ledge, half-in, half-out of the car. He tugged off his new driver's helmet, pulled the ever-present rag from the rear pocket of his jeans, and wiped the sweat from his face. That's when he noticed for the first time since he had been sitting there on the pit road, impatiently waiting for practice to start, that it was even more stifling hot inside the race car than it had been then, and that he was drenched with sweat.

Neither Joe nor Bubba said a word to him but instead raced around to the right side of the car to inspect all the damage that would surely be there from where the car had slammed into the wall time and time again. They both simply stood there gaping, mouths open in shock. The only damage they could see was a small dent from Jodell's initial contact with the rail, then a few dings and a narrow stripe down the side of the car where all the paint had been rubbed off the fender.

Joe leaned across the Ford's roof and looked hard at Jodell.

"Gaw, what in the world happened out there? We thought you were going to tear this thing into forty million pieces the way you were cozying up to that fence. What broke on the car? You were all over everywhere."

Jodell grinned and wiped at his forehead again. The rag left a long oily streak there but he didn't seem to care.

"Naw! That's just the only way to get around this darn place if you want to do it in a hurry. That corner is so tight, the rail seems like it wants to reach out and grab you all of a sudden when you get in the center of the turn."

"I know. I know. But can't you maybe run lower there, darlin'? You gonna tear the whole side out of the car before long at the rate you're going. That might be one nice way to get a breeze blowin' through but not real good for the race car."

Jodell grinned at him some more. He could still feel in his feet, his gut, his hands, the tingling vibration of the engine and the rumble of the tires as they rolled along underneath him on the track. And it still felt good. He smelled his hands. They still carried the aroma of the steering wheel.

"That track seems like it's not ten foot wide or so down in that turn," Jodell said, pointing toward three and four. "It seems to narrow down real fast and then the wall just kind of jumps out at you. You know how that old red bank cutback is on the county road back home, just before you hit the top of the mountain at Bethel Church? Same way here. Except the thing is, if you hit the rail just right, it will straighten you back out like a big old hand giving you a gentle shove. The car never even slows down."

"You don't say! That's what I kept seeing on the stopwatch but I sure wouldn't have believed it if I hadn't seen it with my own two eyes."

"Watch some of the other drivers. All the big guys like Petty and Fireball and them get right up there next to the guardrail and they even kiss it every so often, too. I reckon it's worth it to give up a little paint and sheet metal."

"I see what you mean now," Joe said. He was watching a couple of the cars still on the track as they, too, ran tight into the rail. "So when you weren't trying to knock down the wall, how'd the rest of the track feel to you?"

"Man, I tell you. It's like riding on the widest highway you've ever seen. After some of these rough old dirt tracks we've been running on, it's about as smooth as can be. A few bumps here and there, maybe, but at least there aren't any ruts anywhere!" Jodell finished his report at a yell to be heard over a passing couple of practicing cars.

Joe turned then to time Speedy Thompson as he roared off down the front stretch.

"Say, where did Bubba put that cooler? It seems like it got hot all of a sudden."

"Over there behind the toolbox," Joe said, nodding in that direction.

Jodell found the red Pleasure Chest ice cooler beneath a tarp, grabbed the Mason jar filled with water out of it, and took a deep swig. It was as good as anything he had ever tasted.

He found Bubba on his back on the dirt beneath the right side of the car, trying to figure out what was wrong with the suspension that had caused the car to keep slamming into the railing.

"Danged if I can see anything wrong under here," he said as he slid out from under the car, still shaking his head. His face was covered with sweat, dirt, and dust, but his perplexed expression was still clearly visible through it all.

Jodell smiled. Without even knowing what he had been doing, he had earned his "Darlington stripe." He'd figured out the fast way around this legendary track without even realizing it. But he had noticed early in the practice that the veteran drivers all kissed the wall just slightly as they hit the center of turns three and four. It had only taken him four or five laps to figure out that whatever those guys did would almost certainly be the fastest thing to do.

And true to form, that was what Jodell Lee wanted to do. Whatever was fastest. And if a driver was too scared to run on the frazzled edge, or was reluctant to do whatever it took to be the fastest one out there, then that driver had no business being on the track in the first place, taking up space and getting in the way of the real race car drivers.

Jodell Lee was more sure than ever that he belonged out there. And now, he had his "stripe" to prove it.

UNFINISHED BUSINESS

Supper that night consisted of tins of Vienna sausages and cheap sardines and a box of soda crackers, food they had bought earlier from a roadside store, and bottles of pop from the track concession stand. Later, they would bed down on the seats inside the cars. But for the time being, and despite the clawing fatigue they all three felt from the all-night drive and the busy, tiring day at the track, Jodell, Bubba, and Joe were too primed to go to sleep after they had eaten. Instead, they were content to sit back and finish their simple meal while they talked over their first day at Darlington, seated in the stomped-down grass around the campfire they had built.

Finally, full and more than a little sleepy, they grew quiet, pensive. That's when their thoughts, and eventually their words, inevitably turned to how far they had come, how big a step they were about to take.

"Can y'all even believe we're here?" Jodell asked softly, talking as much to the flames as to the other two men. Joe and Bubba only nodded sleepily as they stared into the glowing embers of the fire. "Heck, it seems like yesterday that Bubba and me loaded the last of the whiskey and I drove it over to old Augustus. Who would ever have guessed how that last 'shine run would have turned out?"

The other two nodded drowsily again, the dying fire reflecting off their faces. But what Jodell was saying was true. That last whiskey run had taken an odd turn that had ultimately made possible the Darlington trip and the continuation of their racing exploits, just when it appeared the cold realities of life would throw a roadblock squarely in the path of their dreams.

It had been only a couple of months before, though it seemed to them like years. The late evening darkness had already ascended most of the way up the mountainsides, with night imminent, but the early June heat had still remained smothering, sultry, especially hot for the mountains. Jodell and Bubba had struck out with his late grandfather's team of mules close behind them, making their way up the mountainside in the direction of the family still. There was one last batch of moonshine whiskey left hidden there, a mixture that Grandpa and Jodell had made up the night before the old man had died. It had sat there in its barrels, aging perfectly, waiting patiently for them to eventually come and draw it out. Now, out of necessity, the two of them had taken on the task of loading it up so Jodell could deliver that final batch to one of Grandpa's oldest and best customers, Augustus Smith, who lived across the mountains and over the state line into western North Carolina.

The family whiskey business had died along with Grandpa the night a sudden, sneaky heart attack had claimed him. Faced with the ultimate decision, Jodell was forced to finally admit to himself that he didn't have the ability to make the whiskey as good as his grandfather had, nor the desire to try to learn how. And besides, times were changing in the mountains. Knoxville was selling beer already, and several nearby counties were trying to go "wet." More would surely follow. Some bootleggers were already buying the legal brew and hauling it into "dry" counties to slake the thirst of their customers. It was certainly not any cheaper that way, but it was easier and safer. And it was a far cry from the family tradition of whiskey-making that had been passed down from generation to generation in those dark, deep hollows.

Farming wasn't much of an option for Jodell either. His grandfather's place was good for little more than small row crops, and even then, it grew weeds and rocks much better than corn or tobacco. It was always said that their scrawny cows grew with their legs shorter on one side than the other from grazing on the steep hillsides. It would be hard to support himself and his grandmother trying to squeeze out a living from the stony earth.

That's when Jodell had decided his best option would be to give up dirt farming and whiskey driving and pursue automobile racing seriously. His cousin Joe and best friend Bubba had enthusiastically agreed to help. Unfortunately, their only race car had been destroyed early on, the victim of the

Hickory wreck in their first real race. They needed to find some creative way to get back into racing and the final whiskey load was to be a means to that end. If not the total solution, it was, at least, a piece of the puzzle.

Although most of Grandpa's customers, including Augustus Smith, had already lined up other suppliers, the old man had agreed to take what was left on hand as a final favor to Jodell's late granddaddy.

"Heck, fire!" Smith had said. "I ought to put that stuff up on a dadgum shelf and save it for posterity. Show 'em how they used to make liquor around here! They'll never be a better whiskey distilled in this part of the country than what your granddaddy brewed up, son. Shoot, I'd take that load for my own self, even if I didn't have plenty of folks that would pay a premium for it. Bring it on. Bring it on!"

So, with Bubba's help, Jodell had done just that.

By the dim light of a three-quarters moon, Jodell and Bubba had filled the Mason jars two nights before to ready the cargo for the run. All that remained for them to do was to load it up and haul it down the mountain from the still and get it delivered one last time, exactly the way Jodell and his grandfather had done so many times before. Just as Jodell's father had helped his own daddy do in his day.

They had made quick work at the still, carefully loading the jars onto the mule sled so they wouldn't clink together and break, and had gotten the sleds snaked back down the mountain to where the car waited. It was the same car Jodell had used to deliver loads for his grandfather. The old Ford Jodell had driven to outrun revenuers who had chased but had never caught him. The same old car they had used for their first race at Meyer's farm without bothering to tell Grandpa what foolish thing they were about to do. The same car they had now used as the tow car to Darlington.

The old Ford had waited for them in its usual place, parked in the weeds along the overgrown logging road at the base of the mountain. Thanks to Bubba's muscles and Jodell's experience, the two of them had quickly and silently loaded the boxes filled with jars of liquor into the trunk and the backseat of the 'shine car until it seemed the rear bumper might touch the ground.

"Bubba, you've missed your calling. You ought to have been a moonshiner," Jodell told him when they had finished. Bubba had only grinned at the praise. He had heard plenty about the whiskey-making business, but this had been his first real experience at it. He had not realized there was so much heavy lifting involved. "It'll probably be after midnight or so before I get back tonight. Old Augustus does like to tell those long-winded stories, you know."

"Okay, but you know I got to get up and go to work at the mill in the morning, so hurry back as quick as you can so I'll know you made it all right."

"I will. That is, if it's not my dumb luck that the Feds finally catch up with me on this last run. Wouldn't that be a hell of a note?"

"Knock on wood!" Bubba had said, and tapped a nearby sycamore with the knuckles of his meaty fist.

"I expect you'll be at the barn working on what's left of the race car?"

"Yeah, that lazy cousin of yours is supposed to meet me there directly. We're going to see if Joe can salvage the motor at least. That thing is burned up pretty good."

"Well, way I figure it, we still got the four hundred

dollars we won at Hickory in the bank. We can use that toward getting us a car for the Strictly Stocks. With what old Augustus will pay me tonight for this 'shine, we might get us something no more than a couple of years old."

"Old and won't run, that's all," Bubba had said, sadly shaking his head. "We need a new car if we're going to race them Strictly Stocks. An old junker car will just break on us and cause us worry and grief and probably get you hurt bad in the process. We need to figure us some way to come into some serious money."

"Well, we'll do what we can do. Let me get on the road before it gets any later or I'll need what cash we got saved up for bail money."

Bubba held on tightly to the reins of the mules to keep them from spooking while Jodell cranked up the '50-model Ford's flat-head V8 engine. The big motor roared to life, echoing off the nearby hills like close-by thunder. Jodell quickly brought it down to an idle to try to keep the noise down. Revenuers could hear a flat-head's growl for twenty miles, it seemed like.

He threw Bubba a quick wave and began to roll down the logging road toward the highway, letting gravity do most of the work while he steered clear of the saplings and bushes that were already trying to claim the roadway now that it was used so seldom. The rumbling of the engine, the tinkling of the glass jars in the backseat, the gentle sloshing of the whiskey all brought back familiar memories of so many nights before. All that was missing was his granddad's, "Be careful, boy," as he had waved a goodbye and then slapped the mules on their rumps with their traces and started the walk back down the other side of the mountain toward home.

Jodell eased out onto the highway and kicked down hard on the gas. The surge of power pushed him back in his seat and he instinctively tightened his grip on the steering wheel. While he was truly glad that this was to be his last run, he knew he would miss the thrill he got from racing along the highway with a full load. And he knew he would miss the danger it entailed, too.

That was where the racing would come in. It would fill his need for the organic thrill he felt from the speed and danger without having to worry about spending time in the federal pen if he got caught. And in the long run, he hoped, it would pay better, too.

For some reason, the drive over the mountain seemed as if it took no time at all that night. There was little traffic, no Feds to be seen, and when he came upon anything slow he would always be at a good place to pass and would quickly make his way around. Even the climb up through the mountains with the heavy, fully-loaded car seemed swift and effortless, the car behaving beautifully with little urging from him.

Before he had even realized it, Jodell was steering past the pile of limestone that stood beside the highway, marking the turnoff to old man Smith's place. He had to slam on the brakes so he could turn into the narrow country lane and then he had sped toward where he knew the old, dilapidated mansion sat waiting, its windows darkened, nestled among the grove of oak trees on the distant hillock.

The house had been exactly as Jodell remembered it from the last run. Maybe it was a little more run-down, maybe the weeds were just a little higher around the deteriorating front steps, a little less flaking paint left on the giant front columns, and maybe a small tree or two he didn't remember from before had now poked up through rotted boards on the front porch. But it was still clear that the place had once been a stately mansion.

The front door had been opened halfway as he rolled into a patch of weeds in the yard. A single bare low-wattage bulb that hung from the remains of an elegant light fixture inside was the only illumination to be seen. From past experience, Jodell knew that somewhere in those deep shadows, old Gus stood waiting patiently with a double barrel shotgun in hand, watching until he could be certain that Jodell was who he was supposed to be, and that no one who wasn't supposed to be might be following him.

Jodell opened the Ford's door and stepped out into the sticky night. It was extra quiet with the engine now off. Even the crickets seemed to be holding their breaths.

"Why, if it ain't old Jodell Bob Lee come to call on poor old Augustus!" The man's strong voice boomed out from the ink-black shadows. "How was your nice drive over the mountain this fine evening?"

"Oh, it was great, Mr. Smith. No problems at all."

"Good. Real good." Gus Smith stepped from the darkness and leaned the shotgun against one of the towering front porch columns. He was old, his beard all white, and the mane of hair even snowier. He was licking his lips with anticipation. "Man, I can taste your granddaddy's fine brew already. Let's make quick work unloadin', then we'll pour us out a little taste and talk a minute about the weather or

the guv'mint or somethin' else we can't do a damn
thing about."

"Don't worry. I can get it," Jodell said, already
pulling the first cardboard box of half-gallon jars out
of the trunk. The last thing he needed was for the
old man to drop dead with a heart attack lifting the
heavy boxes before he could get paid.

But Gus pitched right in and helped him stack the
boxes on an old hay dolly so he could easily roll
them around to the back of the house and out of
sight. Ten minutes later, Jodell was stuffing the cash
money for the load into his front shirt pocket. But
before he could make a clean getaway, he heard Augustus say the words he had hoped to avoid hearing.

"Sample time! Come here, boy, and let's twist
open one of these jars and see how good your poor
old grandpa's last batch turned out to be, God rest
his whiskey-makin' soul."

Jodell simply sighed and settled down on the
shabby old couch while Gus fell back into an obviously well-used parlor chair. Two glasses materialized from out of nowhere.

"Here you go, son," Gus said, handing Jodell a
glass half-filled with the clear liquid and then pouring
himself the other glass full to the rim. "Here's to
your grandpa, the best damn whiskey maker I ever
knew. And that rarity among rarities, an honest man
to boot!"

"Thank you," Jodell said, graciously accepting the
offered toast. He had not doubted the old man's sincerity.

For the first time in his life, Jodell took a deep swig
of the fiery liquid instead of his usual sip. It went
down surprisingly smoothly and immediately settled

just below his breastbone and lit a warm, tingling fire
there. Old Gus took a massive swallow, his Adam's
apple bobbing as he downed half the glass in one
gulp, then he licked the side of the glass to avoid
wasting a few droplets of the whiskey that had spilled
over the top. The old man smacked his lips and
shook his head up and down with obvious approval.

"May be the best batch yet!" he proclaimed. "And
as you well know, I have proudly sampled every
danged one of them." Then he leaned forward, low-
ered his deep voice, and spoke conspiratorially.
"Son, I know whiskey is not your game. Am I right
that this is the last of this sweet, sweet brew to ever
come out of that wonderful still?"

"Yessir," Jodell had answered quietly. He had
dreaded telling Augustus that he would not be following in the family whiskey-making tradition. But
the old man had obviously guessed as much.

"Look, I know you ain't interested in making
whiskey. It's a dying art anyhow. And with your
Papa Lee gone, your grandma couldn't get by for
long by herself if the Feds caught you and sent you
up the river. And they would, you know. You drive
as good as your daddy ever did, from what folks tell
me: But someday, odds are your luck would run out
and they'll catch you one way or the other. You
know they got them gizmos now that reach out from
their car and latch onto your rear bumper. Them so-
and-sos are tenacious enough, they'll catch even the
best eventually."

"Yessir."

It wasn't easy to admit, but the old man was right.

"And from what your granddaddy told me, you'll
have a hell of a time making a living off that dirt

farm, too. What you planning to do, you don't mind me askin'?"

"Well, to tell you the truth, me and some of the boys have been doing a little stock car racing." It must have been the whiskey talking. Jodell didn't know why he was telling Augustus Smith about their wild dream. Just saying the words out loud to him made it all seem sillier somehow, a bigger pipe dream, an even longer shot. But somehow, he couldn't hush once he started. "We won four hundred dollars in a race last week. Bad thing is, though, we tore the car up pretty bad at the end. We're going to try and get us a new car to race with as soon as we save up the money." His tongue seemed to have a mind of its own, wagging, talking, spinning out all sorts of things that wouldn't interest old Gus at all. But he couldn't seem to stop it. "We are planning on getting us a new race car and working on it so we can go down to that place in South Carolina . . . Darlington . . . you heard of it? We want to be able to run down there on Labor Day if we can."

"Son, how much did you say you won in that race?" Gus asked with obvious surprise in his voice.

"Four hundred dollars. We had to pay the taxes on Grandma's place with some of it but we're planning on using the rest of it for the new car. That and what you just gave me for the whiskey."

Gus was studying the alcohol left in his glass against the light of the naked bulb. He took another slow, deep draw of it and savored the taste for a moment. Then he looked at Jodell sideways.

"Do you have any idea how good your daddy and granddaddy were to me down through the years, son? Never tried to short me a drop like some of 'em did. Always gave me the top brew for the dollar.

Even gave me credit when my own customers were slow to pay. Your grandpa even bailed me out of jail once when it would have been real unfortunate for me if I had not been able to get out long enough to make a delivery or two to some very impatient folks."

Jodell had sat there and listened, sipping the moonshine. In times past, he had dreaded the "sampling," as well as the inevitable storytelling that came along with it. He had always been anxious to be back on the road, on the way home before it got any later.

That night, though, he had simply sat there, intently studying the lines on the old man's face, and had listened to every word he had to say.

"Your pa was the fastest thing in an automobile around these parts before he went off to the war. If there was a load to run and a time that it absolutely had to be delivered, then he was the man to get it done. Back in them days, making whiskey was an honorable profession, handed down from father to son. It wasn't just bootlegging the way it's thought to be today. Your grandfather would make the brew and then your daddy would run it. That's the only way they kept their heads above water in the hard times we had back then."

"Tell me about my father!" Jodell said suddenly, and leaned forward in his chair. It had been the first time he had ever encouraged the old man to actually go on with his tale-spinning. Gus grinned and poured the boy another half glass of 'shine. "I was just a baby but I know he went off to war without asking Papa Lee first, or even telling my momma. And I don't think Papa Lee or Grandma ever got over it when his submarine came up missing. Like most of us Southerners, they tended to not talk much about something so hurtful, but I know it still ate at them. Still does Grandma sometimes. And it drove my momma crazy, I hear."

Upon his father's death, Jodell's mother had left home, gone to California, and soon faded away completely, never to be heard from again. The boy had been raised by his grandparents.

"I didn't really know your father that well. Except, of course, that he could drive a car like nobody else around and was just as impatient with the tastin' and my damned old storytellin' as you are." Augustus winked and grinned to let Jodell know it was okay. "There was that night back in 1940 when he had a half dozen revenuers chase him for better than seventy miles and him with a full load of 'shine and four bald tires. He outrun every one of them, though. Folks in these mountains talked about that little escapade for years!"

"Grandpa told me that story many a time."

"Well, he may not have told you that your daddy was on his way over to deliver to me that night and the highway was not near as good as it is today. He's lucky he didn't go off the side of that mountain at least a dozen times. And here's the kicker. The load he delivered me that night actually saved this farm, things were so tight back then."

"I never heard that side of the story."

"Yeah, the revenue people were thick as flies that summer. They had been hanging around everywhere for months and really putting a damper on business. I had been dry, pretty much out of business for several months. I don't mind admittin' that I was at the end of my rope when your daddy come drivin' up between them oaks out yonder with that big old pretty load from your grandpappy's still."

"Gus, I didn't realize it was you he was delivering to."

"Well, it was, and the damn fool risks he took that night saved my rear end. I don't know if I ever properly thanked your daddy. Or your granddaddy, either, for that matter. But like everybody else, I figured they'd be a time for that later. Now, they both done gone on and it's too late to tell them how much I appreciate all they did." Augustus studied the glass again and took a final quaff, draining the last few drops on his poked-out tongue. He stood then, and Jodell figured the old man was stepping out to secure another jar so they could sample some more of the whiskey. Instead, he motioned for Jodell to stand and follow him. "Come with me into the back parlor, boy. I got something I need to give to you. Something I should have done years ago."

Jodell stood, a little surprised that the small amount of liquor had already left him a bit swimmy-headed. He followed the old man down a wide hall-way to a large parlor filled with dusty, chipped, water-stained furniture that had obviously been fine, expensive pieces at one time. Gus had lead the way to a massive china cabinet against the back wall. Its filigree-covered glass and hand-carved woodwork were in bad shape, but it was filled with what appeared to be expensive china from what must have been the farm's better days.

Gus opened one of the doors on the cabinet and reached up high on a shelf to bring down an old tea pot. He lifted the lid, reached inside, and withdrew a breathtakingly huge roll of money. Jodell had never seen such a thing.

Gus had slowly turned toward Jodell and then

started to peel twenties off the roll as if denuding a head of lettuce.

"Here, son. This ought to help y'all buy a car so y'all can do this racing thing right. Don't do it half-assed. Buy what equipment you need to win them races. I won't settle for nothing less. I always promised your grandpa that he could count on me if any of you needed something. This is the first opportunity I've had to make good on that promise."

"Mr. Smith! I can't take this. We'll come up with the money we need somehow. I'll find myself something to do. We maybe can fix the other car up enough to race it."

Augustus Smith suddenly got a deadly serious expression on his face, his eyes narrow and his mouth set. Whiskey-loosened tongue or not, Jodell had known to shut up then.

"Now you listen to me, son. I don't mean to debate about this with you. You take this and you buy what you need. Consider it a loan if you want to, but y'all only need to pay me back when you win enough money in those races. Neither your grandpa nor your daddy would settle for running second. Something tells me you won't either. And neither will I, boy. Neither will I."

And that had been that.

Augustus Smith had been determined that night to settle some unfinished business he had with a couple of dead men. And in the process, Jodell Lee had been put right back into the racing business in a big way.

HUNGRY TRACK

For a moment, when he first awoke, Jodell couldn't remember where he was. Wherever it was, the place was stifling, there was a light bright as the sun in his eyes, and his back ached from sleeping on something hard and slanted. Then he knew. He was in the backseat of the old Ford, and they were still in Darlington, South Carolina, one day closer to their first serious big-time race.

And then, with a start, he remembered that they still had two-thirds of his mental checklist to work down before the last practice and the qualifying began for Monday's race.

"Joe!" he screamed. "Wake up, Joe!"

"Shut up. Hear me, Jodell? Just shut up!"

The sleep-drugged voice had come from the front seat and it sounded seriously irritated.

"We gotta get going. You know what all we got to do?"

"There I was, lying back on a blanket at Indian Bluff, a full moon overhead, the crickets singing a beautiful love song, and me with my arms full of a Thompson twin. And she was about to plant one big old wet kiss right square on my mouth. Then, there you go, screeching like a banshee back there and that beautiful woman, she disappeared like a ghost. Did I ever tell you how much I hate you, Jodell Lee? Did I?"

Then, a shadow passed over the backseat. Rain? Was it clouding up? There was something that sounded closely akin to distant thunder, but Jodell knew at once it was Bubba Baxter's stomach growling, and that the big man was standing at the window, staring in at him still stretched across the seat.

"I'm starving tee-totally to death, Jodell. Y'all got the money. I'd give about anything for a stack of my momma's flapjacks. Lord a'mercy, I would!"

So that was the beginning of their second day at Darlington.

The practice session had given Jodell plenty of time to get used to the track, but he would have only one more session to work on driving in traffic. And then, they would have to qualify. If they weren't fast enough, they couldn't race. Or they would have to start at the tail end, behind most of the others.

It was frustrating because, by rule, there was little they could do to modify the car now. While he munched on a biscuit and sausage they had bought from a vendor behind the stands, Bubba worked a bit on adjusting the front end, but other than that, there was not much they could do to the car. They would have to dance with the girl they brought to the hop.

It seemed strange to them. They had always

worked and adjusted and tweaked on the race cars right up until they had had to crank them up and drive them out onto the track. Joe's magic with a motor was legendary around Chandler Cove. Everyone knew about Bubba's ability with suspension and setup.

But they had stepped up a notch with this trip. With the motor inspected, they could not legally make any major modifications to it. Other than adjusting the settings on the timing and fidgeting with the carburetors, there was little left for them to toy with. That frustrated Joe and Bubba to no end. Jodell figured it was up to him, then, to get all he could from the car once he had it out there on the track.

But there was one big, ugly problem that suddenly reared its head in their last practice before qualifying. This asphalt track was going to be hungry for race car tires. And that almost turned into a disastrous lesson to learn for them, too.

Once they got the car out onto the track for the practice session, Jodell began working on getting a good rhythm going as he tried to run consistent laps in the midst of traffic. Smooth driving was easier on the equipment and usually was the faster way around a track. He had learned that early on, watching the likes of Junior Johnson and Lee Petty.

As he had worked to pick out his marks on the fence for the points where he would get in and out of the gas, he had run the car deeper into the turns than he would have liked. He had no way to know that he was putting a staggering burden on the new Ford's right front tire. To make matters worse, the natural crook Bubba had put in the front end to help it ease through the turns was only causing the track surface to chew harder on the rubber.

Until now, they had always raced on dirt tracks. There, the only concern for the tires had been whether Jodell might run over a piece of metal of some kind that might have been clipped off another car. That could have easily cut the tire and sent the car spinning. But wear on the tires was of no concern. It had never occurred to any of them that it definitely would be something they had to watch in this place.

Now, in practice, Jodell made several long runs, unspooling at least twenty or thirty laps before he came in. Joe consulted the timing charts he was keeping on his ever-present clipboard. They were still more concerned about finding the perfect line around the track than they were with the car itself. The line they could change. The car they couldn't.

Bubba would quickly check everything he could see beneath the hood while Joe and Jodell tried to make sense of their times in comparison with some of the other faster cars. Bubba worked to clear the radiator and the air cleaner, the spots where jet-black rubber wearing off the tires tended to accumulate. On the dirt tracks, it had been the billowing dust that found its way into every nook and cranny of the engine compartment. Here, it was the black, oily tire rubber. It had not yet dawned on any of them that the rubber grit might be coming off their own tires, especially since they had already changed a set once.

Jodell continued to drive the Ford hard up through turns three and four, barely nudging the wall the way he had learned to do in the first practice the day before. But then, on one tour through the tight turns, the bump against the wall had seemed to shake the steering wheel slightly as he fought to straighten the car back out. He felt a slight bobble in the steering as he sped back off down the front stretch, directly in front of the covered grandstand. Jodell was tuned to sense even the most minute difference in the way the car handled and he knew at once that something had changed. He didn't know what yet, or if it was important, but he raised his awareness another level, listening, feeling.

He still drove the car hard and deep, plunging down into the first turn. But the Ford seemed to want to climb up the banking more than before. He tapped the brakes harder than normal to slow the car and help set its line on the track.

But instantly, before Jodell could even lift his foot off the brake, there was a deafening, explosive boom from somewhere in front of him, but close enough to fill him with instant dread. The car jerked sharply to the right as it sailed wildly upward, seemingly of its own free will, dashing headlong toward the outside rail. In a flash, Jodell saw their hopes of making the race coming to a screeching, grinding halt against the dreaded outer rail of Darlington.

Luckily he was almost in the center of the corner and down low. That gave him a little room to work with as the car sailed toward the outside railing, Jodell reacted instinctively, standing on the brakes and twisting the steering wheel with all his strength. His years of running moonshine paid off handsomely. He imagined he was careening for one of the sheer drop-offs along the Goodner Mountain road, loaded down with flammable liquor, with nothing but cool night mountain air beneath him if he went over the cliff. Nothing, that is, until he ultimately landed in a pile of boulders and a pine grove at the bottom of the gorge. The car seesawed back and forth, bucking and braying as Jodell fought to bring her back under his command.

The tires screeched in protest as the brakes caught and held while the back end decided to come around and try to pass the front. The car wobbled one more time as the speed finally started to scrub off, the locked brakes and the friction of the tires on the pavement finally holding her back from her mad dash to the fence.

And then, there was the rail, so close Jodell thought he could easily reach out and give it a slap if his hands had not been gripping the steering wheel so tightly. With a quick, natural jerk of the wheel, he brought the car around in a one-hundred-eighty-degree spin and the machine suddenly veered away from the rail as if propelled by negative magnetism. The car had missed the rail by a foot or so before it spun back toward the inside of the track. The steep banking had helped. It allowed simple old gravity to pull the sliding car away from the guardrail. But the rest of it had simply been Jodell, doing something as instinctive to him as breathing.

Jodell had still held his breath, hoping another practicing car wouldn't come zooming along and run all over him. No one did. Sometimes luck was as important as skill.

The car slid innocently down to the grass on the inside of the track, apparently none the worse for the wear, There was only one flat tire, maybe some fender damage, some smoking brakes, and a scared race car driver. Jodell's heart was thumping like one of the pistons in the Ford's V8 engine. His racing career to this point flashed before his eyes. His hands were still locked in a death grip on the wheel as if letting go too soon might yet allow the car to head back toward the unforgiving outer rail.

Then, when he finally allowed himself to breathe again, he was suddenly aware of how hot it was inside the car. And he almost choked on the sick, burning smell of hot metal and tire smoke.

The car had slid to a stop in a fog of dust and smoke, the engine dead, because Jodell had forgotten to push in the clutch as the car had slalomed toward the outside wall. His face flushed with embarrassment. That was a rookie thing to do. As he tried to control his breathing, he made a mental note to try to push the clutch in next time to keep the engine running, no matter what. If he killed the engine in a race and it vapor-locked, he would be finished, even if he had not damaged the car in whatever catastrophe had caused him to spin out in the first place.

Now, the yellow flag was waving over the practice session, telling the other drivers to be careful while Jodell got the Ford re-fired and back underway, and while the track crew cleared off the remnants of Jodell's shredded tire. Thankfully, the engine finally caught and he limped back around to the pits on the tire rim. It would have been doubly embarrassing to be towed back behind a wrecker.

He was careful not to tear the car up any worse than it already might be. As he drove past a clump of spectators, he could see that they were cheering him, giving him a thumbs-up for his work in saving the car. Somehow that didn't make him feel much better.

Bubba stood there already, waiting with a tire ready to stick on the car so they could get back out and practice some more. Joe scrambled from where he had been timing the cars, hurrying over to see if there might be any damage other than the shredded rubber. The miraculous save Jodell had made apparently had kept the car from suffering an even more serious injury. Jodell eased the car to a stop, the remaining shreds of rubber flapping dully against the fender, slowing down their rhythm as he eased to a halt.

Jodell killed the engine and climbed out of the car, still a bit shaky from the wild ride he had taken. Bubba and Joe surveyed the damage, shaking their heads and pointing. The exploding tire had dented the sheet metal severely around the wheel well. That could be uncrumpled. The rim was bent from the hit when the tire first blew and where it had rolled along the track as the car slid up toward the wall. It could maybe be hammered back into shape and another tire could be mounted on it but then they decided they would do better not taking the chance. An out-of-round rim on this track would be a definite hindrance.

Jodell joined them on the right side of the car, wiping the sweat from his eyes with the rag from his hip pocket. He was surprised to see that his hands shook uncontrollably. He stuck them into his jeans pocket so the other two wouldn't notice.

In all his days of running moonshine, in the wrecks he'd already had in his racing adventures, he'd been scared several times before, but nothing had shaken him as much as this close call had. As he looked over the damage, it occurred to him that it actually wasn't the physical danger, the risk of injury that had affected him so. It was merely the realization of how close they had just come to having their racing quest abruptly halted in the blink of an eye. It would have been over if he had wrecked the car before they even had a chance to win some prize money. All the work, all the sardine-and-cracker lunches, all the lack of sleep, the money Augustus had loaned them, it all would have been for naught if he had crashed into that damned rail.

Their heady dream of making a go of racing would have been over, rudely interrupted as sure as Joe's sweet fantasy with his girlfriend had been cut short earlier that morning. Or at least it would have been postponed for an interminable, expensive length of time.

Joe noticed then that, from what he could see of the blown tire, it had already worn very badly, and so had the other right-side tire. They had been practically new when they put them on fifty or so laps ago. A quick survey of the left side tires confirmed that they, too, were wearing extensively. All four tires would have to be replaced before they could race on them.

Jodell stood there shaking his head while Bubba and Joe quickly jacked up the car to get the new tire on the right front.

"Boys, we're gonna have to change that right rear as well. It's practically worn out and it's got some flat spots from the spin. A few more laps and it'll be worn down to the cord!"

"Man! I figured the tires would have lasted a heck of a lot longer than that," Joe grunted, straightening up and stretching after helping Bubba wrestle the new tire up under the right front wheel well.

"It's that banking over there. It eats tires like Bubba does butterbeans and cornbread. Looks like we might be having to buy a lot of tires before this race is over. I hope they don't cost all of what we are planning on making by winning this thing!"

Jodell said, already trying to do the calculations in his head.

He knew having to buy too many tires would break the bank on the carefully planned budget for the trip. They had never dreamed it would take more than a single set of tires to finish a mere five-hundred-mile race. Certainly no more than an extra tire or two if they ran over something and cut down one. If they had not suspected it before, all three men were beginning to realize that there was a lot more to this racing thing than simply driving the car 'round and 'round real fast!

"I need some help here!" Bubba hollered as he wrestled to get the back of the car jacked up. "It would go a lot faster if you two would quit yapping and come back here and help me with this other tire!"

The two men looked at each other. Bubba could get downright irritable if not fed every hour or so and it had been a while since he had eaten. Still, they hopped to and helped him get the blown right front tire changed.

Then they moved around the car, checking the other tires more carefully, and ignoring the curious spectators who had gathered around to get a closer look at the driver who had so brilliantly saved his car out there. The three of them had unanimously agreed to bite the bullet and switch out all the other tires as well, even if it did stretch their budget. There was no reason to risk wrecking the car to try to stretch the life of the tires, all to save what little money they had left.

"Penny wise and a dollar foolish," Joe dubbed such false frugality.

Wrecking the car at Hickory had taught them a

valuable lesson. It was hard to win races if you didn't
have a race car! The cost of a tire would be a small
price to pay to keep the Ford out there, circling, in
competition.

Jodell had left Joe under the hood of the car tin-
kering with the timing and Bubba trying to straighten
out the bent sheet metal of the fender, getting her
ready for qualifying. He wandered off toward the
closest concession stand to get them each a soda. As
he passed the pit of the "42" car of Lee Petty, he
noticed the crew was swarming all over the car,
checking then re-checking everything there. Like
most successful teams, they would be leaving nothing
to chance. Richard Petty was on the far side of the
car, bent over, digging into a toolbox.

"Hey Richard!" Jodell called. "How y'all doing?"

"Aw, we're fine. The cars are running real good
so far. I'm glad to see that you're still kickin' after
that spill you took at Hickory," Petty answered.
That had been the race where Jodell first met Petty.

"Yeah, I was fine but we killed the car. Won the
race though."

"That's what matters, all right. Second don't count
does it?" Petty grinned, leaning back against the race
car. "You salvage any of that car? It looked like a
good'un for the dirt tracks."

It seemed everyone he met had either been at that
race or had talked with someone who had. And they
all wanted to talk about how Jodell had won in such
a spectacular fashion. At least no one had trouble
remembering Jodell Lee's first racing victory!

"The frame's still good but that's about it," Jodell
said, a bit of sadness creeping into his voice. It had

been his daddy's car, after all. "I never thought about steel burning like that."

"Hey, Daddy has tore up plenty of cars that bad over the years. I don't think he's ever let us throw away nothing no matter what a hopeless pile of scrap iron it turns out to be. It just means more work for me and Chief over yonder when we haul the mess back to the shop!" Richard laughed, pointing toward his brother, Maurice, who was hammering away on something at that very moment.

"Well, our wreck didn't cost us any extra work 'cause there wasn't enough good pieces left on it to work on. Bubba says we could have brought her home in a dustpan."

"Well speaking of ol' Bubba, where are them two cats you run with?"

"They're over yonder adjusting the timing on the new Ford. I volunteered to fetch us some soda pop. We let Bubba get close to a hot dog stand we might not get him reeled back in to help get the car fixed and ready for qualifying."

"What you got wrong with it?"

"We blew a tire out in that last practice and I darn near took out the railing down there in the turn."

"Was that you spinning down there?"

"Yeah, that was me, all right. We're lucky I didn't tear the car up but good."

"Well, Bob Lee, I got to tell you, that was one fine piece of driving to keep that thing out of the fence like you did," Richard said, giving him a sincere nod.

"Thanks, Richard. I do appreciate it."

Such kind words from one of the Pettys was high praise indeed. Jodell said his "good luck"s and "goodbye"s and headed on for the concession stand.

But all the way, he couldn't help but grin. First, Junior Johnson's introduction at the drivers' meeting the day before. Now, someone of the stature of Lee Petty's boy had complimented him on his driving skills. And even the fans around the concession stand whispered to each other and pointed to him as he waited in line for the sodas. He heard snatches of conversation: "Bob Lee . . . won at Hickory . . . saved his car while ago . . . good driver."

It was heady stuff. Jodell drank it in like a long, cold draft of water.

CURTIS AND LITTLE JOE

While Jodell was gone, Joe finished up with the timing change on the Ford and shut the hood while Bubba had the fender back to some semblance of normal. She was good as she was going to be for qualifying. They sought shade then under a tarp the crew of the car next to theirs had strung up. It wasn't much, but any shelter from the relentless early September heat was welcomed.

"If he don't hurry up with those drinks, I may well wither away to nothing," Joe exclaimed, feigning a faint as he settled onto one of the toolboxes in the shade.

"I hope he brings me back some hot dogs. I'm about to starve tee-totally to death!"

"If you'd spend as much time worrying about making the Ford go faster as you do about something to eat, we'd be the Strictly Stock champions already."

"I ain't ate since breakfast. I got every right to be hungry."

"What about them two Dagwood-size baloney sandwiches you inhaled not more than an hour ago? Don't they count?"

"Oh. Them little bitty old sandwiches. I guess I forgot about them, they was so tiny."

"Let's get through qualifying and then you can chow down if you want to. This will be our last shot to get her well up in the field for the race on Monday."

"I think I'm having one of my sinking spells, Joe. I need some food. A couple or three of them dogs and I would be good to go till after qualifying. You know that I think better when I ain't weak from hunger."

Joe gave him a disgusted look and threw a pebble at his ample gut. It was impossible to miss. Bubba retrieved the rock, mocked pain, and tossed it back hard, scowling.

"Hey! Behave, big'un! Tell you what. You be good and we'll find a telephone and try to call the twins tonight."

Bubba brightened immediately. He and Joe had been double-dating a pair of twins back in Chandler Cove and the romance had progressed nicely. That is, until this serious racing thing had gotten in the way. Jodell, too, had a budding relationship with a young woman who, luckily, understood his commitment to racing better than Betty and Susan Thompson did Joe's and Bubba's. Catherine Holt had even worked side by side with the three men in their barn garage a few nights as they fine-tuned the new Ford, handing them tools and asking a blue million questions about what and why they were doing what they were doing to the car.

Jodell had been so focused on the Darlington race that he had not mentioned Catherine since leaving Chandler Cove. But Joe had caught him gazing into space a time or two and knew him well enough to know that he wasn't thinking of compression ratios or front-end alignments.

But Jodell would never admit it. He would only confess to how badly he wanted to win this race.

"You boys stealing our shade, huh? Guess we gonna have to kill you, then."

The crew that had pitted next to them had come ambling up then, laughing and poking at one another and now at Joe and Bubba. This bunch had seemed obviously more interested in having a wild old time there at Darlington than in actually fielding an up-front race car. Joe, Jodell, and Bubba had had no trouble getting friendly with the bunch as they had set up their pits on the first day. They had repeatedly offered them various concoctions to quench their thirst.

"Maybe later," Joe had promised. That alone had seemed enough of a commitment to make them all fast friends forever.

Theirs was a wild bunch indeed. And that was especially true of their leader. The driver was an ex-moonshine-runner like Jodell. But they had seen little of him so far. As soon as he would climb out of the car after a short time practicing, he would give Joe and the rest of them a friendly enough wave and then disappear somewhere for a bit. Eventually, he would reappear just in time to climb into the car again, usually with a blonde on one arm and a brunette on the other and a couple more of each in tow. He called them his "doll babies."

"That's Pops," one of the members of the crew on their other side offered when he saw Joe and Jodell watching the swashbuckling ladies' man, their eyes wide. "Curtis Turner is his name, but everybody just calls him 'Pops' 'cause that's what he calls everybody he meets."

Turner obviously felt comfortable leaving his car to the mercy of his fun-loving crew. And he clearly intended to enjoy his own trip to the races to the maximum, no matter what else got done. But the crew would often disappear *en masse* themselves, tossing a "We'll be back directly" at Joe or Bubba.

"Anybody tries to steal any of our stuff, y'all shoot 'em, okay?" one of them had called back over his shoulder.

"Hellfire," another one of them spat. "They so desperate they gotta steal this junk, y'all let 'em have it and help 'em carry it!"

While they seemed to take a lighthearted approach to racing, Turner and his boys were actually one of the best teams in racing. It was widely known that if you could beat him, which wasn't often, that you'd actually have accomplished something.

On the other side of Turner's chaotic pit was the team of Little Joe Weatherly. The boys quickly learned that Weatherly was Curtis Turner's best friend and preferred running buddy, both men of a like mind and appetite. And as soon as Little Joe had been introduced to Joe and Bubba, they realized that they had inherited a friend for life with him, too.

"Hell, Joe," he had stated. "Me and you got the same name. That makes us like brothers. Put 'er there, brother." And he had offered his big hand.

Admittedly, there had already been a few times when Joe and Bubba had wondered if they should have become such good friends with Weatherly and the Turner crew so quickly. They were, after all, only a couple of hillbillies from the Tennessee mountains and not quite so wise in the ways of the world as their newfound friends seemed to be. At the same time, they were still relative novices in big-time racing, too. That left the two of them easy targets for some practical jokes played by Little Joe, his crew, and the Curtis Turner bunch.

Little Joe had bounced over to their pit late one afternoon, resplendent in white pants and his trademark black-and-white Oxford saddle shoes. He had obviously overheard Bubba whining about how bad he wanted some hot dogs. Weatherly had one in each hand.

Bubba had looked longingly, pitifully, at the dogs as Little Joe took a big bite out of one of them, savoring it as if it were fine filet mignon.

"Man, them things look good," Bubba had moaned. "I been about to starve to death all day and Joe and Jodell keep me so busy I ain't had time to get me nothing to eat."

With a completely straight face, Little Joe obligingly held the other dog out to Bubba.

"Golly, I can't stand to see a grown man go hungry. Here you are, big'un. Enjoy, compliments of Little Joe Weatherly."

Bubba didn't hesitate. He happily accepted the offered sandwich, then plunged half of it into his mouth in one sudden motion. He closed his eyes in anticipated delight, and chewed away happily. But then, a pained look claimed his face as he immediately realized something was seriously wrong.

Bubba half choked before he could spit the half a dog out. It had been garnished with thirty-weight motor oil instead of mustard and catsup. Everybody, including Joe and Jodell, doubled over, guffawing. Bubba's temper flared briefly, but then he realized that everyone was apparently in on the joke but him. He'd have to whip the whole bunch of them. Instead, he stomped off to the other side of the Ford, spitting and snorting all the way.

Half an hour later he was back with the group though, Little Joe right there beside him, telling stories and slapping Bubba on the back as if they were the best of friends.

Nobody could stay mad long at Little Joe Weatherly.

SOLID IN THE SECOND TEN

Jodell finally got back with the three sodas, but he noticed right off the pained look on Bubba's face. The big man had hoped for something more solid than a soft drink.

"Thanky for the pop, Joe Dee, but . . ." Bubba started, then stopped short when he noticed a shadow cross Jodell Lee's face. Bubba and Joe were still sprawled there in the shade of the tarp, swapping stories with a couple of Curtis Turner's crew members.

"I thought y'all were supposed to be setting the timing for the car. Qualifying starts in half an hour and here y'all are, sittin' on your cans in the shade." Jodell threw both of them hard looks, even as he handed them their Dixie cups full of fizzing Coca-Cola.

"Simmer down, Mr. Big-time," Joe said after a big swallow. "We finished up with all we could do and decided we'd take ourselves a breather while you were off letting your fans see you in person."

Jodell took a deep breath and a drink of his own soda.

"Sorry, boys. We just got a lot riding on this qualifying." He managed a smile. "Oh, by the way. I thought you might want these."

He pulled two hot dogs still in their tissue-paper wrapper from under his shirt and tossed them to Bubba. The big man beamed, but still carefully unwrapped, sniffed and inspected each dog before making them disappear in four big bites.

The rest of Turner's and Weatherly's crews drifted in over the next few minutes, still in no particular hurry. Little Joe himself walked up, observed the preparations on his car, then came over to casually lean back against Jodell's Ford as if he had all the time in the world. Jodell and Joe were studying the timing charts on the clipboard.

"Y'all about ready, Tennessee?"

"I guess we better be," Jodell answered. "We're just trying to figure out how to get around this place without blowing out all the tires we brought with us."

"The only way is to buy yourself a whole bunch of 'em." Little Joe laughed but neither one of them doubted his sincerity. "Y'all look a little light for crew members. I expect it's gonna take more than two of you to crew that car come race day."

"We got three other guys coming down to help us," Jodell said. "My girlfriend's brother and a couple of his buddies that work at a service station back home are supposed to be here tomorrow night. We didn't realize how many folks some of these teams have crewing their cars."

"Boys, let me tell you something. To win at this level, you have to be committed to take it serious and willing to do what it takes to win." Little Joe was cold serious now. It was a side of him they had not seen so far in their brief friendship. "Them Pettys, Buck Baker, Fireball Roberts, and some of the others take this racing thing a lot more serious than me and Pops do. Sure, we race to win, but then we aim to have ourselves some fun doing it. You take old man Petty. Now that there is one tough nut, not a bit like them boys of his. He'll run right up your tailpipe to win the purse money."

"Yeah, Richard seems like a good guy. He bailed us out when we had a problem with our car before we won the Sportsman race at Hickory. I'll agree with you on the old man, too. He is one tough race car driver."

"At this level, all the regulars are good drivers or they don't last long. But it takes more than being good, too. You gotta have good equipment and good people to keep it running, too. Winning don't come easy. No sir, not easy at all. There's folks out here who would run their granny into the rail to win a race."

"Well, Little Joe, we kinda figured that," Jodell said, grinning. "But this is still a lot more than we bargained for when we left out of Chandler Cove the other day."

"Hell, sometimes it's more than any of us bargained for! That's why me and old Curtis always make sure we win the award for the best party everywhere we go even if we don't win nothing else. Y'all are coming to our party tomorrow, ain't you?"

"I don't know. We had sorta planned on resting tomorrow." They had reservations in a roadside cottage, figuring they needed and deserved a couple of nights of bed rest before the race. Or at least a room with a shower!

"Curtis has a place rented down the highway a piece. Y'all got to come by for a few minutes. Our parties are always fun, and besides, it'll give you a chance to meet a lot of the drivers and some of the other car owners. Anybody that counts will be there. You can bet on that!"

"Well . . ."

"Some of the boys are barbecuing most of a pig and I doubt if anybody will be going thirsty. I'd say y'all would enjoy the scenery as well, if you know what I mean. That is, if you and that girlfriend ain't too tight." He winked and turned back toward where his crew had just taken his car off the jack. " 'Sides, you don't want to get on Pops's bad side. We'll look for you."

"Uh, what time?"

"Don't matter. You get there, we'll be having a party. Now you keep that pretty car out of that guardrail, Mr. Bob Lee."

Bubba was taking one more look at the front end, confirming that Jodell's wild skid had not ripped anything out of whack. Joe dived under the hood for a quick look-see. All three knew they were about to put everything they'd learned so far on the line. It was time to show all the rest of them that they could race and, in the process, maybe prove something to themselves, too.

Were they simple pretenders? Were they like so many others who thought they could challenge a big-time track like Darlington and then end up a back-marker? Or worse, end up in that storied guardrail, crumpled, battered, defeated?

Jodell climbed through the open window on the car and settled into the driver's seat, buckling the seat belt they had so carefully fabricated back in the shop in the barn at home. Jodell hardly had a chance to reflect on the power of this moment, this last calm in the storm before he again roared out into the vortex of the tornado.

The call to the cars came over the loudspeakers, echoing across the pits and infield and grandstands. The crowd stood as one at the word that qualifying was set to begin. Joe and Bubba spilled from their spots under the car and the hood. Joe stuck his head in the driver's-side window to double-check Jodell's belts, then pulled back as Jodell backed the car out of the pit and moved up to the back of the line of cars, ready to try to qualify.

Joe and Bubba walked alongside the slow-moving car as it pulled up to the line. Eight or nine cars were strung out ahead of them. Jodell squirmed in the seat, getting comfortable, making himself ready, working to calm his nerves. It was hot inside the dark car. The sun bore down through the windshield. Sweat beaded on his forehead and he could feel a trickle work its way down his side, beneath his arm. It itched maddeningly but there was no way he could reach to scratch it with the belts as tight as they were.

Unconsciously, he tapped his hand on the shifter as he watched the other cars whiz by one at a time, already out on the track making their own runs at qualifying.

"Well, Cindy, it's you and me," he told the car. He liked to call her a girl's name but never the same one. That might bring bad luck.

The cars ahead of him inched slowly forward as the first in line would roar out onto the track and make its run. The speeds displayed on the score-board stayed in the 110 to 115 mph range.

Finally, the Oldsmobile directly in front of him was waved out by the track official standing at the head of the line. The Olds peeled out with a cloud of smoke, the tires squealing painfully as the driver gunned the heavy car's powerful engine.

"Old boy's punishing his car, ain't he? I'll go easy on you, girl, if you'll just give me one good lap."

Jodell worked to clear his mind as the Oldsmobile circled the track. He needed to think of nothing but the track: where he wanted to put the Ford on every single foot of its surface, where he wanted to goose the gas, where he wanted to ease off.

Bubba still stood there, leaning against the right rear fender, a rag tucked in the back pocket of his cotton work pants. He watched the crowd, the other cars as they rumbled around the track, the cars gathering in line behind their Ford. He hardly dared to breathe.

Joe had trotted down to stand as near the start/finish line as he could get, one foot resting on the pit rail, and timed the Oldsmobile's lap. He hit the stopwatch button, checked the chart the track had given him, and calculated the lap to be a decent 114.692 miles per hour. Could Jodell and the Ford do that well? He was about to find out.

Jodell shoved the shifter into first gear when he saw the official frantically waving the green flag for him to start his run and eased away, loving the vibration of the engine, the sensation of motion, the heat of the afternoon coming through the window. He caught a quick glimpse of the Oldsmobile streaking past, taking the checkered flag as he felt the slight bump that told him he was now onto the track himself.

He gripped the wheel tightly and jammed the shifter down into second as the car pulled out and straightened to follow the contour of the pavement. Even in second gear, the Ford quickly built speed and barreled off toward turn one.

As the tight banks of the corner quickly approached, he pushed the gearshift up into third gear and drove hard through the turn. Then he jammed it down into fourth as he exited the second turn and raced unfettered off down the backstretch, confident the car had more power than he would ever need. It was all handling and finesse and taking the right line from now on.

Jodell sailed carefully through turns three and four, jumping back into the throttle as he felt the car get a grip off the fourth turn. The car felt perfect beneath his touch, but nothing had counted for anything yet. In a moment, everything would matter! Every nuance, every wiggle or wobble.

Ahead of him in the flag stand, he could see the starter waving the green flag to signify the start of his qualifying run. His foot was now jammed to the floorboard as he flashed down the long front straightaway, a streak as he boomed past the grandstand where the crowd stood cheering for every car taking its qualifying run. He could feel a slight vibration as he barely eased off on the gas while the car glided into the first turn. He hit the line he knew from practice would be the best to run the fastest. The Ford rolled smoothly right on through the corner.

Then, he was hard back into the gas as quickly as he dared as he came up off the second turn. The raw, pounding power of the motor was being transmitted right up through the floorboard to where his foot was keeping the gas pedal pinned down like a boot on the head of a rattlesnake.

The critical third and fourth turn raced up toward him almost too quickly. There was no time to think about it. He would have to deal with the narrow corners the way he had learned how. And through instinct. He kept his mind focused on finding his line and making it through the corner without losing any of his momentum. The car dashed into the left turn and immediately drifted up toward the rail in the center of the curve, just at it had in the practices.

Jodell held on patiently, waiting until exactly the right instant, then feathered the gas as he hit the center of the turn. The ravenous railing seemed to be reaching out, to try to pull him in, to attempt to swallow him whole. He fought the wheel, using all his hay-hauling strength to try to keep the car straight. At the last instant, he felt the rear end break loose on him just as he came up tight against the rail.

And he felt the right rear of the car buss the railing, just enough of a bump to knock him back straight again and send him out of the corner without losing any speed at all. Jodell allowed himself one quick grin, then was instantly all business again.

The Ford had shaken a bit with the slight contact with the wall, but without hesitation, Jodell was back hard into the gas as steered into the stretch run back toward the beautiful checkered flag that was waving for him, welcoming him down there at the start/finish line. Now Jodell was sensitive to even the slightest vibration in the car as he roared down the front stretch to take the flag. And he wrinkled his nose at the heavy smell of burning tire rubber that filled the cockpit. He held his breath as the car flashed beneath the checkered flag.

Joe Banker clicked the stopwatch as the car passed him. He paused a moment, his fingers crossed, before checking the conversion chart they had been given.

Bubba Baxter kept his eyes on the car even as it made its cool-down lap. He wanted to see exactly how she behaved. And he had convinced himself that nothing bad could happen as long as he had the car in his sight.

Jodell took his foot off the accelerator once the car had taken the flag and allowed her to coast into the first turn again. He could see the next car come off the qualifying line as he went past.

Now, he could relax. He had done the best that he could do. The car had run and handled as well as he could have hoped for. He knew it had been a good, clean qualifying lap. Maybe the best he could have hoped for. But he had no feel for how fast it had been, how high up they might have placed. Or even if they had made the race at all.

He guided the car low coming down the backstretch and onto the apron of the track, then rolled on down the pit road, looking for the opening leading back to the area where the cars were parked. Bubba Baxter marked the way as surely as any road sign. The big man was jumping up and down, waving him on in. Joe was waiting back at the pits with a huge grin on his face.

Jodell shut the engine off and climbed from the open window. He pulled the rag from his rear pocket and toweled the sweat from his face. His T-shirt and jeans were soaked, once again from the heat inside the race car.

"Whew! That was something else!" he shouted. He was still half-deaf from the engine noise. "I didn't realize how much fun this could be."

"That was some kind of a great run, Jodell!" Bubba yelped, still dancing on one foot, then the other.

"How'd we do, Joe?"

Jodell was almost afraid to ask, but the grin on Joe's face was a good sign.

"Not too bad for a barefoot hillbilly," Joe said, still staring at the stopwatch that hung around his neck on a shoestring. "Looks pretty good compared to the others that have run so far."

"Well, how fast was it?"

Joe ran his finger along the chart again, making sure he was sighting it correctly.

"I figure you ran about 115 and some change. Most of the others have been running 114 to 115, so unless a lot of these others are really fast then we ought to be okay, solidly in the field."

"Who's left to go out?" Jodell asked. He knew Joe had the entire lineup in his head.

"Well, Speedy Thompson and Buck Baker have already run. Both ran a little faster than you did but not by much. Junior Johnson, Lee Petty, Fireball Roberts, Curtis Turner, Little Joe Weatherly, and Eddie Pagan are some of the ones still left to go. You know all of them boys will be fast."

"Well, we know it will be tough to beat any of those guys. But if we can just run a decent race and get out of here with the car in one piece then we'll have accomplished what we came here to do," Jodell said matter-of-factly.

"No we won't either!" Bubba chimed in adamantly. "Maybe y'all did, but I didn't come all the way down here to 'run decent.' Hell, I came down here to win the danged race. If I'd of wanted to do any less I'd of stayed home!"

Jodell stood there, sheepishly swiping at the sweat on his dirt-streaked face. Maybe he had let the reputations of the other drivers intimidate him. Maybe he had allowed all the talk about how hard winning could be at this level to shake his drive to finish first. He pounded the roof of the race car with his fist and then pointed a firm index finger at his big friend.

"You're right, Bub. We did come down here to win. I can rip and run a car around the back roads at home if all I want to do is drive fast. I want to beat these guys at their own game and I want to own their track when the smoke settles."

Joe Banker stepped between the two and put an arm around each man's shoulders.

"Tell y'all what. Let's just pay attention to what we're doing and don't make any stupid mistakes. We run our kind of race and don't shoot ourselves in the foot then we got just as good a shot to win it as anyone else here. This game looks like it's all about fast cars that don't break. If we stay fast and can keep the Ford in one piece, then we'll be fine."

That said, and with general head-nodding among them, Joe quit preaching to the choir and trotted back over to the pit rail to time the rest of the cars that were qualifying. Bubba and Jodell dropped down and crawled beneath the car to check the tire wear and the suspension.

"Hand me that half-inch wrench, Bubba."

"Need me to hold the linkage?"

"Yeah, I'm gonna adjust it over just a tick to see if that will help the tire wear on the right side."

Bubba scrambled, his back in the dust, trying to

get a good grip on the linkage while Jodell loosened it up.

Jodell twisted the wrench, then reached for the carpenter's rule and measured the distance between the A-frame and the trailing arm. He grabbed the ballpeen hammer and gave the end of the linkage a tap while Bubba held it tight on his end.

Jodell checked the measurement after moving the linkage over a smidgen. Satisfied he'd hit his mark, he had Bubba hold on while he tightened everything back up. He left Bubba under the car doing a sight inspection while he climbed out from under the car to check the alignment from the topside. He heard the cars of Little Joe Weatherly and Curtis Turner pull up from their own qualifying runs while he was still under the hood.

Out there on the track, a sudden, eerie silence indicated that qualifying had ended. Timing was over and the field was set. Back in the pit area, the crews were swarming all over the cars like ants on an apple, checking everything completely and exhaustively.

Joe finally strolled back from where the officials were posting the final qualifying results. He stuck his head under the hood to see what Jodell was working on.

"What y'all hillbillies doing?" he asked. With Bubba's big legs still sticking out from under the front of the car, he had a pretty good idea. He handed Jodell an icy cup of cold cola.

"Still adjusting on the alignment. This tire wear is gonna give me an ulcer." Jodell wiped the sweat from his eyes with the sleeves of his T-shirt and downed half the Coke with one gulp. "And this heat and humidity is about to give me a heat stroke to boot.

Man, what I'd give for some of that cool mountain air from back home right about now."

"That's their secret weapon, cuz. I think they bring us mountain boys down here and then watch us sweat to death."

Bubba looked like a huge crab as he tried to sidle out from under the car. He kicked up a cloud of dust as he slid along on his back, then sat up and gratefully took the offered pop and slurped it down.

"So how did we do?" Jodell asked.

"Not bad. We're solidly in the second ten, starting sixteenth. Eddie Pagan got the pole. I couldn't believe how fast he ran. He got around this place in that Ford at 116.952 miles an hour."

"Damn, that was fast! I didn't know a Ford could run that fast."

"Ain't just him, Joe Dee. There are going to be a lot of fast cars in front of us. We got our work cut out for us."

"If we can keep out of the fence and if this car don't break, we can give them a run for their money. Like old Bubba says, there ain't nobody out there who can keep up with us. They may have a little more experience but there ain't a one of them who can out-drive old Jodell Bob Lee when I can smell that checkered flag. Right Bubba?"

Bubba swelled up with pride, then suddenly remembered an earlier promise.

"Joe, reckon we can find that telephone now."

Joe winked at Jodell.

"Bubba's missing his sweetheart."

"Gotta admit so do I," Jodell said through his grin.

"Then let's go get us a stack of dimes and see if we can talk all the way back to Chandler Cove, Tennessee. Then I want to find the biggest, juiciest cheeseburger I can get. And we can get us a good night's sleep so we'll be well rested for that party coming up."

The three of them got busy, packing up for the night, ready to enjoy the first off day they had had in weeks.

POPS'S PARTY

Sunday dawned even hotter than the day before had, the humidity so thick it seemed even the June bugs and occasional stray crows had trouble batting their wings fast enough to keep themselves airborne. It was so sultry by eleven o'clock that morning that most of the male churchgoers had long since shed their suit coats, loosened their neckties, and rolled up their shirt sleeves above their elbows. The ladies fanned themselves vigorously with the funeral home fans from the backs of the pews and wiped daintily at their upper lips and foreheads with their lace handkerchiefs. The deacons had opened the big floor-to-ceiling windows on each side of the church, but there was hardly enough cross-breeze to make it worth the effort.

Jodell Lee had stood and sung with the congregation, bowed his head when the preacher prayed, dropped a quarter into the collection plate when it passed by, and even offered a hearty "Amen" when the minister made a particularly cogent point. But he was still relieved when it came time to stand and sing the invitation and to finally march outside the suffocating church house.

Jodell made it a habit to always attend church if it was at all possible. There was actually no debate about it. It had been so firmly instilled in him by his grandma that he had never considered not going when he was able.

"There is nothing so important that you can't thank God for letting it happen!" she had always told him, her eyes shining and her prominent McKenzie jaw set firmly. "And the place to do that best is right there in His house."

Racing had ultimately gotten in the way far too often to have ever suited her. Therefore, Jodell had deliberately not shared such sacrilege with his grandmother. She might still whack him over the head with her straw broom and tell him to let go that devilish racing if it was coming between him and church.

He couldn't help but grin as he thought of her as he strode back toward the Ford, parked in the shade of big live oak in the churchyard. He had come alone this morning. Bubba usually went with him, but this time he had decided to sleep back at the roadside cottage. So had Joe Banker, but that was not unusual at all. When they all three slept in the car the night before races, Joe would ride with Jodell and Bubba right up to the church house, then pull the car into the nearest shade and go right back to sleep in the backseat while the other two men went inside.

"The Lord knows I need my sleep. He understands I'll pucker up and just wilt away if I don't get my rest," Joe would say.

Jodell got the Ford cranked and moving as quickly as he could, then used his hand at the open window to scoop in some of the air onto his face as he pulled away, just the way he often did out there on the track. The preacher's sermon that morning at the little country church had been better than most Jodell had heard. He couldn't help rerunning the words in his head as he steered the Ford back toward the room.

Usually, the ministers spent too much time on the evils of cigarettes and moonshine liquor or the jealousy that ate away at the members of the church, or they blatantly begged for money to build this new building or that. But the handsome young preacher this hot Sunday morning had talked instead of the uncertainty of life and the sureness of death. He had even used a few racing metaphors to effectively make his points. The preacher knew what was already on the minds of most of those in his congregation.

The dozen or so ramshackle tourist cottages hid in a grove of tall pines just off the main highway. The trees did all they could to keep the sun turned away, to mitigate the heat, but Jodell could easily smell the hot resin in their trunks and the fragrant straw at their feet when he turned into the narrow, unpaved drive to the place.

Clearly, everyone staying in the cottages had come to town for the races. The Chandler Cove crew had met most of them around a big bonfire the night before and had spent the better part of the night swapping racing stories with them. Several of them waved to Jodell from the sheltering shade as he drove past, proud to know a real, live race car driver.

Their room was exactly the way he had left it just over an hour before. Joe Banker was still sprawled on the cabin floor, spread-eagled on a rough pallet. Bubba Baxter still occupied one of the room's two twin beds, and he still snored like a gutted muffler, and, in his boxer shorts and nothing else, he most closely resembled a beached whale. Or at least what Jodell assumed such an animal might look like. He had never seen a body of water any bigger than the Tennessee Valley Authority lakes back home.

As he entered the room, Jodell was not nearly as quiet as he had been when he had left for church. He allowed the screen door to slam shut loudly behind him. Neither of the two sleeping men moved or broke rhythm with their breathing.

He then closed the inside door with enough force to make the abandoned shoes on the floor dance around. After all, if Jodell didn't wake the two sleepyheads, they would certainly miss the rest of the day. And besides, Curtis and Little Joe's party was supposed to start in only an hour or so. At least, that's what they had been told by the two men's pit crews. But the folks gathered around the bonfire the previous night had informed them quite convincingly that the party would likely still be going full tilt from the night before, regardless of whatever time they might show up.

Still, neither one of the two sleeping beauties offered to stir.

Jodell unknotted his necktie as he gave Bubba a sharp kick in the rear. All that drew was a bearish groan, like a grizzly with the colic.

"You planning on sleeping all day, big boy? I thought y'all wanted to go to a party."

"Hunh? What time is it by now?"

"It's mighty near noon," Jodell answered. He pulled off his Sunday dress shirt, sniffed at his

T-shirt, and tugged it over his head. "Here I was, thinking that the two of you wanted to get there when it started."

"Go away." The muffled voice came from beneath a pile of pillows on the floor.

"What time did you two birds finally get to bed last night?" Jodell asked. He had given up early, worn out from the day at the racetrack, but he had seen the first bottles of beer and the jars of moonshine being passed around the campfire before he had turned in.

Bubba turned over onto his back and shaded his eyes from the bright sunlight that spilled through the room's dusty, streaked window.

"Several hours after you did, I'm afraid. Danged if that Joe can't stay up all night. I ought to know better than to try and keep up with him. Let me rest my eyes for another hour or so!"

"Get up!" Jodell yelped and gave the big man an even sharper kick. "I heard you promise Little Joe you'd help him with the barbecuing. You lay up in the bed all day and your new best friend's gonna forget who you are."

The mention of food did the trick. Bubba rolled over and sat up in the bed. He rubbed the sleep from his eyes and stretched his lumberjack arms over his head.

"I almost forgot about the barbecue. We better get cracking. I got dibs on the shower. You better wake up your lazy old cousin while I rinse off."

That was going to be a tougher row to hoe. The mere mention of food wouldn't likely be enough to get the job done with Joe Banker. Jodell poked the inert body of his cousin with the toe of his shoe.

"Go away and don't never come back." The voice

was weak, raw, and gravelly. Joe was obviously paying a tough toll for the previous night's festivities.

"All right. Me and old Bub'll go on without you, but I don't know what we'll tell that blonde you were talking to yesterday. I reckon she's gonna be there. But listen. You go on and get your nap out. We don't want you to get all tuckered out."

The lifeless body slowly began to move, then carefully sat upright. Joe's face was still all screwed up, his eyes tightly closed against the painful sunlight.

"What time is it? I swear I just went to bed a half-hour ago!"

Joe stumbled to the shower while Bubba slicked down his crew cut in the tiny mirror above the sink. Jodell waited impatiently, his hands hooked in his rear pockets, watching the two men primp. He was anxious to get to the party, not so much for the food and drink and inevitable carrying on, but for the racing talk he knew he would hear there. He was convinced he could learn plenty from the likes of Curtis Turner and Joe Weatherly, despite their seemingly cavalier attitudes toward most everything but cold drinks and hot women. They were veterans of the race tracks all over Virginia, the Carolinas, and Georgia.

Turner's room was in another tourist court a few miles down the road toward Florence. There were already at least two dozen cars parked around the motel when the boys pulled into the side yard and parked. They could hear the music and happy crowd as soon as they climbed from the car and they gawked at three good-looking women who were climbing the steps to the front door of one of the cabins that stood at the back of the group of buildings. The party was obviously well underway already.

The cottage had a small living room, bedroom, bath, and kitchen. Little Joe Weatherly was staying in one close to it. Luckily, the buildings were located in the back of the court, near a small branch creek, better than a couple of hundred feet from the motel office.

"I told the owner me and old Joe was gettin' old and that we craved quiet and solitude, so he put us way back yonder next to the crick," Pops had told Joe. He had somehow managed to keep a straight face as he talked.

The cottage's front door stood wide open. Jodell led the way as they dove into a swirling mass of people, some with familiar faces from the track, others complete strangers. Every one of them held a glass or bottle. And there were good-looking women everywhere.

Once their eyes were accustomed to the darker interior of the room, Jodell and Bubba worked their way through the mass of people toward the kitchen. Bubba had his nose in the air like a coon dog on the scent of prey. Joe Banker had spied some prey of his own, a couple of women he had picked out the day before in the Darlington infield.

Something cold and wet hit Jodell square in the stomach. It was a bottle of beer.

"Well, I'll swear! We can finally get this party a'goin'! The Volunteer boys are here!" It was the unmistakable voice of Little Joe Weatherly from the back corner of the kitchen. "You fellers been gettin' your beauty sleep or what?"

Jodell took the offered beer from the stranger by the doorway but immediately passed it on back to

Bubba. He reached into a washtub full of ice water, beer bottles and soft drinks and fished out a Coca-Cola.

"The boys ain't running on all cylinders yet this morning," Jodell laughed.

Little Joe stood up from his chair and stepped toward Jodell. He carried what appeared to be a large flower vase, but it held no bouquet, only a generous amount of some kind of brownish liquid. He shook Jodell's hand vigorously and gave Bubba a big bear hug.

"Come on, boys! Let's mingle and I'll introduce y'all to everybody that's done beat you here. These two lug-nut heads here work on the '27' car. Mike here works with Fireball. Them guys yonder talking to the redhead work with Speedy Thompson. Them drunks out there passed out on the living room floor are reporters with a couple of the newspapers. And this ugly old thing is . . ."

Jodell waved and acknowledged and shook hands with each introduction as they worked around the room. Bubba simply followed along and nodded. Some of the names were familiar, others not, but Jodell was certain they could have fielded a pretty fair race from among the party guests that Sunday.

Little Joe had his arm around Jodell's shoulders as he explained to yet another clump of strangers who this newcomer was.

"Folks, this here is that boy that give old Junior such a good race a couple of times. Old Junior tells me that 'White Lightning' here comes by race car drivin' naturally. Not like me, that had to work so hard learning how to beat all them other pecker-woods." Little Joe laughed heartily and downed some of the liquid in the vase. "You know, Jodell

Lee, you and Curtis and Junior all got something in common in your background. Before this night is over, I might need you to teach me how to outrun the law once this party gets good and cranked up. Or maybe send you out to one of them hollers for some more something good to drink."

Jodell grinned at all the praise.

"My days of running from the law are over, Little Joe. You get the cops after you tonight and you're gonna have to be on your own."

He opened the Coke with a church key that had materialized from nowhere, then handed it over to Bubba to open his bottle. The big man smiled as he pulled deeply on the cold amber liquid, but then he stopped suddenly, remembering his earlier quest.

"Where is the barbecue pit?"

"Aw, shucks, my giant friend. What kind of party host am I?" Little Joe asked in his ribbon-cane-syrup Virginia drawl. "Let me top off the old vase here and we'll go out back. You're about to see the prettiest sight ever. That old hog and all them little chicks are ready to go on the grill. Shoot, it might make a big fellow like you break down and cry like a baby just by looking at them."

Little Joe gave Bubba a big wink.

While Little Joe filled up, Jodell took time to look around. There were easily thirty people inside the cottage and he could see plenty more outside. Still more folks drifted in and out the front and back door.

Just then, someone came through the front door with a case of beer on each shoulder. It was clear that the party may have been idling along all night but it was about to kick into third gear!

Jodell finally spied Joe, perched in a corner with a

striking blond-haired girl sitting beside him and a cute brunette resting on his lap. Joe was busy, using his hands and a cluster of empty beer bottles to describe to them some hair-raising racing incident he was claiming to have witnessed, and the tall tale seemed to have his lovely new friends mesmerized.

With a wave of his hand, Little Joe Weatherly signaled for Jodell and Bubba to follow him on outside where the serious partying was taking place. With his curly red hair, his cherub face, and a kitchen towel slung across his shoulder like a sash, he looked for all the world like royalty, maybe a king surveying his realm. Before the day was over, the "Clown Prince of Racing" would have certainly further justified his nickname.

Outside the back door of the cottage, a large pit had been dug in the ground not far from the little creek. A hickory-wood fire already burned smokily beneath a large welded metal grate that someone had laid across the bed of coals. A whole split pig already lay on the makeshift grill, sizzling as its juices dripped into the fire. Nearby, a dozen or so chickens were waiting, iced down in an old number ten washtub. Beside it sat another larger tub, filled to overflowing with crushed ice, beer, and soda.

Little Joe waved his flowerpot mug at Jodell and Bubba as he addressed the assembled crowd around the pit like a king addressing his subjects.

"Boys, this here is Bob Lee. And this big old mountain of a man with him answers to 'Bubba.' Bob is the feller what drives the '34' car and old skinny Bubba is his wrench."

It was clear that many of those at the gathering were drivers, car owners, and mechanics. But most of the other people staying at the tourist cottages, mostly race fans, had been invited to the party, too. That lessened the chance of anyone calling the cops should the festivities get out of hand. And besides, Little Joe and Curtis operated on the principle of the more the merrier.

Wait. This party was missing somebody.

"Hey, Little Joe! Where is Curtis anyway?" Jodell asked.

"Don't know. I ain't seen him since about four this morning I reckon it was. He said something or other about going into town to find something to eat. He left out with a couple of girls on the back of the bike with him." Little Joe gave a big wink. "I expect he'll be back directly, though. He only had one drink with him and he ain't likely to find any more anywhere else around these parts on a Sunday. That is unless he decides to ride clear to Atlanta to quench his thirst."

Little Joe cackled then drifted off, bouncing along from person to person, greeting each one in his wild, staccato voice.

Jodell could only shake his head and laugh at the man. He had never seen anybody like him. Meanwhile, Bubba was staring longingly, lovingly at the roasting pig, unconsciously licking his lips. He had missed breakfast already and lunchtime had come and gone as well.

"Joe Dee, I'm gonna have to go find me something to gnaw on to tide me over until that beautiful thing is ready," he whined. "I'm feelin' weak already."

Jodell waved him on and then pitched in to help some of the others with the barbecue. He grabbed some of the chickens and began to skewer them and put them on the spit. As he worked, he struck up a conversation with some of the mechanics helping around the barbecue pit. They seemed more than willing to share some tips with him.

Meanwhile, back inside the crowded cottage, Joe Banker was hard at work, but not at cooking chickens or gathering up racing pointers. He was sure that he had died and gone to heaven. He'd never seen so many good-looking women in his life! It had taken him no time at all to begin a lifelong relationship with a couple of them. If this was a fringe benefit of big-time stock car racing, then danged if he wasn't going to take advantage of it!

"Honey, while you're up would you mind getting old Joe another cold beer?" he asked the blonde. The brunette was still perched on his lap with her arms tangled around his neck.

This certainly wasn't Chandler Cove. Back there, a fellow had to go all the way to Kingsport to meet anybody who didn't already know his whole life story. And a guy had to know a girl for years before she would sit on his lap. And even then, never in public.

Nope, this was a million miles from Chandler Cove, Joe thought as he stole another kiss from the girl.

Bubba had wandered into the kitchen but the only thing edible he could find were the lemons, limes, and olives intended for the drinks. He helped himself to another beer out of the washtub and grabbed a handful of olives and settled down on the back steps to wait for the barbecue to be ready.

From that vantage point, he could keep an eye on the pit and be the first to know when the pig was done. He could see Jodell, basting the lineup of chickens with some dark, mysterious sauce. And he could tell that Jodell was having a good talk with the other men who were helping out. He was having no trouble fitting in with the racing people. Jodell had clearly won their respect on the track already and they were more than willing to welcome him into their fraternity.

As Bubba popped open the beer and took a long, thirsty swig, he thought about how hard it was to believe that they were actually here, enjoying this party with these people, many of them drivers they had read about in the papers, heard about on the radio as the races had been broadcast. And here they were, hanging out with them, sharing drinks with them, on a first-name basis with some of them, being welcomed into their circle easily and openly.

Just then, Bubba felt a hand on his shoulder and someone stood between him and the sun.

"Mind if I sit down?"

Startled, Bubba jumped, spilling some of the cold beer on his hands.

"Uh . . . sure," he stammered. "I mean no. I don't mind."

He wiped his hands dry on his dark khaki trousers and scooted over to make room on the step.

About the most beautiful thing he'd ever seen settled down next to him. Dark black hair. Black as the coal that rolled down from Kentucky on the railroad that ran through Chandler Cove. And tall, too. Easily close to six feet. Thin and lithe. And perfume that smelled like the gardenias that grew around his momma's porch. Bubba felt the need to say something else, to be glib and suave before she decided he was a total dolt and moved on, but nothing would come out of his mouth when he tried.

"Hi, I am Joyce Anderson." She offered her hand and he actually managed to take it. "This is all new to me. What about you? I came down for the race with a few of my friends. One of them has a cousin who lives outside of Florence and we're staying over there with her. You here with somebody?"

"Umm-humm. My best friend." Bubba croaked, pointing over to Jodell, still deep in conversation with one of the mechanics he'd met. Jodell was using his hands to illustrate his story about two cars racing side by side into a high-banked corner.

"Y'all down for the race, too?"

"Uh, yeah. We been here for a few days." For some reason, Bubba's tongue felt thick and unresponsive and he had had only one beer so far.

"Who are you pulling for? We want Lee Petty to win. My cousin actually met him at a race last year and he is so nice," Joyce said innocently.

"Uh . . . well . . . uh . . . see, Bob Lee drives a car," Bubba stammered, nodding again toward where Jodell stood next to the barbecue pit. "I'm his chief mechanic."

Joyce Anderson's mouth fell open and she looked at Bubba wide-eyed.

"You mean y'all are actually running in the race?"

"Yes, ma'am. We qualified in the second ten."

"That is so exciting! My daddy's a mechanic back home. I guess that's why I like cars and anything that goes fast."

Bubba couldn't believe his ears. A beautiful woman who actually enjoyed cars and going fast? It had never occurred to him that any woman could possibly care for anything mechanical or have more than a passing interest in racing. There had certainly been few back home who did. Jodell's girl, Catherine Holt, maybe, but not many others. Betty Thompson, the closest thing to a real girlfriend he had ever had,

had only wanted to talk about her friends, to gossip about other girls, and didn't give a hoot about cars burning around in a circle, making all that noise and raising such a dust cloud. Bubba doubted she even knew what model race car they ran.

"What do y'all drive?" Joyce was asking. "Ford? Chevy? What size engine?"

And before he even realized it, Bubba was out of his shell. And not giving a thought to the sizzling pig or roasting chickens.

Jodell spotted Bubba talking to the dark-haired woman over on the steps and grinned. But he had to shake his head a half-hour later when he saw she was still there, and that Bubba was talking animatedly to her, no doubt describing one of their exploits. The woman seemed to be hanging on every word, laughing, tossing her long hair.

This was now, officially, a new Bubba record for talking to anyone, and especially to a woman!

Suddenly, there was a loud roar, like thunder. Jodell looked up but the sky was clear, the sun beaming down hotly. But then an old Indian motorcycle came rumbling through the crowd, its muffler long since rusted away. The 'cycle slid to a stop just before running into the midst of a clump of laughing people. And there was the grinning face of Curtis Turner, straddling the cycle, with two women on the Indian with him, one sitting on the gas tank in front of him, the other hanging onto the back.

The crowd parted before the bike as if more royalty had arrived. Turner acknowledged their shouted greetings, then climbed off the 'cycle and headed inside in search of drink. He emerged a couple of minutes later with an iced-tea glass filled to the brim with a suspicious-looking liquid that no doubt contained more than a little Canadian Club as part of the recipe. Little Joe Weatherly was beside him, his flower vase turned up to his lips.

"Hey, Pops," Curtis said to Bubba. "I see you found yourself a nice lady."

Bubba blushed, grinned, then settled back into conversation with Joyce.

Turner stepped off the porch and began working the crowd like a politician on election day.

"Hiya, Pops. Glad y'all could come. Y'all need a drink? Well, run inside and get yourselves one. Hey, Pops! Where you been hidin'? Ain't seen you in ages! Well, hey Pops!"

And so it went.

It must have been around five o'clock or so when Jodell looked up from the barbecuing and turned away from the conversation to see that Bubba Baxter was still sitting there on the porch with his lovely new friend. Man! Bubba had not eaten all day! For all the years Jodell had known him, he'd never known the big man to miss a meal. And Bubba had never, ever talked to a girl for anything like three hours straight.

He'd not seen Joe in a while, either. He hoped he wasn't drinking too much, losing himself in some new women friends of his own.

Jodell shook his head. He didn't mind Joe and Bubba having a good time. But he wanted them to be alert and focused tomorrow, too. They had come here for one thing and one thing only. Fun was fun. But winning tomorrow's race was the reason they had worked so hard on the car and come all the way down to Darlington.

While Joe and Bubba had spent the afternoon improving their love lives, Jodell had been talking to one of Curtis Turner's mechanics and the man who worked on the engine of the "56" car. As they had spent the afternoon tending the fire and saucing the meat, Jodell had picked their brains, learning how they intended to manage tire wear and set up the springs and tune the engines. He pumped them for their impressions on how the cars would feel as the tires wore out and for what they considered to be the best line around the track. The fire and the sun were hot, so the men had imbibed liberal amounts of cold beer while Jodell stuck with pop. The friendship and the brew had made the men more than willing to share all their secrets.

They also confirmed Jodell's conviction that having a fast car was good, but driving a steady, smart race was the key to winning. Run the car too hard and you'd find the fence or break something crucial and be on the way home or to the hospital when the checkered flag flew.

When the barbecue was finally ready, Jodell fixed a towering sandwich and took it over to where Bubba was still lost to the world with his new friend. He couldn't help but worry about his buddy. He might actually starve to death after all. Jodell stopped at the washtub and got three beers on the way.

"Excuse me! Y'all mind if I join you."

Jodell stuck the plate in front of Bubba before he could answer.

Bubba momentarily lost his composure, grabbed the plate, seized the sandwich with his free hand, and started stuffing the barbecue into his mouth. Joyce sat wide-eyed, taken aback by the sudden change in his demeanor.

"Watch your hands and arms, ma'am. If they get in his way he's liable to eat them, too." Jodell grinned and extended his hand to the woman. "By the way, I'm Jodell Bob Lee."

"It's nice to meet you. Bubba has already told me all about you. He says you are the greatest race car driver in the world."

"Well, I don't know about that. This racing thing is still new to us."

"Well, Bubba says you are a sure thing to win tomorrow."

"Bub doesn't lack for confidence. Or an appetite."

Jodell pointed to Bubba who had just finished wolfing down the barbecue sandwich and was sopping up the last of the sauce with a bit of bread.

The three of them sat on the steps, talking, watching most of the crowd get more and more intoxicated. By six o'clock, there were probably a hundred or so people milling about behind the cottage. Curtis Turner had disappeared on his motorcycle again while Little Joe Weatherly played his role as host to the hilt. Jodell watched as he waved his arms wildly, full-bore into some story he was spinning. But as he hit the punch line, Little Joe managed to splash the icy contents of the flower vase on more than a few of the onlookers, including down the front of the blouse of a very attractive young lady standing close by.

She squealed and danced backward, bumping hard into a burly young man who was clearly half looped. He in turn stumbled into another red-faced man who had been standing there, trying to remember his name and which hand held his latest cold beer. With the collision, he lost his drink and, at the same time, his temper.

In an instant, there were slurred words about each man's parentage exchanged, and then fists flew. Neither man was sober enough to actually land blows on the other, but they began waltzing each other across the clearing toward the cottage. Little Joe seemed oblivious to the fracas. He had dived into his next story already.

The crowd parted to give the two fighters room while other partygoers ran over to see the fray. Jodell, Bubba, and Joyce were only half-aware of the fight. Jodell had never seen Bubba exude so much personality. The big man was bubbling, articulate, telling stories like a practiced veteran. And Joyce Anderson sat there, seemingly engrossed in the conversation.

Then, one of the fighters stumbled sideways, throwing a blind punch toward where he thought his opponent might be by then. Instead, it landed hard on the side of Bubba's head, then the drunk fell backward into Joyce's lap, knocking her aside. The other drunk dived in, seizing the opportunity to try to pin his foe while he was down, but accomplishing nothing more than bowling over Jodell and Bubba.

And that was all it took.

Before he knew what was happening, a large hand had grabbed the first fallen fighter by his collar and jerked him upright. A second large mitt latched onto the back of the neck of the other would-be heavyweight champion of the world and pulled him to his feet.

Bubba stood there, holding each of the fighters at arms' length like a couple of recently caught fish. He glanced over his shoulder to make sure Joyce was okay. She seemed to be as she brushed dust from her blouse.

Jodell scrambled to his feet to cover Bubba's back,

but it appeared the two fighters had no friends willing to come to their aid.

But then, one of the drunks made a serious miscalculation. He drew back and threw a roundhouse swing at Bubba, barely missing his head. Bubba pushed the other guy in Jodell's direction, stood the puncher straight, and delivered a massive right hook that dropped the redneck as if he had been clubbed with a two-by-four. The other guy took off at a gallop, his party over.

A couple of the fallen man's buddies finally came and helped him to his feet. Bubba managed to plant a solid kick in his rear as they dragged him away.

At that moment, Curtis Turner came riding up again on his motorcycle like the cavalry coming in to save the day.

"Well, I'll be dogged. I go for some more Canadian Club and I miss all the entertainment."

That's when Joe Banker stuck his head out the back door to see what all the commotion was, the two women so close to him that they seemed attached at each hip.

"Darn, cuz! I leave the two of you alone for a minute and y'all pick a fight with some of Pops's guests! How embarrassing!"

"Put a lid on it, Joe." Jodell said, a hint of irritation in his voice. He suddenly felt very tired.

"Aw, Joe Dee, I'm just playing."

Jodell grinned then.

"Look, guys, I've got a long, hot race to run tomorrow. I think I'll head on back to the cottage. Y'all coming?"

Joe looked at each girl, gave them both a quick kiss on their cheeks, then turned back to his cousin with a silly grin on his face.

"I'll get a ride back in a few minutes."

Bubba looked as if he were drowning, not really wanting to leave Joyce and the party yet but not sure how to gracefully say so without being too forward. Joyce bailed him out.

"We can give you a ride back when you get ready, Bubba," she said.

"You sure?"

"Absolutely. I'm not through talking to you yet, Mr. Bubba. And we have to go right by where y'all are staying on the way to my friend's cousin's."

"I don't know. Jodell might need some help with something to get ready for the race." His words were sincere, but Jodell Lee could read the look in the big man's eyes.

"Stay and have a good time, Bub. Maybe I can get a little sleep before you get there and start snoring."

Bubba was still standing hesitantly, Joyce at his side, watching Jodell leave, obviously torn. But Jodell tossed him a wave to let him know it really was okay. He just hoped Bubba wouldn't be too late, too lovestruck, to give it his best tomorrow.

As he steered back alone toward the tourist cottages and into the fading sun, he realized again how tired he had become. Or was it just nerves in anticipation of what lay ahead tomorrow? He thought of Catherine, too, and how much he was missing her. How lonely it was without her. How lonesome it felt now without the constant company of his cousin and his best friend. Was that distracting him, too, as much as Bubba's and Joe's partying might be diverting their attention from what was really most important?

He decided not. He knew what was most meaningful, and that was getting ready to win the race.

He'd see Catherine again in a day or so. And he'd tell her then about how they had come to Darlington and how they had outrun all the big names and how they had won this big-time race the very first time out.

That's what he would tell her. And if he closed his eyes against the last of the sun, and if he thought about it, he could almost picture the way her face would light up and how she would smile and how her blue eyes would sparkle at hearing the news.

RACE DAY AT DARLINGTON

A few miles from where Jodell Bob Lee was fitfully catching his last few minutes of sleep, the world was coming awake early for a holiday morning. The sun quickly cleared the tree line and tried to get a free peek over the top of the metal roof shading the long grandstand that framed the front straightaway of the Darlington racetrack. Even shy of full daylight, there was bustling activity beginning everywhere. Already a cordon of cars was strung along the main highway and into the dusty parking lots around the track. Soon, local cars trying to cross the main road would have crude, hand-lettered signs their drivers could wave that said "LOCAL," simply so they could get themselves a gap in the traffic to get across the choked highway.

The air was warm already, threatening to get downright hot when the sun had had time to work on it some more. Down in the pits in the middle of the pear-shaped track, a few men were already beginning to scramble around with purpose, to crawl beneath the frames and under the hoods of the race cars.

Jodell came awake that morning with a start, interrupting a sorry dream in which he was trying to win Darlington with four flat tires and an engine that could only cough, spit, and smoke, while Junior Johnson and Lee Petty and the rest of them circled and passed him by time and time again, grinning and waving each time as they scooted on past. As soon as he realized where he was, he fumbled for his watch he had left on the floor next to his bed.

Six in the morning. Thank goodness. For an awful moment, he had been afraid he had slept all the way to time for the checkered flag. He blinked and looked around the still-darkened room.

Bubba Baxter snored lustily on a pile of blankets on the floor. Joe Banker was nowhere to be seen.

Jodell quietly showered, giving Bubba a few more minutes of sleep. But when he stepped out of the bathroom, Jodell saw that the big man was already awake, standing, his eyes still closed, his massive body swaying slightly as he scratched his belly and yawned.

"Where's Joe at?" Bubba asked, his voice thick, like a record played at the wrong speed.

"Don't know. I thought you might have some idea."

"We left him back at Pops's party."

"Well. You better get cleaned up. We need to be on the road before the traffic gets any worse. We got lots to do."

Jodell pulled on his jeans and T-shirt and packed up the rest of his duffel bag, grabbed up Joe's old cardboard suitcase and headed out to the car to stow them. They would have to check out of the tourist court before going to the track and he hoped he and Bubba could come up with enough money between them to pay the bill without Joe's help.

When he stepped onto the cottage's porch, he saw a familiar car, a dusty old Hudson Hornet parked in the shade of the building, almost at the steps, its windows opaque with dew. It belonged to Catherine Holt's brother, Johnny. Jodell had given Catherine the name of the place they were staying when he had called her, just in case her brother and his two friends made it to Darlington early, but he was actually surprised to see them here already.

Pleasantly surprised. That had been something else he had worried himself sick over. What if they didn't make it? How could they crew the car with two people?

He threw the bags into the Ford's trunk, walked over to the Hudson, grabbed the rear bumper and gave the car a good shake. Heads popped up inside the car, roused by the motion. Johnny Holt rolled down the driver's side window, leaned out and stared at him sideways.

"Hey, Jodell! That ain't no way to say good mornin' to somebody done drove across hell's half-acre to help you win a race."

"Sorry, Johnny, but I didn't want y'all to come up shootin'. How was the trip?"

"Fine," he said, crawling slowly from the car. He was tall, muscular, and looked as if he could still run pass patterns, just as he had a half dozen years before on the same football team with Jodell, Joe, and Bubba. "We left out yesterday about three and got here a couple hours ago, I guess it was. Everybody but me was asleep when I pulled up so I just decided to catch a nap myself out here in the car. I didn't see no need to wake y'all up."

" 'Preciate that. Glad y'all had a chance to sleep some. It's gonna be a long day and we got beaucoups to get done."

"Where's everybody else? Joe and them?"

"Bubba's in the shower and I ain't seen Joe since last night. I expect he's still hanging out at this party we went to. Y'all need the shower or the bathroom before we get going? We need to beat the traffic."

"I'm fine. What about you boys?" Two forms were groaning and stretching as they poured from the car's backseat. They said something that sounded like, "No. Reckon not." Johnny looked back inside the car. "How 'bout you, Cath? I know how you women are."

There was someone else in the car Jodell had not noticed, curled in the passenger-side seat. She opened the door, stood and grinned at him across the top of the Hudson.

"Mornin', Jodell," Catherine Holt said. Her hair was tangled, her blouse wrinkled, her eyes swollen and red. She was the most beautiful thing he had ever seen.

Jodell didn't hesitate. He danced around the rear of the car, grabbed her up and hugged and kissed her long and hard. The three men whooped and curtains parted on several of the nearby cottages as their inhabitants checked to see what was going on. When he finally came up for air, Jodell looked deeply into her blue eyes.

"I'm so glad you're here! But I never . . ."

She hushed him with another kiss.

"You know how stubborn she can be, Jodell,"

Johnny was saying. "I kept telling her that this was no pleasure trip."

It had never occurred to him that she might come along with her brother and the others. She had not mentioned a word about the possibility when he had talked with her on Saturday night. But now that she was here, he felt his spirits lift considerably. Merely having her present seemed to be the ultimate good-luck charm. Somehow, he felt as if he drove better, had better racing luck when he knew that this beautiful woman was watching him out there running around in circles.

They collected Bubba, said their howdies all the way around, and then headed for the track. Jodell had a pre-race drivers' meeting and there was still plenty of checking and tweaking to be done on the race car. John and the boys quickly set to arranging the tools and spare tires where they could easily find them, just the way they had practiced in the field out behind Jodell and Joe's grandmother's barn back in Chandler Cove. Catherine had stayed back with the car, making sandwiches for their lunch.

Jodell looked up from the Ford's exposed engine to scan the busy pits, looking for any sign of Joe Banker. Joe's womanizing was a source of much amusement when so much was not at stake. This morning, in the middle of the pits at Darlington, there were far more important things to be concerned with. Joe Banker should have been there. Too much was on the line. Too much work. Too much money. Too many dreams.

Bubba read his mind.

"He'll be here, Joe Dee. This is all as big to him as it is to you and me."

"We got a race to run in a couple of hours and

our chief engine builder is still out God-knows-where doing God-knows-what with God-knows-who."

"Aw Jodell, Joe ain't gonna be late to the Southern 500. Quit stewin' about old Joe and start worrying about how you gonna be at the front when the checkered flag falls!"

Jodell grinned but he still had an ache deep in his gut. He had planned for this day for too long to remember. He couldn't stand the thought of anything being misaligned, of this special day not running on all cylinders from the very start. Standing here with a key cog of the machine missing was not part of the intricate blueprints he had mentally drawn up for this day.

"That's better, driver. Now, let's get this buggy ready to win us a race!"

Johnny Holt and the other two men, Randy Weems and Clifford Stanley, quickly made the pits their own domain. They swept the area clean with a whiskbroom and stacked up an extra couple of sets of tires that had already been mounted on rims. Joe had bought the extra rims off Curtis Turner's team after they had kindly pointed out that it could be dicey trying to win the race with only one complete extra set of mounted tires. Joe and Jodell had assumed that if they had a flat, they would have time during the race to mount a new tire for a full set, that they could get it done before it was time to change the whole set again. Curtis had pointed out that in the scramble of the race, they might need another set of four ready to go before they could get even one new tire mounted on its rim.

"It gets like fruit-basket-turnover sometimes out there, boys. You don't want to be caught with three tires when you need four," Turner had advised. It had made sense, even if it had cost them money they didn't need to spend.

Finally, it was time for Jodell to head off for the drivers' meeting. Bubba tagged along as his crew chief. Jodell was fuming now, more than simply irritated with Joe Banker. The two of them had spent the better part of the last hour inspecting the car from stem to stern. It had turned out that they had not put a wrench to a single bolt. Everything seemed fine. But Jodell had wanted Joe to do some fine adjusting on the carburetors before the race started. He grumbled to himself all the way to the meeting while Bubba tried to take his mind off his annoyance.

"Man, look at all the folks up yonder in them stands," Bubba said, trying to claim Jodell's attention. "I ain't never seen so many Confederate flags in my life. You ever seen so many good-looking women in one place in your born days? Wonder how many cars they can squeeze into this infield?"

Jodell successfully ignored him. Now, when they should be planning race strategy and concentrating on the car, Jodell was dangerously distracted, worrying about his useless cousin, his mind not on the Ford, and, more importantly, not on winning this race. Jodell stormed into the drivers' meeting, his focus fast fading.

Little Joe Weatherly bounced up beside him, chipper as ever despite his own late night, and slapped Jodell heartily on the shoulder.

"How goes it, Tennessee?"

Jodell squinted with pain and turned to face him.

"Little Joe, you seen my cousin?"

"Matter of fact, I think I saw him leaving the party about seven this morning with those two girls he got tangled up with."

"I don't care who he was with," Jodell snapped. "I need him here. We got a race to run in case nobody has noticed!"

"Sure, Tennessee. I done figured that out. We got a race to run and I intend to win it. You might as well pack up the toolbox and head on back to them mountains of yours. I hate to tell you, but the word is that I got this one in the bag. You might try to race for second place with Lee and Fireball and them if you want to, with or without that rascal cousin of yours."

"I ain't in no mood for you this morning, Little Joe."

"Hey, lighten' up, Mr. Bob Lee. You gotta learn to have a little fun in this business. You have to party hard, have lots of fun, then you'll have ample opportunity to get serious in here on race day. This racing stuff will eat you up alive if you let it. Relax. Have a little fun along the way or you'll dry up like an old prune. Don't take it as serious as old Lee Petty over yonder. See how it's done got him all scrunched up and old looking. Danged shame."

Jodell grinned back sheepishly. He should have known better than to take out his irritation on Little Joe.

The meeting went quickly as they reviewed the now-familiar caution rules, specific situations to look out for, and what to expect over the course of the race. Bubba and Jodell sat there and soaked up every word though, trying to ignore the banter and horseplay going on around the fringes of the meeting.

Once back to the car, Jodell stuck his head under the hood and helped Bubba visually check every nut, bolt, belt and hose once more, as if something that had been perfect an hour before might have suddenly and spontaneously punctured or split or loosened itself in the meantime. But that was the only way to avoid the creeping nervousness. Keep busy. Force themselves to do something, anything, to occupy their hands and, at the same time, their minds. Jodell had noted some of the other drivers, stretched out on blankets in the shades of their cars, taking a catnap before climbing behind the steering wheels. He envied them their calm.

No way, he thought. No way.

Johnny and Clifford were still hard at work, setting everything up and matching the sets of tires. Randy had taken off with the gas cans in a wagon they had borrowed, headed for the Pure Oil filling station in the infield, behind the pits. It was his job to make certain they were filled to the brim. Catherine was still back at the car, building a huge stack of sandwiches and other food and distributing it all on an old Army blanket as if she was dealing cards.

Bubba was busy, pointing out to Jodell some minor adjustment he had made on the front suspension. Jodell was leaned so far over into the wheel well that his feet were off the ground. Suddenly, he felt something icy cold on the bare skin between his T-shirt and jeans. Instinctively, he came squirming out from the wheel well, cracking his head on the hood, dancing in the dust as he struggled to get the piece of ice out of the seat of his pants.

He rubbed his head, feeling for a bump, then squared around, fists up and cocked, looking about for Little Joe Weatherly or Pops Turner or one of their zany pit crew members, ready to clock the nearest one he could reach.

"Hold on, cuz. You just a little bit touchy this

morning, ain't you?" Joe Banker stood there in the bright sunlight. Except for a slight droop in his cowlick, he looked none the worse for wear from his prolonged night of partying. "Maybe you didn't get enough shut-eye last night."

"I ought to kick your sorry butt all the way . . ."

Then Joe tossed a garment of some kind to Jodell. "I picked these up for you. Put 'em on!"

"What is it?" Jodell looked warily at what appeared to be a pair of white coveralls.

"This, Mr. Lee, is your official racing outfit. I picked it up off some of the boys last night. They got to telling me about the danger of fire in these old race cars and how they soaked these surplus coveralls in fire retardant to make a flame-resistant driving suit. Well, I says to myself, Ol' Jodell needs one of those. It turns out the boys had an extra one about your size that they'd soaked and here it is. Put it on."

"I ain't wearing this thing. I don't need no racing suit!"

"Come on, Jodell. Most of the guys are wearing them. Hey, look, I want to win, too, but hell, if you get burnt up in a wreck then we can't race no more. And I'm the one what's got to haul your ashes back to our grandmaw and show her what's left of you."

"This is a long race. It's too darn hot. This T-shirt is all I need."

"Well, at least think about it."

"Tell you what. I'll think about wearing these overalls while you adjust this carburetor so the jets are set perfect. I don't know why I ask, but where the hell have you been anyway?"

"What do you mean where have I been? Y'all missed the best party I have ever been to in my life.

Even old Bubba here was making out with a fine lady. You seen Joyce this morning, Bub?"

"Urrgh!" was all the response he could get out of Bubba. The big man was now entirely focused on the race, his new girlfriend apparently out of his mind for the time being. He had not even groused about being hungry yet.

"Okay, okay. A touchy subject I see. I thought you were having fun anyway."

"It was okay. Fix this carb so we can go get us some lunch, how about it?" Bubba growled, then stalked off.

"Aw, I'll have this baby purring like a kitty in no time," Joe bragged, reaching into the toolbox for a couple of wrenches and screwdrivers.

Johnny hopped in the car and started the engine while Joe tweaked the setting on the jets in the carburetor. They worked the engine up through the RPM ranges while Joe listened intently to the pitch of the motor, cocking his head like a piano tuner trying to get the perfect chord. Finally, satisfied with the melody he was hearing, he sawed his hand across his throat in a cutting motion, signaling Johnny to kill the engine.

"Hey, Jodell! How's she sound to you?" Joe asked.

"You're the engine man. When you tell me it's right, then it's right."

They moved the car to the end of the slow-moving inspection line and left Clifford to ease it up a few feet at a time as the queue moved at a crawl, then they headed to where Catherine would certainly have the picnic ready. It was the first time Jodell and Bubba had allowed themselves to think of food since the barbecue the night before. There was fried chicken, plenty of bologna and ham sandwiches, a cake Catherine had made the morning before, and a huge jug of sweetened iced tea. A separate cooler held Mason jars full of water and a dozen or so sodas. The men devoured the spread of food as if they had not eaten in days.

Jodell caught Catherine watching him eat. He smiled at her and she beamed right back.

"Have I told you how glad I am that you came?" he asked her.

"Yes, but it's still good to hear. I know how big this race is, Jodell. I don't want to get in the way."

"Don't worry about that. In fact, you could help if you want to." Her eyes grew wide. She had only come to watch, to fix the lunch, to offer encouragement. "We are going to need a scorer again and you have experience. Do you mind?"

"Really?" She had scored for him in the past, at some of the small dirt tracks they had run, but it had never occurred to her that they would allow her to do that here.

"If you want to."

"I would love to. Where do I go?"

She didn't know how to explain to him that when she scored, it made her feel that she was somehow helping Jodell around the track, giving him a better chance to win, that she most felt a part of what he was doing as she marked each succeeding lap.

"Joe can take you over to the scoring stand in the fourth turn so they can get you set up and show you what to do."

"Thanks, Jodell," she said excitedly. Then she stepped closer and hugged him tightly. "Thank you, Jodell. Thank you for letting me be a part of something that's so important to you."

"Just make sure you mark every lap," he said, grinning. "We don't want to have to run any of them twice."

Then a strange look crossed Catherine's face.

"Be careful out there, Jodell. I love you."

She had whispered the words so only he could hear them. Before he could answer her back, she gave him a deep kiss.

And then she was gone. Jodell could only stand there, his head spinning, unsure if he'd heard correctly what she had said. He watched as she and Joe disappeared into the milling crowd. Catherine Holt was unlike any girl he'd ever met. And she had a knack for causing the strangest feeling in his chest where his heart should be.

But at least the butterflies were gone now. And with Joe there, with the makeshift pit crew apparently getting the job done, with Bubba and his race face on, he now felt that they might could actually do some good out there on the storied asphalt of Darlington.

He couldn't wait to find out for sure.

"START YOUR ENGINES."

You going to humor me and wear the suit or not?"

Joe stood there watching Jodell, an unusually serious look on his face. They had pushed the car through the inspection area and then out to where the rest were lining up for the start. The crowd was roaring, ready to see some racing, moving toward a frenzy now that they could actually recognize some of the name drivers climbing into their cars.

"I ain't going to wear that old thing."

"I am serious, cuz. Fire is one of the things you don't what to run into out there. I don't care how good a driver you are, you still gonna burn like a stick of kindling. Now put on the damn thing before I pin you down and me and Bubba put it on you like we're diapering a baby."

Jodell couldn't remember a more intense look on his cousin's face.

"All right, all right. But if I sweat to death and wreck this car it'll be your fault."

"I will kick your butt if you wreck this car that Bubba and I have spent all this time working on."

Jodell went quickly to the men's room in the infield and changed into the driving suit. Once in it, he had to admit it did make him look more the part of a professional driver, though. He liked the looks he got as he walked back through the crowd and then climbed into the car and strapped himself in. Bubba, Johnny, Randy, and Clifford gave the car a final wipe with their rags and then headed back to their stall along the pit road. Joe reached in and checked the belt harness as he always did, making sure it was secure and tight, then gave his cousin a pat on the shoulder.

"Now you remember what we talked about and you watch for Bubba with the chalkboard. Remember, he'll give you the lap count every ten laps and tell you when it's time to come in for a stop. If you understand what the board says give us a thumbs-up. If you don't get it, then shake your fist. Got it?"

"Got it. Now let's go out and win this thing!"

"You got that, cuz."

The crowd was standing, ready, screaming, while the drivers sat tensely in their cars, trying to ignore the heat and concentrate on the task at hand, hoping the engine would start, that the clutch cable wouldn't snap, that a gear wouldn't shatter, that the engine wouldn't explode into flames when fed gasoline. In the motor pits, the tension was as real as the smell of oil and gas, as thick and ponderous as the humid air.

"Gentlemen, start your engines."

It was a politician or a singing star or a local car dealer who gave the command over the PA system. The drivers were unaware of exactly who it was. It didn't matter. Before the tinny, screeching sound had even stopped reverberating around the grandstand, the powerful engines roared and rumbled with a sound like some long-dormant volcano had suddenly decided to erupt beneath this particular spot and in front of all these people.

Jodell hit the starter switch and couldn't actually hear his own motor awaken to his bidding. Instead, he felt the vibration in his seat and saw the gearshift lever shimmy so he could tell it had come alive. He ran the engine up through the RPMs, and felt it go smoothly as the pistons moved faster and faster beneath the hood in front of him. Joe reached in the window, checked the belts one last time, then shook Jodell's hand before the cars rolled off the line. Jodell gave him a thumbs-up and gently eased out on the clutch pedal, rolling off the line behind the cars in front of him and following the pace car.

Jodell shifted in the seat trying to get comfortable. The smells of the cars and the track drifted in the open driver's window. The rubber, the burning oil, the gasoline, even the aroma of hot dogs wafting over from the crowd, all hitting his senses at the same time. Once again, it struck him that he was actually at Darlington, on Labor Day, in line behind cars piloted by legends he had read about for years.

And it was time to race.

As they made the pace laps, Jodell strained to pick out Bubba amid all the color and motion in the motor pits. But then he found he didn't have to strain at all. There he was, standing tall as an oak, holding the chalk signboard marking their pit stall high over his head. Jodell pointed to him as the cars slowly rolled by and Bub dipped the board in his direction. Jodell could even see him wink as he gunned the engine.

As they rolled beneath the flag stand, the flag man held up one finger indicating one more pace lap. Jodell watched the furled green flag the man already held high over his head.

Catherine sat in the scoring stand, fifty feet above the outside rail in the fourth turn. She had gotten a quick lesson in scoring and, much to her relief, it was being done much the same way she had scored other races for Jodell and the boys in far smaller and less important places.

Her only reservations had come when she had learned exactly where the scoring stand was. She had assumed that they would sit at the end of the stands, but the rickety wooden structure sitting high over the fourth turn was the actual scoring stand. There was a line of precarious steps leading up and some of the other women who would be scoring wondered out loud whether the thing was sturdy enough to hold them all.

But there was no choice. Catherine had to do it for Jodell. She had bravely climbed up the steps and settled into her chair, then laid her clipboard across her lap and waited for the race to start. The friendly lady next to her introduced herself as Margaret Baker and pointed to her husband's car, the number 87 Chevrolet of Buck Baker. The scorer for Fireball Roberts sat on her other side and she introduced Catherine to all the others, mostly wives, girlfriends, and a few men who scored races as a hobby and to be a part of the action.

Then, the cars rolled out of the third turn, came directly toward them for a bit, and, just when it appeared they might actually career right into the stand with them, they steered into the fourth corner. Catherine could feel the stand vibrate beneath them, as if shaken by a windstorm, and smell the exhaust and rubber from the cars. She picked up her clipboard and fingered her pencil nervously as the cars moved off toward the start/finish line that was waiting for them on down the track. Even from there, she could see that the pace car had begun to accelerate away from the lead car, the Ford of Eddie Pagan that was rolling along on the inside of the front row.

Jodell had an even better view than Catherine. He watched intently the cars in front of him as he waited for the green flag to flutter from the flag stand. From where he sat, trapped on the outside row, Jodell knew he couldn't jump down to the inside immediately. He would have to wait patiently for an opening to the inside to make any kind of immediate dash toward the front. Already, he felt claustrophobic, confined. Patience was not a virtue that came easily to Jodell Lee. He longed to break out, move to the front of the pack, and lead this race from the get-go.

He tightened his grip on the wheel and reached for the shifter with his right hand. He pulled the car down into second gear as he hit the center of the fourth turn and felt the car buck. He could see the crowd in the stands rise in unison, as if yanked up by a giant puppeteer as the field lined up obediently coming through the fourth turn. Hats held high in the air, the spectators all waved wildly as the cars approached the green flag, urging on their own favorites.

Jodell could only imagine the roar from the

collective throats of the crowd as the flag was held high. The bellow of his and all the other powerful engines drowned out the sound completely. In the track's infield the rebel flags snapped in the breeze while those who watched from there held their beers high in a thousands-strong salute.

Jodell was still in the exit of the fourth turn when he saw the green flag wave. He jammed the accelerator to the floor as hard as he could and rammed the shifter up into third gear. He felt the raw power of the engine working away in front of him as the car came quickly up to speed and flashed across the start/finish line. But sure enough, he was boxed into his outside position as all the cars ran down into the first turn two-by-two in a cloud of smoke and dust.

The smells and sensations of the Ford soon merged into a blur as the cars raced around the track, side by side, inches from each other, in a mammoth struggle. Jodell knew he would have to concentrate every single second, every inch of asphalt, on every lap. With all the cars on the track and as bunched-up as they were, an accident was a certainty at any moment. The slightest bobble, an instant's inattention, a mechanical glitch no matter how minute and all hell would break loose, and, in the close quarters of door-handle-to-door-handle racing, there was nothing anyone could do to steer away from trouble. He renewed his squeeze on the steering wheel and leaned forward a bit more, his nose only inches from his white knuckles.

As the second lap unwound, Jodell found himself still trapped on the outside, though he had managed to move up a single spot. The car felt a bit loose, its rear end tending to slide upward in the corners of the race track, and that made it treacherous to try to

pass someone on the outside line. He was able to
keep the RPMs up in the motor and that gave him
a jump coming out of the turns, but then he'd lose
that advantage as soon as they approached the next
left turn. Instinctively, he knew he had to get down
to the inside quickly if he had any hopes of moving
up through the field.

By the fifth lap, the field had finally begun to string
itself out, the slower, poorer-handling cars lagging
back while the ones to beat moved ahead. As the lap
counts reached the teens, Jodell could see the lead
group and picked out the cars of Pagan, Fireball Roberts, Lee Petty, Junior Johnson, Joe Weatherly, and
Curtis Turner. And it was clear they were having
some fun up there. They raced each other as if every
lap was the final one, the checkered flag ready to fly
the very next trip by.

Back where he was, it seemed to Jodell that it was
all he could do to simply hold on every lap, to keep
from being passed by cars driven by people he had
never heard of before. This was much tougher competition than he had seen in the bull rings and on
Friday and Saturday night dirt tracks back up in the
mountains. The large number of cars and the length
of the track made it all the more difficult to pass the
others and get up to the front to run with the leaders.

But that was why he was here. To run with the
leaders.

"Mabel, let's see what we can do," he told the car
beneath his breath. She seemed to hear him and
roared her approval as they spun out of the fourth
turn and headed together down the front stretch of
Darlington.

Jodell gritted his teeth, watched intently for the
smallest of openings, and finally managed to drive

the Ford into a sliver of daylight to the inside. Immediately, he was able to start picking off some of the other cars one by one. By the twentieth lap, he had swerved and tapped and slid his way up to thirteenth place. Everything inside the car was a haze. He could feel every vibration that might be a tire going flat or a spring coming loose, smell the burning oil smoke even when there was none, and hear every rattle and knock that might suddenly explode into a smoky ball of fire beneath the car's hood. He could feel the tension grabbing the muscles in the back of his neck and the butterflies having a party in the pit of his stomach. With each car he passed, his concentration level seemed to intensify and there was no chance to clear his focus. Soon, he had lost any sense of how many laps might have wound out so far and he completely forgot to check the count on Bubba's blackboard in the pits.

Each turn became a battle of its own as he tried to set his line or make a pass. He tried to imagine himself the only car on the track as he concentrated on hitting his throttle points. The car had soon re-acquired the Darlington stripe on her right flank, the distinguishing mark that Bubba had spent so much time beating out of the sheet metal and spot-painting after the last practice lap on Saturday.

Soon Jodell had settled into a nerve-wracking routine, watching the mirror at the exit of the turn, giving a quick glance down at the gauges, stomping the accelerator down the straightaway, risking another glance in the mirror, then finding the throttle point to get off the gas, and all the while making for certain that the car was set in the proper line it needed to take it safely through the corner without tangling with any car that might be on the outside or, worse, with the guardrail. And so it went, lap after lap.

It actually became monotonous after a while and he felt his concentration begin to waver. He became aware of how hot it was in the car, how bad the shoulder straps were chafing his chest, how his head was aching from the constant g-forces that pulled him outward in the corners.

And the maddening thing was that even though Jodell kept passing cars, improving position, he also continued to fall farther and farther behind the leaders. Those guys seemed to be having their own private race up there, and Jodell Lee had not been invited!

The traffic that remained ahead of him, and even the slowest cars that had already been lapped, simply refused to allow him to go around them without a struggle. It seemed that, no matter how hopeless, no matter how far down they might be, getting passed by yet another race car on the narrow track was a personal insult to the drivers. But his struggles with all this traffic were allowing the leaders to put more and more distance on Jodell.

He couldn't help it. He felt the frustration building inside. And he felt almost desensitized by the repetition, distracted by the heat. Despite himself, he felt his attention wander even more, his vision to blur.

Suddenly, he felt a sharp jolt on his rear bumper. In the mirror was a '57 Chevy planted so firmly on his rear end that it might as well have been chained there.

"Where in tarnation did he come from?" he wondered. He had certainly not been there when he'd glanced in the mirror the last time. Or had he? Maybe he had missed checking the mirror for a while when he had been tussling with a Hudson that seemed to be all over the track blocking his way. Admittedly, the heat in the car and the strain of the g-forces on his neck were beginning to make him foggy in the head. He forced himself to collect his thoughts.

As Jodell shook his head, the black Chevy's driver apparently decided he was waiting no longer. As Jodell dove hard into the first turn, then got off the gas to once again set up his line, the Chevy steered in a little deeper, its right front no more than two inches from the left rear of Jodell's Ford. Then, as Jodell came down to run his line through the corner, he clipped the Chevy. The cars kissed slightly, the left rear tire of the Ford momentarily catching the right front of the black car. The two cars grabbed each other for an instant with a sharp screech before the rear end of the Ford kicked outward in the direction of the guardrail.

In the cockpit of the Ford, Jodell had felt the two cars touch for an instant, and only then did he realize how far the Chevy had driven past him. He felt the bump, the grab, and then the slide as the Ford yawed sickeningly toward the high side of the racetrack.

He reacted as if by instinct, the moves learned first on dark, foggy mountain roads, then reacquired on a series of dusty racetracks over the past few months. It was the same, whether on the spotty blacktops back home, in the cornfield track at Meyer's farm, or here in the first turn at Darlington. He sawed hard at the wheel, trying to get the Ford back under control, to keep her out of the fence.

It worked. He was able to catch the car a few feet from the railing and slide her none-too-gracefully back onto a straight line. He heard the tires scream in protest, but felt them as they finally caught traction and propelled the car forward instead of sideways.

Jodell rammed his foot back down on the gas pedal once he knew it was beneath him again and roared out of the exit of turn two. He tried to catch his breath in the stifling heat of the car but there didn't seem to be any oxygen left to suck in, no matter how hard he tried. The seat belts were starting to bite deeply into his shoulders from the sudden short detour and his neck hurt worse than ever.

He was well into the third turn before he felt his heart start beating again. By then, the black Chevy was gone, eaten up by the traffic ahead of him.

Down on the pit road, Joe, Bubba, and the rest of their pit crew were suffering their own frustrations. From where they were, they could actually see very little of the race. About all they could do was count off the laps and time the cars as they rumbled past. They could only get a brief glimpse of their car as it came past them on the front straightaway. Bubba dutifully scrawled on the chalk board every ten laps and then held it up for Jodell to see as he blew by, keeping him updated on how many laps of the race had been run.

Joe perched on top of a toolbox with a stopwatch in each hand. He timed every lap Jodell made with one watch and clocked the lap of the leader with the other. What he was seeing was especially frustrating to him. Jodell was dropping farther back from the leaders with every lap, losing a couple of tenths of a second each time past. It had to be the traffic. He knew they had a fast car and a faster driver than they were showing so far.

Then, on the thirty-seventh lap, Jodell's time was off by over a full second. Joe shook the watch and gave it a second look. No way! He looked at the watch a third time to make sure. Then he felt someone tugging on his arm.

"Joe!" Bubba screamed, cupping his hand over Joe's ear when he bent down closer. "Looks like Jodell's fender is pushed in on the left rear."

"What?"

"The left rear fender is pushed in. Somebody has gotten into the side of him."

Joe whipped around to try to catch the Ford while it was still in the fourth turn. The dark blue paint job on the Ford was similar to several of the other cars on the track so it made it hard to pick it out from all the traffic. As it zipped by though, he could clearly see that Bubba was right.

Joe stepped down off the toolbox.

"Looks like the fender is pushed in close to the tire. It could be rubbing."

"I don't think so or it'd be smoking. But I can't really see it down in the corners. Could be rubbing there and okay on the straights," Bubba said as he stood on his toes, trying to follow the car all the way around the track.

"See anything, Bub?"

"Naw. I can't tell. How's his time?"

"He's down just a little." Joe tried not to show any worry on his face.

High in the scoring stand, Catherine had been following Jodell around the track until she was dizzy. She could not miss marking a single lap on the clipboard she held tightly in her left hand. She had been surprised at how fast the cars were running here and how dangerous it looked out there on that coiled black snake of hot asphalt. But she knew that all she could do was continue to follow him, keep marking his progress on the score sheet, and pray under her breath. Somehow, she felt that if she took her eyes off him, she would be letting him down, that as long as she watched him she was like his guardian angel.

She had seen the black car of Dash Rockford run up quickly on the rear end of Jodell's Ford, then watched as the Chevrolet stayed glued to Jodell's bumper, unable to pass, and saw him bump the rear of Jodell's car. Then, to Catherine's horror, she saw the two cars touch. Dash's car had hit the side of Jodell's Ford, knocking the back end loose and sending the car sailing directly toward the fence, but somehow, miraculously, Jodell had brought the skidding car under control and narrowly missed the fence. It had taken her a moment to catch her breath and she almost missed scoring that lap. Even then, she had to get a new pencil. She had broken the one she held in two.

All the while, the crowd behind her had screamed their approval of not only the bump but the way Jodell had saved the car. Catherine was sure she would be proud of him, too, when she was able to breathe again.

The leaders had sailed past Jodell while he had struggled to bring the car under control. His blood pressure was up and, if nothing else, the incident with the black car had gotten his mind back where it should have been, on the race instead of the heat and his aching body and how uncomfortable he was. He chased futilely after the leaders, trying to run along with them, but, try as he might, they continued to pull away.

Just then, down at the opposite end of the track, a couple of the slower cars crunched together and went spinning in opposite directions. Finally, the yellow flag was being waved all around the track. Jodell wound his way through the wreckage on his way back to the start/finish line to take the caution flag. He was unable to catch the leaders and that meant he was now officially one lap down to them. He didn't like the feeling.

When he came back around past the pits, he saw the towering figure of Bubba holding the signboard. On it he had written in chalk "-1" signaling that he was one lap down. Joe studied the lap count. They still had forty or so laps to go before they needed to come in and fill the car up with gasoline. By the way the car was driving they were not that far from needing tires. On the next pass, Jodell could see that Bubba had scratched a big "X" on the board, telling him not to pit yet.

The caution flag had come at a good time. It gave Jodell time to catch his breath in the hot car. He had had no idea it would be this blistering. He was completely soaked in sweat and the fireproof jumpsuit that Joe had pushed off on him was causing him to itch all over. He pulled a rag out of a pocket and tried to wipe off his face. Only the goggles he wore kept the sweat out of his eyes.

As he circled the track another time under the caution, Jodell had two thoughts. First, he wanted to catch the idiot who was driving the black Chevy that had tried to wreck him. If he got a chance, he would show him a thing or two, and if, in the process, it sent the dumb so-and-so into the outside railing, then so be it. Secondly, he had to do a better job keeping his mind on the business at hand. He had seen how quickly somebody could become hypnotized by the repetition and that had almost put him into the wall. To do it right, a driver had to run each lap as if it were the last, and always be aware of everything going on around him.

The destruction in the fourth turn was finally cleaned up, the wrecker hauling away the last of the smashed cars. They got the signal for one more lap before the green flag, but as the cars tightened up behind the pace car for the restart, Jodell noticed his car was suddenly feeling a little spongy. He discounted that feeling to the slow speed of the car. To try to make sure, though, he wiggled the car from side to side. Everything seemed to feel okay so he shrugged it off as the pace car dropped down onto the pit road, clearing the way for them to race again.

The lapped cars rode on the inside lane while the cars on the lead lap were on the outside, nearest the wall. Several of the lapped cars were fast though, and they were trying desperately to get a lap back. At the green flag, they raced the leaders hard into the first turn, trying to get the advantage.

Being a lapped car himself, Jodell ran deep down into the first turn on the inside, too, trying to outdrive the lead cars on his outside into the corner. He yanked hard on the wheel and tapped the brakes as he set the car up for the turn. The front end dropped as the car set for the corner, but then, all of a sudden, he felt the back end get soft for an instant before the rear of the car sailed around as if it was intent on passing him all by itself. He wrestled desperately with the steering wheel, but he knew at once it was too late. The car was gone.

He spun up through the outside line of cars and, miraculously, didn't hit one of them. Then, not knowing anything else to do, he locked down on the brakes and turned the steering wheel hard to the left, trying to turn the car to the inside. It looped around on him as it sailed through the outside line of traffic, swerving dizzyingly up toward the outside wall. The locked-up brakes kicked up a billowing cloud of tire smoke, blocking the view of the track for the cars behind him.

As the car spun, Jodell was amazed at how quickly everything had happened, yet he had been able to see it all unfold in his mind as if in slow motion, like some bad movie he and Catherine might have watched together without actually seeing. He could feel the jolt of the steering wheel in his hands, sense the wild skew of the rear end, and smell and taste the gritty rubber from the locked-up tires. He braced for impact with the rail, but the car only nudged up against it gently before sliding back down to the inside.

Thankfully, as Jodell had jammed on the brakes he had had the presence of mind to push in the clutch to keep the engine running, even as the car spun of its own free will. The Ford came to rest down on the bottom apron of the track with the front end facing the wrong way, back into oncoming traffic. Jodell didn't even take the time to catch his breath. He threw the shifter up into first gear, jammed his foot down on the gas, and spun the car around getting it headed off into the right direction.

Even as he spun around, Jodell could tell his left rear tire was flat. He limped the car around to the pit road as fast as he dared to go, feeling it shuddering beneath him, seeing shreds of the tire peel away in the mirror. He had to struggle with the steering wheel, twisting it back and forth to keep the car going in a straight line as he rolled slowly through the fourth turn and on to the front stretch pits.

Joe had realized Jodell must be in trouble when he

didn't come around with the rest of the field. Johnny had pointed to the smoke over in turn one about the same time they all heard the screeching of complaining tires.

"Hope Jodell ain't caught up in whatever it is," he had said, echoing all their thoughts. There was no way to know that Jodell *was* the smoke in turn one. Bubba was the first to see him come limping through the fourth turn.

"Boys, here he comes. Let's get ready to change the tires," he yelled.

Bubba stood on the pit road and held the chalkboard high over his head waving it back and forth as the car came slowly down the pit road so Jodell could see where to stop. Meanwhile, the leaders roared by, putting another lap on Jodell as he pulled into his pit space. Bubba jumped out of the way as the car came to a stop and headed for the back of the car. Sure enough, the left rear tire was in tatters. The boys jumped over the wall and went to work changing all four tires and filling the tank with gasoline.

In the car, Jodell sat tensely, trying to gather his emotions. He stretched his arms and rotated his neck as he felt the right side of the car rise up on the jack. Then he felt something cold on his neck. It was an old Army canteen Joe had shoved his way, along with a rag that had been soaked in the ice chest. His cousin was also giving him a thumbs-up. Jodell could only grin back at him sideways and shake his head sadly.

While the boys worked with the tire irons to get the rubber changed, Jodell drank the icy water and wiped his gritty face with the wet rag while he ran over the first part of the race in his mind. He knew he was allowing the track and the heat to beat him more than the other cars out there. He was too worried about the heat, about his discomfort in the car, and was generally being nice to the other drivers. If he had any chance to win, he was going to have to focus on the track, his car, and on going fast. If someone got in his way, then he would simply have to run over him, exactly the way he had been run over by the black Chevy.

Bubba loosened the tire iron on the lug nuts as fast as his big arms could twist. Johnny stood with the handle of the jack raised ready to drop it so Bubba and Clifford could go around and change the left side tires. Clifford had worked feverishly at the right rear while Randy stood there, holding the two new tires that were ready to go on. The jack finally dropped and the four of them ran around to change the tires on the left side. Joe had finished cleaning the windshield and was inspecting what was left of the flat rear tire as they came around. Randy raced to grab two more tires while Bubba and John went to work on the lug nuts. Meanwhile, out there on the racetrack, the leaders kept coming past, putting more laps on them.

The cold water had refreshed Jodell so he turned up the canteen and drained it. He pitched it out the open window and reached down for the shifter. He revved the engine to keep the plugs from fouling, impatient to get back out on the track and try to gain some ground back. He watched out the window, keeping his eye on Joe, waiting for him to wave him off and back onto the track. Johnny finally twisted the jack handle and the car settled back down onto the asphalt. The boys backed away from the car and Joe waved frantically for the car to leave the pits.

In the scoring stand, Catherine finally had time to take a sip on the Coke somebody had passed to her while her driver's car sat on pit road. She needed the cola to settle her nerves after she'd watched Jodell spin wildly down there in the first turn. How all those other cars had missed him she would never know because she'd had her eyes closed the whole time he was spinning. She had not wanted to watch the horrible crash that she had known was a certainty.

When the smoke cleared, she had pried her fingers off her eyes and saw Jodell stopped on the track, the car facing the opposite direction toward the oncoming traffic. She had finally started breathing again when she saw the car spin around quickly and take off back around the track. Her joy had quickly turned to concern when the car did not come back up to speed as it headed through the turn and down the back stretch.

She saw the car come to a stop and the boys scramble around it. When the crew appeared to be working on the car with a purpose, she felt better, even if all the scorers around her were still marking laps on their score sheets while she could only sit and watch her driver in the pits. She continued to sit, watching helplessly until she saw the deep-blue car begin to roll back down the pit road and onto the track.

At least Jodell was okay. But she knew him well enough already to know how he must be suffering, not being able to get to the front.

Jodell smoked the new tires as he spun out, heading back toward the track. He ran hard up through the gears as he pulled out into traffic just as Fireball Roberts came roaring past him. Fireball zipped right on by in his number 22 as if Jodell was standing still.

However, with fresh tires and a desperate new outlook, Jodell was able to quickly catch up and hold his own with the 22. As he followed Fireball down the front straightaway, he glanced over and saw the towering figure of Bubba holding the chalkboard, signaling "22L." That meant the 22 car was the leader! He could save a lap right here if he could only concentrate.

He focused on getting his rhythm back, hitting his throttle points on the track. The clear mind and fresh tires allowed him to pull right up on Fireball Roberts's back bumper. He followed him around the track for two laps, mirroring his every move. He checked the line the experienced driver took, watched how Fireball just nicked the wall between turns three and four every lap, working on his Darlington stripe. Jodell felt he was watching one of the masters at work and he took it all in.

Finally, when he felt the time was right, Jodell got a fender up beside the 22 going down the front stretch and drove him deep into the first turn. Fireball gave him plenty of room and allowed Jodell to move on around him. There was no way, at this point in the race and on worn tires, that Roberts was going to race a lapped car. For Jodell it was a chance to get one of the six laps back that he had lost to the leaders.

After Jodell passed the leader, a strange calm came over him. He and his car were as good as any of these other drivers and he could hold his own with the best of them. That realization gave him a new determination, a new shot of confidence just when he needed it most, and he began to focus in on the next task at hand.

He would go high, low, drive deeper into the corner, or rub a fender if that was what it took. He zoomed past car after car and he felt his conviction building with every position he gained. This was what racing was all about. Passing cars and heading to the front.

But he was smart enough to know, too, that he needed a bit of luck. He actually needed the leaders to have to pit under green-flag racing so he could make up the laps he had lost while he had been forced to stop to change the flat tire. Without that, it wouldn't matter how fast he ran, he could never make up the laps unless most everybody else ahead of him wrecked or broke.

But it wasn't to be. At least, not yet. The caution flag came out twenty laps later when someone dropped a fender in the middle of the third turn. The leaders all pulled in to pit, only allowing Jodell to have gained back one lap instead of the five he had lost on his own stop. That left him still five laps down and still re-starting on the inside with all the other lapped cars when the green flag waved once more.

As the cars came out of the fourth turn and as Jodell saw the flag man raise the green flag high over his head, he was able to get an even jump with the leader and out-raced Fireball Roberts down into the first turn. That let him pull out in front of the leader by the time they had circled back to the start/finish line once more, making up yet another of his laps. Then, he pushed the car hard, trying to stay out in front of the leader. It seemed now that every lap Jodell ran, he ran better than the last. Surprisingly, the heat and the fatigue were no longer factors. Running the right line, picking the time and place to pass, those were what kept his mind occupied.

The race stayed green for a long stretch then and Jodell could eventually feel his car start to skate through the turns, the tires beginning to wear. The leaders passed him a time or two again as he did all he could to keep the car on the track. In the pits, Joe Banker could tell as well, since his driver's times had begun to drop off. Finally, he sent Bubba out to the pit wall with the chalkboard. Scrawled on it was the single-word question, "Tires?"

Jodell saw Bubba with the signboard and knew exactly what he was asking, even before he could read it. The car was getting more and more loose, starting to move all over the track, denying him the ability to do some of the things he knew he had to do to get back in the race. He flashed a thumbs-up sign, signaling that he understood.

Jodell sailed off into the first turn one more time, trying to keep the wheels under the car. Once again, the tires had so little traction left that they would not hold their grip and the rear end began to skate around on him. He was forced get out of the gas to gather the car back up.

No doubt about it. They couldn't afford to wait for another caution period. It was time to come in for the tires.

Suddenly, up ahead in the fourth turn, the pole-sitter, Eddie Pagan, broke loose and rammed hard into the outside retainer, hitting almost head-on, shearing the seemingly indestructible metal of the rail itself. Even from where he was, Jodell could see that it looked like an awful lick and when he steered past, he could tell that indeed, it had been. The entire front end of Pagan's car was crushed back all the way up to the windshield.

The caution flags quickly waved all around the track and the field slowed down accordingly. Clearly, this was going to be a long caution while the car was pulled away and the railing was repaired.

Finally, Jodell thought, a break!

The boys did an even better job on this stop now that they had one real live one on their résumés already. They had also watched some of the other teams and had made adjustments based on what they had observed.

Bubba signaled that they were done with the tires and the gas and Joe quickly waved Jodell off so he could take his place in the field.

"Go! Go! Go!" Joe yelled, even though there was no way Jodell could have heard him inside the car.

"Good stop, guys!" Joe said as he patted each of them on his back. "That's what we need to be doing every time."

"We're just trying to win us a race is all," Johnny said, grinning.

"Yeah, Joe, how we doing anyway?" Clifford asked as he took a big drink of ice water from the water cooler.

"I got us six laps down. What you got Bubba?"

"I got the same."

"Well, we hadn't lost a lap in a while before the tires went on us so I'd say he is finally getting the hang of this."

"Yeah, that busted tire just killed us. Without that we'd be running up at the front," Bubba said, kicking what was left of the tire in frustration.

"With the race Fireball is running, he's gonna be tough to beat. The only way anybody's gonna get him is for him to break something."

"Yeah, the only ones who seem like they can even

give him a run for his money is Little Joe and Curtis."

"Them two is plumb crazy. You see 'em? They have run the wheels off those cars."

"I'd say Fireball is making them run the wheels off trying to keep up. I bet he'll know who old Jodell is as well after the way he ran him the last forty laps or so."

"You have got that right," Bubba said proudly. "He knows old Jodell showed up to race!"

Jodell jockeyed hard for position with the cars around him when the race began again. There were fenders rubbing and bumpers touching as the cars, tightly packed together, rolled through turns one and two. Little Joe and Curtis pressed Fireball hard at the front but were unable to do anything with him. The cars sailed through the third and fourth turn with the faster cars running right up against the rail working on their Darlington stripes. Jodell had gotten good enough at it that he could now hold his own with everyone on the track but Fireball Roberts. Even that had a positive side, though. He studied how Roberts made his way around the track, how he drove and where he drove. He could think of no better education than riding along behind one of the masters of this sport, watching his every move.

The heat and fatigue were really beginning to wear on Jodell as the laps wound down. It had never occurred to him that he needed to be in athletic condition to drive a race. But now he knew. That, too, was something else he needed to work on.

Then, before he realized it, they were inside thirty laps to go. Little Joe Weatherly and Curtis Turner had long since dropped by the wayside, victims of mechanical problems. They had pushed the cars as hard as they would go until their race cars could take no more punishment and had finally surrendered. With them gone, Fireball Roberts's nearest competition was laps and laps behind.

Jodell had seen Bubba's chalkboard with the "thirty laps to go" signal but he had been so tired, it took half a lap for him to realize they were near the end of the race. By that time, he had been passing cars at will, even though he was still six laps behind, and was in tenth place in the field. When he had seen that fact go up on the sign board, a big smile crossed his face as he blew past.

He kicked the accelerator even harder and roared on down the back stretch, passing more cars that were simply limping around on the inside of the track, just trying to hang on till the finish. Then, up ahead, he spied the black Chevy of Dash Rockford. Apparently, Rockford wasn't running as fast as he had been before. Jodell pulled up tight on the Chevy's rear bumper, then eased down to pass him on the inside.

As he did, Dash moved his car downward on the track to cut Jodell off as he ran beneath him going into the corner. The cars touched slightly as Jodell was forced to get hard on the brakes to keep from running into him.

"Uh oh. Here we go again, Mabel," he said, suddenly as alert as he had been all day.

Jodell got back into the throttle in the middle of the turn and quickly made up the lost ground as they exited the corner and headed back down the front straightaway. Once more, Jodell planted himself on Dash's rear bumper as he went through the broad sweep of the corner. He tried to pull up next to him coming off the exit of the corner and get a good run on him down the back stretch so he could pull away.

But as Jodell eased out and tried to accelerate past Rockford down the back stretch, the driver once again cut down on Jodell, trying to block him from passing.

"What is this guy's problem?" Jodell thought as he swung even farther toward the inside, trying to keep the cars from touching and possibly spinning out of control. "Get out of the way!" he yelled in the noisy cockpit. Never mind that the guy could never hear him.

Jodell got an especially good jump on Dash going into the third turn. He out-drove him hard into the corner, which allowed him to finally get past, but his momentum carried him high through the turn, allowing Dash to get back under him. That's when Jodell smacked his Darlington stripe a lot harder than he meant to. Dash was able to maintain his side-by-side position as they swept on through the fourth turn. But being on the outside, Jodell was able to keep his momentum better and he managed to pull ahead by half a car-length as they exited the corner.

Dash was pinched down coming out of the corner, Jodell having the line. The worn tires on the black Chevy lost their grip and the back end slid out from under Rockford. He must have twisted suddenly at the wheel, trying to correct the car, but the rear tire caught unexpectedly while he had the wheel turned toward the outside. Basic laws of physics came into play and the black car shot upwards suddenly, straight into the side of Jodell's Ford.

Catherine, from her seat in the scoring stand, had a perfect view of the tangle all the way through the corner. Somehow, she managed to mark the lap as the two cars flashed past the scoring stand, locked together in a dangerous hug.

Bubba was watching for Jodell to come out of the fourth turn.

"Joe, you see him?"

"Yeah, there!" he said, pointing. "He is on the outside of that black car. Coming there. See?"

"Okay, I got him. Ain't that the same car that he got tangled up with while ago?"

"I believe it is, Bubba. And he still ain't giving him no room."

"Whoa! Watch it!" Bubba danced up and down as the black Chevy spun into the side of Jodell. "Oh no!"

Jodell felt a sharp jolt in the side of his car as they ran side by side toward the first turn. Fortunately he spun down toward the inside when Rockford crunched into him. This time, he kept his foot on the gas and the car started to come all the way around. He let off the gas just as she was completing the three-hundred-sixty-degree spin and felt the tires start to grab. He locked down hard on the brakes and was able to keep the car under control. Once he gathered the car up he was actually surprised to see that it was pointing in the right direction. He threw her up in gear and rolled slowly off, appearing to the screaming crowd as if this crazy spinning around in the middle of a stock car race was something old Jodell Lee did every day just for fun.

Dash wasn't as fortunate. The impact with Jodell pushed the right front fender hard into a tire. He had used Jodell's Ford like some sort of cue ball to bounce off of and send him straight on down the track. The car trailed a heavy plume of smoke and sparks from the damaged front end. Miraculously, no parts fell off either car and, though damaged, they were able to move without use of a wrecker. That kept the yellow flag in the hands of the starter instead of waving over the field.

As Jodell got his speed back up going into the first turn, he could hear the sickening thud and screech of a tire rubbing badly on metal. He could only hope it would hold air until he could get back around to the pits so his crew could change it and punch away the sheet metal. He ran the car gingerly the rest of the way around the course as he struggled to make it back to the pits.

The boys were ready as he came limping in. Bubba was the first out to the car with a ball-peen hammer and a pry bar to work on the fender. Clifford and Johnny helped him with the fender while Joe and Randy checked over the rest of the car for any damage.

When Jodell left the pits, he twisted the car from side to side, checking to see if the front end might have been knocked out of alignment. It didn't seem to be, so he vowed to run the car as hard as he could. He still wanted to pick off some more places but he didn't want to destroy the car trying to move from seventeenth to sixteenth.

Finally, there it was. The white flag. One lap to go.

Jodell Lee could not remember being more exhausted. Even his brain ached from the strain of concentrating so hard for so long. The final lap was almost surreal as he circled as fast as the battered car would go. He could feel every vibration in the wheel, jarring his entire body all the way down to the bone.

The spin had cost Jodell several more laps, leaving him in seventeenth or eighteenth place as the checkered flag fell on Fireball Roberts in the number 22 car. For Jodell, the last twenty laps or so were anti-climatic as he simply tried to hold his own on the track and to keep his temper in check. What had been a superb start on the famed track had all gone for naught thanks to a stubborn, reckless driver. He didn't know who drove the black car but he sure aimed to find out.

For the fans in the stands, the sight of the checkered flag brought them all to their feet. They cheered wildly as Fireball took the checkered flag and made his victory lap. The winner circled the track slowly, arm raised in victory out the window. It had been a six-dollar ticket and no one left the stands feeling that he had not gotten his money's worth.

As Jodell pulled into the pits, he rolled to a stop and sat there exhausted, still trying to squelch his anger. This racing business was simply too expensive to have somebody out there wrecking cars for no reason. After all, this wasn't some short track populated by cars more fit for a junkyard. This was the real thing, bona fide racing, and the seven or eight places they lost from the useless sparring with the black Chevrolet was going to cost them a couple of hundred dollars, easy. That would be enough money to make a difference between breaking even and coming out ahead, to have enough money to make it to the next couple of races or have to sit home until they could save up enough to get back to the track.

The crew was waiting for him. Jodell cut the engine but was too used up to climb out the open driver's window for a bit. Joe and Bubba had to finally help haul him out and lean him up against the beaten and battered side of the car. A big jar of ice water appeared from somewhere. He took a deep drink, poured the rest over his head, and slumped back against the car again. Joe Banker slid down next to him and sat in the dust.

"Jodell, that was some race you ran," he said quietly.

"Yeah, that was tough. Not at all what I expected. Where did we finish?"

"I don't know. You had just made top ten when that cat in the black car spun you out, though."

"You don't say! Top ten, huh? I don't know what that guy's problem was anyway."

"Some of Little Joe's boys were saying that he causes nothing but trouble wherever he races. They said he would just as soon run over you as look at you."

"I believe it. That cat clobbered me twice for no reason. I was racing him clean and he just ran over me." He wiped his face again with the cold rag. Then he remembered somebody. "Where's Catherine?"

"She is supposed to meet us over here . . ."

Suddenly, a dark figure rushed into the midst of them, bent over and grabbed Jodell by the collar, pulling him to his feet. Jodell hardly recognized him without his goggles and helmet, but he knew it could only be one person, and some of the vile words the man was using were new, even to the boys from Chandler Cove.

Dash Rockford had the open collar of Jodell's driving suit clenched in his fist. Jodell tried to get loose and in the process, the two of them began to wrestle.

Bubba Baxter's back was turned when Rockford came running up, but he heard the grunts as the two of them struggled. He closed the distance in two giant steps and gave Rockford a roundhouse punch to the side of the head.

That was enough to cause him to let go Jodell's collar.

Jodell managed a nice uppercut of his own as he dropped to the ground. Rockford was left staggering as race officials with their armbands and a couple of state troopers came running in to break up the brief fight.

Things were still being sorted out when Catherine got there. She ran up and gave the thoroughly exhausted Jodell a bear hug and a kiss for the ages. That's when she spied Bubba, towering over the crowd, his neck puffed up and a menacing scowl on his face, pushing everyone back from his driver. The rest of the boys, urged on by Joe, were busy, trying to get everything packed up as quickly as possible so they could get out of there before any more trouble started.

That's the exact moment when Joyce, Bubba's new friend from Curtis and Little Joe's party the night before, found their spot and came rushing up to hug the big man and give him a kiss on the cheek. He blushed an even deeper shade of crimson, unbulled his neck, dropped his fists, and then grinned sheepishly.

They all laughed, the tension broken. But Jodell watched the troopers escort Rockford all the way across the infield to his tow car before he relaxed.

There would be another day, more and better races to run, with far better finishes for them. And Jodell was certain they had not seen the last of Mr. Dash Rockford either.

* * *

It was close to full-night dark already at the high end of a mountain cove nearly three hundred miles northwest of Darlington. The sun seemed to set early there, blanked out by the trees, their leaves already gone multicolored, and eclipsed by the rocky bluffs of the undulating Smoky Mountains.

In the dusty, dark parlor of a ramshackle mansion, an old man sat alone in the duskiness, listening to the last laps of the race spill out through the static and atmospheric interference on the big radio in the corner. Augustus Smith's face carried a broad smile as he heard a familiar name called in the finishing order.

Slowly, he rose to his feet, got his arthritic knees beneath him, lifted the Mason jar from where it sat on the top of the radio, and tilted it up to his lips.

"Here's to you, Grandpa Lee," he spoke in a respectful whisper after he swallowed the brew. "Looks like you flat raised yourself one fine grandson, you old devil you!"

He turned up the jar once more and took another deep draw, then reached over and switched off the radio before they could start spinning one of those loud, bumping rock-and-roll records he despised so much. Jar in hand, he walked out onto the wide front porch, leaned against one of the columns, and gazed wistfully out across the hollow where the evening haze was already dropping a curtain.

For a moment, he thought he heard something off in the far distance, an eerily familiar noise echoing off the sides of the mountains. He turned his head and listened harder. There it was! The bass-voiced grumble of a whiskey car, the tenor yelping of tires at high speed, grabbing pavement. But then, he could tell it was only the engines of an airplane high overhead, vectoring into the airport at Knoxville or Asheville, and the high-pitched shriek of an old barn owl out there somewhere in the woods anticipating supper.

But Augustus grinned again anyway, then took himself another blissful sip of old man Lee's smooth, sweet brew. With a contented sigh and a smack of his lips, he leaned there against the column and watched peacefully as the dusk slipped inevitably into deep darkness.

GETTING DOWN
TO SERIOUS BUSINESS

I t was Wednesday evening already, but none of them had quite recovered from the weekend yet, from the trip, the race, the party. Grandma had fussed because Jodell had begged off church that night, but he knew the rest of them would be over soon to talk about what had happened, what they could have done differently, what they would do now. Sure enough, Bubba and Joe had shown up shortly after supper. Catherine and her brother, Johnny, were close behind. They claimed some sodas from the refrigerator, Bubba found some leftover biscuits and fried chicken, and they migrated to the shop in the old barn.

Jodell settled down, prone on the dirt floor on one of Grandma's old quilts, stretching out to ease the ache in his still-sore muscles. It had been a long ride back across the Carolinas and over the mountains. Jodell had spent most of it in the backseat asleep, his head in Catherine's lap. Bubba and Joe, fighting drowsiness all the way themselves, had taken turns driving the Ford, towing their race car home. Johnny Holt and the other boys had followed along in the Hudson.

They were surrounded by tools, parts, cars there in the barn. The Darlington race car. The half-rebuilt sportsman car. The old Ford tow car, the whiskey car that had belonged to Joe and Jodell's grandfather. The talk quickly turned to the race the past Monday, and they dissected the whole show, from practice to qualifying to the race itself, the wrecks, the moves, the pit stops, and even to the fight that had wound down the day.

One subject was inevitable, though. And it was Jodell who finally brought it up.

"I don't think I ever considered how expensive it is to go real fast."

"No two ways about it. Speed costs money," Joe agreed.

"Then we are slow as Christmas, 'cause money is one thing we are definitely short of right about now," Jodell said sadly.

"Okay then," Bubba chimed in through a mouthful of biscuit and drumstick. "Let's just give up and throw in the towel and forget about ever winning a big race. That what y'all are saying? 'Cause if it is, I don't want to have a blame thing to do with none of you."

"Whoa, Bub! I don't think we're talking about quitting. We're just trying to figure us an angle here. I could start doing some driving for some of Grandpa's old competitors. That would be risky, considering how tight the Feds are nowadays. And some of those characters don't exactly do business the way Papa Lee did. There's some mean folks in the business these days, I hear."

Catherine's eyes had grown large with the mention of Jodell whiskey-driving again but she stayed quiet for a moment while the conversation turned to the cost of tires, of parts, of replacing crumpled sheet metal, or of simply traveling to races in far-flung foreign places like Atlanta and Charlotte and way down there in Daytona Beach, Florida. Finally, frustrated, the talk faded and they drank their pop quietly and considered the financial magnitude of their need.

Catherine finally broke the silence.

"What we need is a solid sponsor."

Johnny Holt squinted at his sister. He couldn't resist chiding her the way brothers are duly obligated to do their sisters.

"Well, Cath, reckon we can find one hiding out yonder behind the barn or somewhere, waiting to write us a big old check?"

"Yeah," Joe chimed in. "I don't know how it would look to have 'Augustus Smith Bootlegging Company' wrote out on the side of the car in big old white letters."

They all laughed but Catherine had a determined look in her eye. Somehow, they knew instinctively to hush and hear what she had to say.

"I sat with Elizabeth Petty and Margaret Baker in the scoring stand. They told me they would take a sponsorship from just about anybody they could get as long as they were honest. That was the only way they could begin to make all the races."

"Well, honey, we'd take on about anybody, too, but old Gus is the only one so far who has actually peeled off some bills and handed them over," Jodell said.

"Look at it this way," she said, her jaw set. "Gus may have given you the money to buy the car and get you headed to Darlington, but he is not the one who got you to run there and to build the car good enough to qualify it and to finish as well as you did. That you did on your own! You and Joe and Bubba and Johnny and the boys." Catherine's blue eyes were shining now. "You didn't sit around in this old barn and wait for somebody to show up and build you a race car. Y'all went to work and got it done. Now, if you'd work as hard at getting somebody to sponsor you, you might actually get to make some more races."

Joe Banker stood up and dusted off the seat of his jeans as if he were about to go out that very minute and get some money.

"You know what? She's right. I bet I can get the garage to help with a few dollars and some parts if we can run some races around here close by."

"Shorty's filling station up on the highway might give us some tires and gasoline and a few dollars if we'd put his name on the car somewhere," Johnny offered.

"Look, all we need to do is get enough to get me into some races and I can win enough to get us some money to pay the bills." Jodell had forgotten his stiff legs and aching neck. He sat up straight on the quilt. "And if we win enough, it'll sure as shootin' make it easier to find more sponsors."

The conversation got steered then back to the race at Darlington and all they needed to change on the car based on what they had learned there. Joe and Jodell were talking steering geometry while Johnny Holt listened intently. So did Bubba, but he chewed vigorously on a cold chicken wing while he did.

Catherine stayed quiet, letting them talk of tow-in and camber and tie-rods. Suddenly, she cocked her head and spoke, interrupting Joe

"I have an idea."

"Oh, Lord. What now?" he asked, clearly irritated.

She threw him a dark look but went on.

"I was about to say that Daddy knows Mr. Williams at the Bubble Up bottling plant over close to Kingsport. He owns the plant. I know his daughter, Cissy, too."

"So? We got plenty of soda pop already," Joe said impatiently, showing his mostly empty soda bottle.

"Wait a minute, Joe," Johnny interrupted. "I think I know where she's going here. We do know the Williams family real well. They come down to our church most Sundays. Daddy's gone fishing a time or two with Mr. Williams."

Catherine had a smile on her face now.

"Jodell, you know that case of soda you got when you won the race at Meyer's farm? Well, that was Bubble Up. Remember?"

Jodell still had a quizzical look on his face. What did Bubble Up have to do with front-end alignment and steering box setup?

"All I remember is Bubba drinking up most of them before I ever got a taste of one."

"Look, it means they are at least interested in stock car racing if they kicked in a case of drinks for a prize. We could talk to Mr. Williams. He might be willing to do something. I know they spend money advertising on the radio and at the high school football games. They might want to try to hit the crowds at the races. As hot and dusty as it gets out there, that would be the perfect place to see an ad for something cold to drink."

Only two days later Jodell found himself sitting on a plastic-covered couch in the carpeted reception area of the offices of the Bubble Up bottling plant. He could hear the roar of equipment and the distant chiming of bottles clinking together and the whole place smelled of lemons and some kind of disinfectant. But at least Catherine was there with him, sitting next to him on the bright-orange couch, nervously fingering the straps of her black purse.

She looked beautiful, her hair pulled back, dressed in a black skirt and flower-print blouse and wearing the necklace he had given her for her birthday. Jodell felt as if he was choking, though. He wore the same white dress shirt and tie he put on every Sunday morning for church, but today, they seemed like a noose around his neck. He had intended to wear his Sunday suit but Catherine had suggested that he not.

"We need to look as if we are serious, businesslike, but we don't want to look like we are putting on airs," she had said.

Jodell tried to collect his thoughts, to go over in his mind the points he wanted to make with Mr. Williams. The big clock in the shape of a soda bottle on the wall behind the receptionist's desk showed it was past time for their appointment already, but the woman kept typing away at something, looking over the tops of her funny-shaped glasses at the paper in front of her. She had been polite when they came in but had paid them no mind since.

Maybe Mr. Williams was simply too busy to see them. Mixing up all that pop had to be a demanding job. Maybe he would simply laugh at them, tell them to be on their way, that he had soda to make and sell and didn't have time to listen to somebody begging for money for a silly race car. He was about to suggest to Catherine that they leave, get out before they embarrassed themselves, coming with hat in hand, pleading for money.

But then, something buzzed on the woman's desk and a tiny voice squawked something they couldn't hear.

"Mr. Williams will see y'all now," she said. "Right through there."

Jodell stood awkwardly then helped Catherine to her feet. She smoothed the front of her skirt, then smiled at him and he instantly felt better. After all, the worst he could do was say "no."

They walked over to the large oak door and Jodell turned the polished brass handle. Behind the door was a surprisingly cluttered office. There were files and papers strewn everywhere, even piled on top of cases that held dark green bottles of soda.

Homer Williams waited for them behind a large partner's desk. He was clearly finishing up a conversation on the telephone so he motioned them to have a seat in a pair of chairs facing the desk. Jodell sank down uneasily and waited nervously, tapping his fingers on the arm of the chair. Catherine surveyed the clutter in the office, thinking how well she could organize everything if she had a chance.

Williams finished his conversation with a quick laugh and "goodbye," dropped the phone back into its cradle, rose and stepped from behind the desk with a friendly-enough grin on his face.

"Catherine dear, it is so good to see you again." He gave her a "best uncle" hug. "And you must be Robert!"

Jodell took the offered hand and gave it a firm

shake. He had to study a moment to think who "Robert" might be. His name was Jodell Bob. Not Robert. Mr. Williams must have assumed Bob was short for Robert.

"Yessir. Most people call me 'Jodell,' sir."

"Ah, then, Jodell it is. Catherine, how are your mother and daddy?"

"They are fine, sir. He's always complaining he never has time for fishing."

"I know, I keep telling him that I'm going with him one day but this business keeps me way too busy as well." Williams sat back behind the desk, leaned back in his chair and put his hands behind his head. He wasn't even wearing a tie. Jodell was thankful he had not worn the Sunday suit now. Williams nodded toward a stack of blueprints on the desktop. "We're getting ready to expand the plant and that's taking up too much of my time. I don't have time to get out and sell the product like I need to."

"Well, we don't want to take too much of your time," Catherine said hastily.

"Don't be silly. I can surely take a minute to visit with the daughter of an old fishing buddy. Helps to break up the day. Now, what I can do for you?"

Catherine took a deep breath and dived into deep water headfirst.

"Well, Jodell is a race car driver, Mr. Williams. He just drove at the big race down at Darlington on Labor Day."

"You don't say? I listened to that race on the radio," Williams said, interrupting her. "You ran in it?"

"Well, yessir, I did. I got spun out late or I would have had a real good finish."

"Was that you that got bushwhacked by that old Dash Rockford there at the end? That so-and-so is about the dirtiest driver I have ever seen, pardon my language, Catherine. Bob Lee! Now I see. That was you!"

The man was clearly getting excited now, leaning forward with his hands on the desk in front of him. Jodell could feel his nervousness melting away as he quickly gave Williams a cockpit view of the race with all its bumps and spins. Catherine sat back and let the two of them talk like two old friends telling each other racing stories.

"Well, I sure didn't know anybody from around here was racing in the big Darlington race," Williams said, finally sitting back in his leather chair. "I'd of certainly been pulling for you, Jodell."

"I could have certainly used it."

Williams stood suddenly, stepped to a big plate-glass window that overlooked the machinery where his company made its own brew. He rocked back and forth for a moment, his back to them, obviously considering something. Catherine and Jodell exchanged looks but they knew now was not the time to interrupt the man's musings. He had a thoughtful look on his face when he turned around toward them again.

"I've been fooling around with racing for a while now. I've been giving away cases of soda for prizes at some of the tracks around here. Not much of an investment but it gets me a little exposure at the finish when they present it to the winner."

"Jodell won a case of your soda out at the Meyers speedway last year," Catherine proudly offered.

"Is that a fact? So, tell me, Jodell. Are you

planning on running any more of the Grand National races?"

"Well sir, I sure hope to if we can afford it. We are going to save the car we ran at Darlington and take it to Daytona for the opening of the big new track down there in February. You know they're not going to run on the old beach course anymore. We have a sportsman car we wrecked a couple of months ago that we almost have fixed up enough to run it again. We plan on running it as much as we can before all the tracks close down for the winter but it's a mighty expensive proposition, even on the local tracks."

"Well, looky here. I don't want to be presumptuous or anything but there's something I'd like to propose to y'all if you'd be willing to listen. It's my opinion that stock car racing is set to take off big time. I think it is the best sport to appeal to the common man and there's a lot more common men out there than there are those who play golf or tennis. Football, now that's a good game but you got to go to college to really do any good at it. Baseball's fine but it's hard for a man to put himself in Mickey Mantle's place, hitting a ball being thrown at you like that. But stock car racing, that's different. Any manjack of us can imagine ourselves behind the wheel of a car that doesn't look so different from the one in the garage out back. And it's simple. Whoever can drive the best car the fastest and avoid getting wrecked up can win the whole race. Yessir, I'm convinced this sport is about to take off like nobody's business." He turned back to the window and watched his plant at work again for a few seconds. Jodell and Catherine swapped looks again, not allowing themselves to think it would all be this easy.

When he talked, he spoke to the glass in front of him. "What if . . . maybe . . . that is if you wanted to . . . we could work something out where you could run all the races you needed to run?"

His words seemed almost hesitant, as if he were reluctant to make his offer.

"Well, Mr. Williams, we . . ."

"Now don't say 'no' yet, Mr. Lee." Williams spun from the window and seemed to transform into full salesman mode. "We are about to triple the bottling capacity of this plant. That means we are going to have to sell three times as much soda as we do now. And it seems to me that all the folks . . . especially young folks . . . who go to stock car racing would be prime prospects to buy our product. Now, I could go out there to the tracks and hire me some old boy to wear a sandwich board and advertise my Bubble Up on it. Or I could put me up a billboard on the way to the track or hire me a crop-duster to pull around a banner up there in the sky. But you know what? Every eye in every single one of those tracks is going to be on one thing for the entire race. That's the cars down there on that track. Am I right?"

"Yessir. They do watch the cars . . ."

"And I can't think of any better place to have my name plastered than all over the side of one of those race cars where everybody is looking in the first place when they get hot and dusty and thirsty. Can y'all?"

"Well, no sir, I . . ."

"But not just on any car. I need to be on a car that's going to run the whole race and not spend it up on a jack in the pits where can't nobody see my name on the side of it. Somebody that intends to be out front where everybody will see it and down there in victory lane with all the folks watching and the flashbulbs going off from all the newspaper reporters and the newsreel cameras rolling for the television. Can y'all picture that? Talk about advertising! I gotta figure that would be about the best advertising a man could get right there! And well worth whatever it cost to keep the car and the driver out there. And just imagine being in that winner's circle down there in Daytona! What do you think, Jodell?"

The man had hardly paused for a breath. Jodell was nodding excitedly through the entire spiel.

"That's exactly how I feel, Mr. Williams. And I certainly intend to keep my car at the front. That's why I race. To win. Shoot, far as I'm concerned, there's no such word in the English language as 'second.'"

"Well, bottom line is I got to sell triple the soda I been selling. We got to get all the exposure we can get to do that. And seems to me you got a perfectly good rolling billboard out there making circles for the whole danged race."

"I don't know if I can sell soda but I can sure get the Bubble Up name into the winner's circle."

"Well, here's my proposal. If you were good enough to win the races you won and to do as well as you did at Darlington with no sponsor, then I expect you will get my name on victory lane more often than not. Or at least have it up front enough so some of them folks will develop a powerful enough thirst for my soda. I would consider it an honor if you would allow me to sponsor you in the races you need to run between now and Daytona. Then, I'll sponsor you to go down there and teach that Dash Rockford a thing or two. We'll see how it goes for the rest of the year after that. What kind of money you thinking about?"

The question caught Jodell off guard. He had a rough figure in mind but actually saying such a stu pendous number out loud at that very moment would certainly queer the whole deal. It was Catherine Holt who reached into her purse and pulled out a set of typewritten sheets of paper and handed them to Williams. Jodell's mouth fell open.

"This is what we figured it would cost to get us going and to be ready to compete in Daytona," she said, matter-of-factly.

They had talked among themselves about what and how much they needed and had even scrawled some rough figures on the back of an envelope. Catherine had obviously put those numbers into a formal proposal.

"Looks like y'all did your homework. I appreciate that. I love racing but this is a business investment for me. I still have to justify what I do to my partners and stockholders. I won't have any problem selling this." He paused for a moment as he studied the columns on the last page, then looked up with a frown. Jodell's stomach turned over. Oh, Lord. What had Catherine tacked on that would blow the whole deal? And when they were so close, too. "I see two problems here, folks. First, I suspect you will need at least twenty percent more than you think you will. That's a small price to pay to make sure you have what you need to compete. Let's just up that across the board. Skimp here and you'll not win like we need for you to. And there's one other big thing missing."

Once more, Jodell and Catherine exchanged glances. Catherine was sure she had put down everything Jodell and Joe and Bubba and Johnny had talked about.

"What's that?" Jodell finally asked.

"How you going to live for the next half a year? Even with my help, you'll still need to plow that purse money you're gonna win back into the cars. Look, I got a job here for you if you want it. It's hard work and I expect you to get it all done, but you can be off when you need to be, and it'll sure get you in shape to be inside a hot old race car for three or four hours at a time."

Jodell couldn't believe it. They were getting all they had intended to ask for and more.

"Absolutely! I'll take it."

"Good! Now, all we need to do . . . shoot, listen to me, rambling on. I haven't even asked y'all what you came here to talk with me about today. Where are my manners?"

He had a curious look on his face when Catherine and Jodell burst into laughter. In the course of the next fifteen minutes they worked out the basics of a deal that would let Jodell get the sportsman car fixed so they could run a few races, then get the '58 Ford they had run at Darlington ready to race at the new Daytona speedway the middle of February.

Now Jodell could concentrate on racing and winning. The only other prospects had been to drive loads of whiskey for wild-eyed outlaws that now ruled the roost in that business or go to work full time in the mill with Bubba. Neither would have left much time or heart for racing or preparing to race. Now they had a means to an end they could only have dreamed of a few days before. As he left the Bubble Up plant, hand in hand with Catherine, Jodell couldn't wait to crawl under the sportsman car, to line it up and drive it off the first turn at speed somewhere, to climb into the Ford and zoom around the amazing new track rising up from the sand a few miles off the beach in Florida.

But for the time being, he could only hold Catherine close to him as they drove back to the barn to tell everyone the great news. Hold her and kiss her and tell her how much he loved her, how much he appreciated all she had done to help him live his dream.

The next several weeks were busy. The wrecked sportsman car was repaired and made ready to race, then tested on the same mountain roads where Jodell had learned to drive. Bubba spent several evenings painting the Bubble Up logo on the side of the cars and spiffing up the number 34 that was written on each side door. Homer Williams gave it his hearty approval and had three rolls of pictures made of it with Jodell proudly standing by it. He would use some of the photos to show to all their customers and to put on the calendar they would distribute in the new year.

Now, they needed to find a race so they could take the car to the track and try it out. Jodell caught wind of three events that would be run on a Thursday, Friday, and Saturday night at a series of small tracks down around Asheville. They could make a quick trip of it and maybe clear a few dollars after expenses if they won.

"When we win," Bubba kept reminding them. "When we win, boys. Y'all need to get used to winning 'cause we're about to do some of it."

These races would get them used to running several nights and days in a row, experience they would need when they seriously followed the Grand

National circuit the next year. And as good a driver as Jodell was, he still was short on experience compared to Curtis Turner, Little Joe Weatherley, Junior Johnson, Fireball Roberts, the Pettys, and all the others they would be trying to out-race. He could use the next few months to go to school on the smaller tracks before they jumped into the really deep water down in Daytona. They knew that the brand spanking new two-and-a-half-mile-long wonder would be a tough sea to sail for someone with little experience.

At least everyone would be on equal footing on such a radically different kind of track. Jodell hoped to use his own hard-won knowledge of high speeds and hairpin turns to great advantage once they hit the high banks of the new oval.

And the long days spent loading the cases of soda onto delivery trucks at the plant in the last hot days before autumn set in didn't bother Jodell in the least. Every case of drinks got him closer to Daytona. Every bottle helped in its own little bit to get him nearer to the first time he would send the Ford around one of those wonderfully high-banked turns he had been reading about.

Every drop of the sweet liquid he sent out the doorway of the plant seemed an anointing, a blessing that helped get him that much closer to savoring the sweet taste of victory in the biggest shrine to speed on the planet.

DIRT GLORY

I t was a cool, clear Thursday morning, and an early traveler could feel a breath of cooler autumn air already. The leaves along the roadside were glorious by now, too, their canopy of color seemingly set ablaze by the quickly rising sun. Jodell, Joe, and Bubba should have still been sleepy from a late night beneath the older sportsman race car, but the cool air and the Technicolor light show Mother Nature was providing for them and the prospects of finally getting back on a racetrack had them wide-eyed. They had pointed the tow car southeast, to the highway that eventually led to a dirt track they had heard about that was tucked in the bowl between two mountains about an hour north of Asheville. It was appropriately dubbed "Twin Mountain Speedway."

The track was a third of a mile in diameter, was said to have a good surface, and drew respectable crowds, even on a weeknight. But most importantly, it also drew some decent competition and paid a hundred and fifty dollars to the winner of the main event. The experience and the money made the half-day drive through the vividly colored mountains well worth their while, and it was on the way to two other tracks they could drive to on Friday and Saturday nights.

It was midafternoon when they rolled up to the track gate, the race car in tow behind them, and there were already a number of others ahead of them, both in line to pull in as well as in the middle of the track in the area that served as the pits. The information they had gotten on the track was right. The dirt surface seemed smooth, was obviously well prepared, and should be fast.

Jodell smiled. That's the way he liked it.

As soon as they had located themselves a spot in the pits, Bubba Baxter was off on a quest to find the nearest open concession stand. He had finished off the picnic lunch Grandma Lee had packed for them while the farm was still in their rearview mirrors. Jodell had only managed to claim a chicken wing and a biscuit. Joe Banker had only gotten a single biscuit.

When they had stopped in Rocky Fork, near the state line, to swap drivers, Joe had immediately gone to the basket in search of a breast or thigh once they were on the road again. He came up empty, his face an anguished mask in Jodell's mirror.

"Bubba, what on God's green earth happened to our dinner?" he whined.

"Sorry, Joe. What? Did you say something?" Bubba said, cupping a hand around an ear as if he couldn't hear above the roar of the big Ford's engine and the wind whipping past their rolled-down windows.

"Shoot fire! Grandma fixed enough for dinner and supper!"

"You mean that little old snack?" Bubba said, winking at Jodell. But he still kept a wary eye on the mirror, fully expecting a gnawed chicken bone to the back of the head at any minute.

And the feast still wasn't enough to keep Bubba from setting off in search of sustenance. Jodell and Joe got busy unhooking the race car and unloading the trunks of both cars. First were the stacks of tires, a result of their Darlington experience. While they had never had tire trouble on a dirt track before, they had learned at Darlington that it paid to be ready for anything. Tires that weren't needed could just as easily be loaded up again and hauled to the next race. It had become quite clear that they had been spending too much time and worry trying to chase down tires and spare parts and in redoing things on the car when their efforts would have been better focused out there on the track, learning how to consistently go fast.

They were well into getting things organized when Bubba showed up with a big stack of hot dogs cradled lovingly to his chest like a baby in a blanket. He gave Joe a couple of the dogs as a peace offering and passed another one over to Jodell then settled down in the shade of the race car with the other half dozen. Jodell extracted three bottles of Bubble Up that rested in crushed ice in the red Pleasure Chest cooler Joe had just pulled out of the trunk of the tow car. Those dark green bottles were the first perks of their new sponsorship. They would get all the free pop they wanted when they went to the races from now on.

Lunch finished, Jodell climbed through the window of the '38 Ford and began to strap himself in for his first spin around the track. He fired the engine and revved it up, listening to the bass rumble as if it was sweet music. He shoved the shifter into reverse and backed the car out of its slot, kicked the car up into first gear, then rolled out onto the track. He took a slow lap, getting a feel for the surface.

The car felt good beneath him, like a well-trained steed pulling at its tether. They had tested it out as well as they could on the back roads around the farm but that was a poor replica of an actual track. The car responded beautifully to his commands as he took the second lap a tad more aggressively. He picked up his speed at the end of the third trip around but still did not open the car up fully. With only three other cars on the track with him at the moment, he had plenty of time to get the car up to speed.

After the fourth lap he was ready.

He steered out of the fourth turn of the tight track and finally stood hard on the gas. The Ford literally leapt beneath him as if she was ecstatic to finally be freed. Almost immediately, though, he had to stand on the brakes as the first turn came up fast. He stayed in the brakes only long enough to get the car's front end down and to set its line through the corner. The smooth surface of the track allowed him to hold the desired route through the turn without the car bouncing all around on him as it had done on some of the rougher tracks they had run.

Joe clicked the stem on his stopwatch as the car flashed in front of him and wrote the time down on his clipboard. After five laps under speed, he noted happily that each circuit had gotten faster, but by the tenth lap the times had begun to level out. That would be their top speed with the current setup. With that, he had Bubba swing out the signboard and bring Jodell in.

"How'd she feel, Joe Dee?"

"Real good. That motor is perfect."

"Good thing. We couldn't do a lot about it now if she turned up sour. You improved times on every lap till here then you leveled out." Joe pointed to the rows of figures on the clipboard.

"Yeah, I was about flat-out by then."

"What about the handling?"

"The track is great. This is some of the smoothest dirt we've been on. It's gonna be a fast track all right, and we got a fast car to run it."

"What can we do to make it faster?" It was Bubba, asking the pertinent question in his usual flat delivery.

They looked at each other, then got busy, hashing through their options, looking for extra speed and better handling, yet not wanting to make something worse while trying to make it better. With the track as short as it was and the motor as nearly perfect as they thought they could make it, there was not much else they could do. They settled on a tweak or two on the front end. A little more camber might do the trick.

And so it went for the balance of the afternoon. Another of their lessons from Darlington was to attack anything they did in a logical, methodical way. Set a baseline and then work the changes off the known benchmark. If experimenting wasn't done in a logical sort of way then it was more difficult to learn what worked and what didn't, and where mistakes had been made. Most drivers and crews showed up to have fun first and try to win the race second. Jodell and his crew had made a sacred pact that if they were going to make their living at this racing thing, the fun would be in the winning and they had to be serious and professional about the way they approached it.

By the end of practice they had the car dialed in about as solidly as they could get it and Joe's stopwatch confirmed they were among the fastest cars there, in a group with only two or three others. One of the cars was the local hot shot. Another was a regular from a track they would run on Friday night. Those drivers' experience with this particular track was reflected in their lap speeds. The rest of the field would be made up by drivers that Jodell instinctively knew he would best try to avoid. Get too close to some of those cowboys and his day as well as his payday would be a bust.

Darkness fell on the speedway early, the effect of fall already, and the primitive lights were switched on. Surprisingly, they did a better job than Jodell had expected, illuminating the track fairly well with no apparent shadowy spots that could play tricks on a driver's depth perception. The stands had already begun to fill up with spectators. The next time they looked up from the all-over inspection they were doing on the car, the crew from Chandler Cove saw that every nook and cranny of the racetrack was filled with fans, impatiently waiting for the action to begin.

The first sound of engines brought the crowd to its feet. The "limited" cars or "junkers" were lining up for the first race of the double header. The cars themselves appeared ready for the junkyard already, merely painfully loud, rolling piles of smoke-belching, backfiring sheet metal and cracked windshields with maybe a roll bar added for safety. But from the dents and crumples in the cars, it appeared there would be plenty of entertainment for the spectators if they wanted to see wild fender-banging.

Bubba took his customary spot by the inside rail while Jodell and Joe crossed over the track to try and escape some of the impending dust cloud. They also wanted to get a good view so they could see how these cars negotiated the track. They managed to wrangle some standing room at the top of the grandstand against the back railing. The junkers pulled out onto the track and slowly began to circle in a motley, pitiful parade. Joe and Jodell grinned at each other. This was a far cry from the spectacle they had a been a part of only a short time ago in Darlington.

The flag man waved the green flag and the cars roared off into the first turn. And roar was exactly what they did. With their unmuffled "straight pipes," they were threatening to render deaf anyone in the crowd without plugs or wads of cotton in their ears. By the second lap, the fans were already getting their money's worth as the circling heaps suddenly accumulated in a huge screeching, smoking pile of debris in the middle of the second turn.

One of the cars had swerved around sideways when the driver got on the gas too quickly in the middle of the corner. In a flash, two other cars spun wildly to miss the first car. In the ensuing dust cloud, a half dozen more cars piled in before everyone could manage to get stopped. The crowd was on its feet, roaring its collective approval for the demolition they were witnessing. The yellow flag came out while all the cars got straightened out and moving more or less in the right direction again.

None of the cars were damaged much more than by the addition of another fresh dent or two among all the others they carried already. The race was restarted and stopped several more times before the twenty-five laps which made up the distance had spun out. The checkered flag finally waved on the cars that had outlasted the carnage and remained running on the track. In addition to the wrecks, a flurry of overheated radiators, flat tires and exploded engines had done in many of the cars.

For the winner, it was a jubilant time. The young lad in 401 overalls, no shirt, and work boots couldn't have been more than eighteen or nineteen. He jumped out of the car and danced around as if he had just won a race at Darlington or North Wilkesboro. His crew, clearly even younger than their driver, came running up, jumping and waving their arms in a wild celebration. The crowd joined in, too, loving the magic of a first-time victory. Who knew where this youngster might end up someday, spurred on by the intoxication of finishing first?

Jodell and Joe quickly made their way back across the track and found Bubba there already, slapping a fog of dust off his clothes.

"Well, boys, y'all ready to go out there and kick some butts?" Jodell asked. He reached through the driver's-side window and retrieved his helmet.

"We're ready!" Joe yelped. The fender-banging in the preliminary had his adrenaline pumping.

"Ain't nobody out there can catch us," Bubba offered, then sneezed lustily from all the dust he had inhaled.

"We're starting fifth so I'm gonna just have to be

patient. If I can avoid the wrecks then maybe we can bring this thing home first."

Jodell swung his right leg in through the window, slid in, sat down, and fumbled for the belts.

"That's exactly right!" Joe said as he slapped the top of the car with his palm. "I got to go and see if they have a scorer that we can use. I want to try and watch the race from the pits."

They pushed the car to the starting line and Bubba cleaned the windows and the front of the radiator one last time, for all the good it would do. The dust from the first race still hung suspended like a haze in the lights.

The crowd waited impatiently while the officials tried to get the field lined up and ready to go. They were mostly working folks, out on a weekday night to see some racing, but they had to climb out of bed early the next day for work. They were ready to see more action and right now. The drivers were finally given the signal to start their engines and the crowd joined the thunder as the cars began to roll slowly off the line.

Jodell revved the Ford's engine as they rolled away and the car felt good to him, its pulsing motor, the way the tires spun through the dirt, the stiffness of the steering beneath his hands, all a natural symmetry he had come to recognize and appreciate. The big unknown would be how much the track might have changed since the last afternoon practice. The spin-fest of the first race had churned up a lot of dust and dirt into the corners. What effect it would have on the handling for this race was an unknown. The answer would come in two more laps when they received the green flag.

Jodell tightened his belts, making sure he was

secured in his seat. He reached up and gripped the wheel tightly with his left hand and the shifter with his right hand. He looked at the cars around him then up at the flag man standing on the platform next to the outside railing. He was signaling that the field would get the green next time by as the pace car pulled off the track.

As they rolled in close tandem down toward the first turn, Jodell could see the huge form of Bubba Baxter standing in his usual spot during a race in which there would be no pit stops, closely studying each car as it rolled past. It was a comforting sight. Joe Banker, ever mindful of the dust, perched on top of the tow car in the center of the tiny infield. That vantage point would help somewhat but there would be no escaping all the dust.

Jodell booted the gas pedal the instant he saw the fluttering green flag. The car directly in front of him never came up to speed and Jodell was into his rear end before either of them knew what happened. The driver had obviously missed a gear and Jodell drop-kicked him out of the way. Instinctively, he twisted the steering wheel of the Ford to the left and simply bulldozed the wide-eyed driver out of his way.

Jodell felt the impact and heard the grinding crunch of sheet metal but he didn't have either the time nor the inclination to worry about possible damage. He was more concerned about avoiding getting run over himself by all the other cars behind as they accelerated toward the first turn.

The car he had tagged spun out of his way but collected two other unfortunate cars before the rest got by. The ensuing dust cloud erased any view of the front stretch as the field came into the third and fourth turns. The leader blissfully stayed on the gas as the cars came out of the corner and drove blindly into the grimy fog.

The second and third place cars followed the leader through the dust. Jodell tucked right up on the third-place car's rear bumper and followed him in, too. He could only hope that driver could see more than Jodell could. He braced for impact but kept his foot on the accelerator anyway.

Then, as they emerged from the other side, Jodell could see the yellow flag waving from the flag stand. He slowed down and caught his breath. If this was any indication of how the rest of the seventy-five laps would go then it was going to be a long, dusty night!

The race restarted a few laps later with the cars in single file. This one went smoothly as Jodell trailed the lead cars off into the tight first turn. The rear end kicked out and slid around as the car took the corner but Jodell kept one foot on the gas slightly to keep power to the rear wheels and tapped the brake to set the front end of the car down. The car bit, taking the corner and staying glued to the rear of the car ahead.

The race settled down then, and several laps unspooled as the drivers got accustomed to the feel of the track. By the tenth lap, Jodell had come around the third-place car, slipping past as the driver went high going into the third and fourth turn. The front two cars, piloted by drivers who were obviously familiar with this track, had pulled away. Now clear of the other car, Jodell took off in pursuit.

On the fifteenth lap, the caution flag was out again as three cars spun coming off the second turn, swerving wildly and bringing the crowd to their feet again. The leaders were stacked up, one, two, three, as they slowed for the yellow flag.

On the restart, Jodell did his best to try to jump down to the inside of the blue second-place car as they headed off into the first turn. He got a fender against the rear of the Buick just as they were setting their line for the turn. The cars rubbed with a screeching grind before Jodell had to back out of the throttle to keep from spinning the car ahead of him.

But he didn't give up. He pulled back up on the bumper of the blue car as they hit the third turn.

"Move over, buddy. Move over and let this old Ford eat some track," he ordered.

But the cars circled bumper to bumper for several more laps before Jodell was able to slip by when the Buick's driver, studying Jodell in his mirror, made the slightest miscalculation and slid a few feet high. Five laps later, Jodell put a fender on the red Ford which was leading the race, loosening him up just a tad as the cars raced into the third turn. Jodell boldly took the lead in the corner and held on as the cars raced through the growing dust cloud which had by then enveloped the track. Jodell deftly wiped the sweat from his brow with his fingers as he finally caught a piece of clear track for the moment. Only the goggles he wore kept the sweat and dirt out of his eyes.

He held the lead by several car lengths, slowly pulling away from the Ford and the Buick. Then, Jodell began to pass slower cars all around the track as they hit the thirtieth lap. Approaching the first turn, though, he suddenly approached a pack of slower cars. He tried to go low, saw no opening, then went high. That's where he found himself, stuck up on the outside, as they came off the corner. He was boxed in by the slower cars heading into turn three when two of the cars suddenly swerved together and locked fenders.

Jodell tried to cut underneath but just as he did, the two cars started to spin, and as he got his front end past them, the inside car broke loose and turned downward on the track. The front bumper of the spinning Hudson clipped the rear of Jodell's Ford just as he was inches from clearing the spinning cars. Jodell's stomach flip-flopped as he felt the car turn suddenly towards the outside of the track. He didn't even think about it as he wrestled with the wheel trying to keep the car under control.

The Ford suddenly spun around and around as he tried in vain to get it back headed straight and going in the right direction. Jodell could only close his eyes and pray that no one would careen into him as he tapped the metal railing that lined the outside of the track. The impact of the rear end against the railing bounced the front end up and into the fence as well. But with the slow speeds they were running on this track, the impact was little more than banging into the wall at Darlington, like picking up his Darlington stripe on Labor Day down in South Carolina.

Jodell used the bump into the rail to gather control again, then threw the shifter up into first gear and gunned the gas. The car's tires spewed dust as they spun and he took off after the rest of the field. The race leaders had zoomed past him during the melee with the slower cars and were already closing up on him again as he worked to get back up to speed and struggled to keep from getting lapped. He kept one eye on the leaders in his mirror and the other on the tail end of the field as the caution flag waved over the track.

When it was all sorted out, Jodell was left in

eleventh place, the last car on the lead lap. The old number 34 had a long way to go with forty laps left. They had all agreed the way to win the race was to stay out of trouble. Now, their worst fears had come to pass. With all the traffic from the lapped cars and with ten cars ahead of him, it would be tough to make it back to the front of the pack. But at least the car was rolling and seemed none the worse for its trip to the guardrail, no sheet metal rubbing against a tire or anything else potentially fatal. Jodell struggled to keep his wits about him, to concentrate on not pushing too hard, not losing his composure and maybe there would still be time. But there was certainly not enough race remaining to overcome another major bobble should he make one. And every position they might finish behind the winner was that much less money they would make.

He was hot, sweating, the cool morning autumn air long since turned to Indian summer hot. His coveralls were soaked all the way through. Under the slow speed of the caution, he tried to catch his breath in the stifling heat of the cockpit of the car, to use his hand at the window to scoop up a little air and send it inside. The primitive shoulder belts dug deeply into his shoulders. Somehow, he never noticed it when he was racing wheel-to-wheel, but the discomfort was certainly there when they circled slowly. As much as he wanted to, for some mighty good safety reasons he could not loosen them. He had heard horror stories of drivers thrown from their cars, run over, killed, when they kept belts too loose or failed to buckle them at all.

Finally, mercifully, the green flag waved and the field charged off once again into the first turn, resurrecting the dust storm. Jodell set his jaw and tightened his grip on the steering wheel with his left hand while with his right, he grabbed the shifter and jammed it down into the next gear. Foot hard to the floor, he felt the 34 respond beneath him and jump ahead. He swung it wide going into the corner as the inside was blocked by a slower car but another driver slid up in front of him, blocking that route as well. He fought the impulse to try to split them, to do something foolhardy, and waited until he saw the opening he needed. When it came, he took it and thanked goodness again for their attention to detail in setting up the car. It did exactly what he asked of it when he asked and he easily put the two blocking cars behind him.

The laps clicked off as Jodell tenaciously made his way back to the front, but, as was to be expected, the closer he got to the leaders, it took more and more track distance to get past each car. The slower cars continued to get in the way, blocking the fast line around the track. Jodell had to steel himself to stay patient in the swirling dust bowl in which he found himself.

With fifteen laps to go there was another wild spin involving four cars. The caution flag was forced to wave again while the track was cleared. For Jodell it was a chance to pull in tight on the four cars that were still ahead of him. It would also give him a clean shot at the front cars without all the slower cars there, getting in his way.

Jodell was confident that if he could set his own line, not one dictated by some slower, inexperienced driver, then he could pass anyone on the track. He forgot about how tired and dirty and hot and dusty and thirsty he was. There would be plenty of time to be miserable after the checkered flag had flown.

As he came out of the fourth turn one more time, he stretched his left arm, trying to get the circulation going again, to work out a pesky cramp that threatened to seize the muscle again like a dog bite. Out of the corner of his eye, he saw the dust-covered figure of Bubba still standing in his spot at the end of the front-stretch railing, one foot propped up on the rail. Jodell wondered if Bubba's fine paint job on the Bubble Up logo would still be visible through all the dust that now coated the car.

Joe stood nervously on the hood of the car in the infield. He held his trusty stopwatch in his hand, trying to time Jodell and some of the leaders, but with all the slow cars on the track it was impossible to get accurate numbers. He was pleased with the way Jodell was driving, with the way the Ford was working, but the four cars were still in the way and several of them were very fast and there would only be thirteen laps to go when they took the green. He was already wondering what fifth-place money might be.

Jodell prepared for the restart. He wiped his grimy face one last time with the rag from his front coverall pocket. The cars zoomed away with Jodell as close as he dared be to the bumper of the number 16 Olds that was riding in fourth place. He tried to get underneath him as they hit the first turn but a car on the inside pushed upward, almost touching the side of the Ford, and Jodell was forced to get out of the throttle for longer than he wanted. The 16 and the car in front of it were able to pull away.

From his unfortunate vantage point, Jodell could watch as the 16 pulled up tight on the 30 car, sitting in third in front of him, only three car lengths behind the front two cars. Two slower cars had kept Jodell pinned out high in the loose dirt and that caused him to continue to lose ground to the four leaders.

But just then, the 16 car dived under the 30, trying to get past him going into the third turn. But the driver had driven a bit too deeply into the curve and his tires lost traction, allowing him to slide upward into the 30 car, and that swung both of them wide, all the way to the outside railing. Both drivers had to get entirely out of the gas to keep from spinning out.

Jodell had just cleared the slower cars and was only six or seven car lengths behind the third and fourth place cars when they slid up the track. He immediately took the inside line and sailed past both cars through the turn, power-sliding right on by below them. Now, suddenly, the two lead cars lay in his sights and Jodell had a clean stretch of track ahead of him as he went to work to try to close in on them.

With nine laps to go, he was locked tightly on the rear of the Chevy sitting in second position, and the Chevy was only half a car length behind the leader. Jodell gently tapped the rear bumper of the Chevy, giving him the universal notice that he intended to come around him one way or the other. The bump caused the rear end of the Chevrolet to sway and almost lose traction. As much out of surprise as from the nudge itself, the driver allowed the car to slide up a bit, just enough for Jodell to blow on by. Not missing a beat, Jodell set his line and made his pass.

He had eight laps left to clear the lead car but there was a large pack of traffic looming ahead of them. Jodell pushed his car as aggressively as he felt he could, standing hard on the brakes and then jumping violently on the gas, all the while making certain not to spin the car out as it slid in each corner.

Jodell tried high and then low, working to get by the lead car, but the driver knew what he was doing and had the car to do it with. Ahead there were three slower cars, riding along virtually side by side, blocking the track. The leader aimed his car low, trying to outrun the slower cars in the corner. Jodell anticipated the move. It was what he probably would have done himself had he been leading. But something told him to take a higher line, edging toward the outside of the track. Just as Jodell committed to the high line, the slow cars continued their own private race and cut downward in the corner, pinching the leader, opening up the high line for Jodell and his Ford.

Jodell sailed by as the leader roughly drop-kicked one of the slower cars out of his way. That car slid round and round, pinwheeling, while Jodell sailed on around the track trying to get to the white flag that indicated one lap left in the race. The driver was able to right the car without bringing out the caution flag.

Now, all Jodell had to do was maintain his concentration for the last lap.

The beautiful checkered flag waved high as Jodell charged down the front stretch to cruise beneath it. He could see the crowd standing, cheering. Inside the car, if the spectators could make it out, they would have seen the big grin on Jodell Lee's face, his teeth shining through the grit and dirt and sweat on his face, his aching, tingling fist pumping in jubilation.

It was wonderful to be up front again. For Jodell, this was what it was all about. Winning.

The money was great. Lord knows, they needed all of that they could win.

Getting his picture made in the victory lane with

a beauty queen and the race officials and being presented a trophy was all right. Getting Homer Williams's Bubble Up logo in the paper.

But there was nothing else that came close to that feeling in his gut the instant when he flashed beneath the flag stand to take the win ahead of all the others, some of whom were just as driven as he was to win. Nothing else mattered.

Who ever remembers who finished second? Who cares?

As he finished the cool-down lap and headed to victory lane to meet an elated pair of partners, Jodell wondered how much more intense it would feel to win a race in the big-time. How it would feel to lead the likes of Junior Johnson and Buck Baker and Fireball Roberts beneath that checkered flag. How it might feel to capture that first win at the awesome new track down there in Florida in a few months.

Jodell Lee was so deep in his fantasy he drove right on past the entrance to the victory lane. He laughed out loud, stomped the accelerator, jerked the wheel hard left, felt the rear end spin past the front, raised a rooster tail in the thick dirt as he stomped the gas again and twisted the wheel back right, and executed a perfect one-eighty spin as the crowd went crazy. "Bootlegger's spin," they called it.

Coolly, he roared right back to the cut-off to collect his trophy, his photo with the beauty queen, and the winner's check, all the time moonshine-high on this thing called "winning."

ROADSIDE COFFEE

Pockets of nighttime fog hid in the gullies and pine woods beside the two-lane blacktop like lurking highwaymen. Except for the occasional sedan, doubtless piloted by some farmer's son on the way home from a late Saturday-night date, there was no other traffic to contend with as Bubba steered the tow car back toward home, the trailer and race car following along behind. Tired as they were, none of the three men had slept. The radio played first one station then another as the low-powered signals on the right side of the dial faded as if erased by the mist. Joe Banker finally twisted the dial until he found a big station out of Chicago that was playing a song by Fats Domino. He left it there and played drums on the dashboard for a while. They had mostly kept their thoughts to themselves but when the song ended and the station began playing commercials for stores and car dealers that were a very long way from the Smoky Mountains, Joe finally spoke up.

"Boys, this was not a bad trip at all." Bubba and Jodell grunted their agreement. "We got us one win, a fifth that would have been a first if that peckerwood hadn't of cut down on you, and a second that would have been a third if that Buick hadn't of blowed up like a H-bomb. And we won, what? A little over three hundred dollars? We're gonna net two-fifty, two-seventy-five after expenses, even counting all Bubba has done eat up, and we still got the car in one piece except for a few dents we can hammer out and some trim we'll need to screw back on, and Jodell didn't get killed or nothing, and that old gal's boyfriend down there in Hendersonville never did catch me stealing a smooch from her. Good trip, I say."

Just then, the dim glow of the sign of an all-night diner drew Bubba off the road like a moth to a flame and Joe and Jodell didn't discourage him. They had only taken time for sardines and crackers and more Bubble Up before the race that night and they were all three ready for a supper stop by then. Even if it was way yonder past suppertime. Jodell had been lying across the old Ford's backseat, trying to unkink the muscles in his legs. Before he could sit up, get the door open and crawl out, Bubba had cleared the screen-door entrance of the diner and was sitting at the counter, surveying the plastic-covered menu.

Joe leaned against the side of the car, waiting patiently as Jodell slowly unfolded like a rusty jack-knife. A couple of other vehicles towing race cars were parked there in the gravel lot already. The place was clearly a regular stop for drivers and crews on the way back home from wherever the racing was on a Saturday night in western Carolina. Inside, the clientele filling most of the booths and tables were obviously racers. Their auto parts store caps and grease-stained T-shirts were giveaways even if their loud, gesture-filled re-creations of every lap of their own races weren't.

When Joe and Jodell eased up onto stools on either side of Bubba, the big man was already imparting his rather involved order to a sweating, heavyset waitress.

Jodell picked his own poison from the handwritten menu then stepped to the washroom to try to get rid of the grime from his face, neck, and hands. He could still feel the grit of that night's dirt track between his teeth. As he dried his face with a rough paper towel, he saw a tired pair of bloodshot eyes staring back at him out of the spotted, cracked mirror. Not even the goggles had been enough to keep the fine dust and sweat from getting into his eyes.

A big mug of steaming coffee waited for him when he hopped back up onto the stool next to Bubba. The waitress was back then with a plate of eggs, sausage, grits, and a cat-head biscuit.

"Here you go, honey. You look like you could use this," she said with a pleasant-enough smile.

"Thanks. How long you been a mind reader?"

"You eat like your little bitty buddy there next to you and I'll be needing to get you seconds. If'n we don't run out first, that is."

"Just don't get your fingers too close to his mouth when he's eating," Joe chimed in.

"Don't worry, I seen his type before. I'm goin' out back and tell the chickens to get busy so's they can stay ahead of him."

She moved off down the counter to see to some

of the other customers. One gaggle of dirt-covered men was beginning to grow a bit loud, apparently gassed by anger and a little thirst-quenching that had gone on already. The three Tennesseeans paid them no mind, concentrating on their late-night breakfast and strong roadside coffee. Jodell finally slid his empty plate back and drained the mug of the latest refill.

"That sure hit the spot. It wasn't Grandma Lee's biscuit recipe, but it did probably save my life."

He spun around on the stool and propped both elbows on the counter, trying to find a position that didn't hurt while he waited for Bubba to inhale his third helping of biscuit and ribbon-cane syrup. Joe looked up from his own plate in time to catch a quick wince on Jodell's face.

"You okay?"

"I'm sore as the dickens and tired as a single-trace mule. Three races in a row and trying to sleep in the car has plumb wore me out and I don't mind admittin' it."

"I hate to be the bearer of bad news, Joe Dee, but if we aim to try to run the whole circuit next year then you had better get used to it. We're gonna have to run two or three nights a week and there's gonna be a lot more distance between some of them than what we done this weekend."

Joe punctuated his words with a noisy slurp of coffee and set the cup down just in time to get it filled again by the middle-aged waitress. Older or not, she winked at Joe, openly flirting. Meanwhile, the post-race discussion down the counter had escalated to the point that a couple of the men were on their feet by now, loudly questioning each other's ancestry.

"Yeah and that's another reason we need to run all the races we can before the tracks all close down for the winter. I need to get in shape. Then I'll have to work hard at the plant over the winter, too, letting all those cases of soda pop get me toughened up."

Joe stared into his cup.

"I been talking to Coach Dupree down at the high school, too. He says he wouldn't mind if we came in and used the gym and the weights some if we lock up behind ourselves. You, me, Bubba, Johnny, and the boys. We run the big-time tracks like Daytona and Richmond we need them all to be in shape, too."

Bubba hardly flinched at the mention of his name. He was still shovelling in the chunks of sweet buttered biscuit and staring intently at the old black cook who was working the griddle on the other side of the counter like a magician doing some involved illusion. And he was apparently not paying any attention to the profane shouting match that was breaking out a few feet from where they sat.

Joe winked at Jodell and turned to the big man.

"Bubba, you hear anything from Joyce lately?"

He knew the answer. He simply loved to needle him. Bubba shifted uncomfortably on his stool but a big grin cracked his dirty face.

"Well, yeah. I have. I got a letter on Tuesday before we left."

"Only one letter this week?" Joe knew for a fact that Bubba usually got three or four letters a week from the girl he had met at Darlington. "You do write her back don't you?"

Bubba ducked his head and stared into his coffee as if looking for something in its murkiness.

"Well?"

" 'Well,' what?"

"Do you write her little love notes back?"

"Joe, you know dern well I write her back. Now leave me alone."

"Well, what does she say in all them letters?"

"Lots of things. Things she's doing at work. The weather," Bubba mumbled.

"So, what else?"

"Yeah, Bubba, what does she say?" Jodell said, suddenly perking up and taking an interest in the conversation.

"Well, okay. She said she thinks she's gonna take a week off in February and come down to Daytona."

"Now, see, Bub. That wasn't so painful," Jodell grinned. The coffee had kicked in enough that he actually felt like gigging Bubba. Then another thought popped into his head. "Maybe she can stay with Catherine and she can help us out some. What do you think?"

"I guess when I see her I can ask her. Her and Catherine seemed to hit it off all right."

"When you see her? You planning on seeing her anytime soon?"

Bubba squirmed some more on the stool and glanced sideways at what was now threatening to be a full-blown fight on the opposite side of the restaurant.

"She's gonna come up to Greenville to see some of her kinfolks in a couple of weeks. I'll ask her then. Are y'all satisfied?" he growled and shut off any other conversation with a huge mouthful of biscuit. There was the sudden clatter of broken dishes and vulgar challenges to mix it up from among a few members of the rowdy group across the diner.

"Come on boys," Joe said quickly. He rose, paid the check and left the dumpy waitress more of a tip than was usual. "Let's get out of here before we get sucked into somebody else's fight. I'm too tired and too pretty for any of that mess tonight."

Jodell nodded. He could add, "Too sore."

And for once, Bubba Baxter turned down a chance to throw a punch or two.

They crawled back into the tow car, turned up the music on the radio again and once more pointed toward home.

BEACH BOUND

The voice on the radio was tiny, distant, but Jodell was sure he could hear the breakers from the Atlantic Ocean in the background as the man talked.

"The stiff breeze off the water is cool but not cold this morning. That's typical for mid-February here on Florida's east coast. And it's also typical that this normally sleepy beach town swells to become a medium-size city for a few weeks as thousands of visitors descend on its motels and restaurants and palm-tree-lined streets."

Jodell had been dialing around, looking for a weather report, hoping a sneaky snowstorm was going to dodge them to the north. They had too much to do, too far to drive, to have snow-slick roads through the mountains make it any tougher for them. But he had stumbled onto the radio report from Daytona so he sat there at his grandmother's dining room table and listened.

"Just west of here on Highway 92, a huge dirt and sand bank suddenly jumps up out of the palmetto, outlining the sparkling new speedway which is being frantically readied for its first week of stock car racing. The track has been carved out of flatlands a few miles inland from the beach where many of the same cars and drivers used to compete on a course marked off on the hard-packed sand and run only feet from the surf. But this new speed palace is nothing like that rough track. The scope of the place is breathtaking in every respect."

As he listened, Jodell could see through the frosty window the dim lights from the barn shop where Joe and Bubba worked at that moment, putting the finishing touches on the race car they would tow to Daytona. They would be leaving the very next morning. It was still hard for him to believe they were destined for the very same place the man on the radio was talking about with such reverence.

"For all the naysayers who claimed this massive project could not be done or that such an undertaking was doomed to failure, the gleaming new speedway is a testament to what can be done when men refuse to fail. And to those who said no one would show up to watch men and their machines run in circles, the builders of this phenomenal place can take some measure of satisfaction in telling them of the thousands of tickets which have been sold already, more than a week before the opening event. This place now will truly become a mecca for stock car racing, the center of a growing sport that had its origins far from here and in a very different locale, in the southern Appalachian Mountains, among moonshine runners and dirt farmers."

Jodell grinned. He wondered what his father and grandfather would have thought of the crusade he, his cousin, and his friends were about to embark upon. But then the reporter's voice dropped an octave and he spoke more ominously.

"But there are those who say the speeds that can be achieved at this new track with its high-banking, wide turns are more than a man or a machine can take, and that the effect will be deadly. Others say the cars, better suited for small-circumference dirt tracks, are not safe enough to run at such velocity. And still others say that the strong desire to win that runs so virulently through the men who drive these cars is so strong, they will push their chariots far harder than is safe or sane to . . ."

Jodell switched off the radio. He didn't want to pollute his mind with any such negative thoughts. And he certainly didn't want to have Grandma Lee overhear talk like that or she would simply forbid him to go.

He zipped his windbreaker tight against the cold and stepped back outside and toward the barn. Joe and Bubba were still at it, jawing at each other as they tied down the race car on their new trailer and made sure they had everything they could possibly ever need. The three of them had spent the better part of two months completely rebuilding and fine-tuning the car. Once satisfied it was well on the way to being as fast and tight as they could make it, they had rolled it out the doorway of the shop and driven it hard along the back roads that Jodell had once run, loaded with white liquor, dodging those who would have happily robbed him of his freedom for such a transgression.

Now they were satisfied that everything was tested and race-ready. Even the tow car had been redone, tuned, shined, re-tired, and made ready for the trip to what amounted to a foreign country to this trio of mountain-raised men.

Jodell stood just inside the barn door and surveyed the race car, resting sleekly on the trailer. She was beautiful! They had trimmed her in blue with the Bubble Up logo meticulously but boldly painted on the rear fenders. Bubba had spent days doing the painting, making certain it was perfect. Over the driver's-side door, he had scripted "Bob Lee" in healthy yellow letters. Jodell had originally shortened the name in the hopes his grandfather wouldn't catch on that it was his own erstwhile grandson who was out there banging around in the whiskey car that helped feed the family. Bubba had also gilded each of the two doors with the number 34 in white, and they seemed to glimmer and glow.

All three of them were excited, but tired. Tired bordering on exhausted. Between working at the Bubble Up plant and then spending most evenings working on the race car till just before Grandma's old bantam rooster crowed, Jodell was flagging. Joe Banker had put in much the same long hours getting the motor freshened up and balanced. Only Bubba Baxter seemed immune to the long hours, first at the mill and then either underneath the car or swallowed up by the motor compartment there at the race shop. Nothing physically demanding ever seemed to bother the big man.

They had torn the Darlington car down almost to the frame and then rebuilt it, further strengthening

every point they could. They had beefed up the suspension and the frame, then had gone back and done
it again, using even heavier-duty parts. They in-
stalled a complete roll bar system in the car. The
driver's seat and a new belt system were configured
so they fit Jodell perfectly, both for comfort and for
safety at the fearsome speeds they would see down
there at the beach. They knew centrifugal force
would make ill-fitting belts or a mismatched seat
nothing but torture over the space of an afternoon,
wearing a driver down as surely as the close-quarters
racing would.

The boys had checked and measured everything,
not once, not even twice, but at least a half dozen
times or more. Joe had joked that Bubba was going
to wear the spark plugs down to a nub if he checked
the gap on them even one more time. The big fellow
ignored Joe as he meticulously welded every joint on
the race car and then ground them down and welded
them some more, making sure they were good and
solid.

As they worked, they gave careful consideration
to the rule book. It would be disastrous to get all the
way down to Daytona after spending all that time
and a big stack of Bubble Up money getting the car
fast and ready to race, only to have it disqualified on
some technicality. The men who ran the sport now
were sticklers for following the rules. It was their
intention to keep the cars as evenly matched as possible, as close to street machines as they could come,
all so the spectators could see an exciting race in
virtually the same cars they could buy off the showroom floor.

Catherine's brother, Johnny, had happened up on
a good buy on the trailer, a mere sixty dollars from

one of his customers at the shop, and it would make towing the car such a long distance immeasurably easier. They could move faster and safer now without having to deal with a tow bar.

"What's the weatherman saying?" Joe asked when he saw Jodell standing there in the doorway.

"Maybe a flurry. It'll likely be slick on the mountain roads but we can take it easy and probably make it okay."

Joe nodded, hopped through the open window of the car and fired up his newly rebuilt motor. He eased out the clutch and pulled the car up onto the trailer while Jodell and Bubba helped guide him. The sweet music of his engine brought a big smile to Joe's face as he eased the front tires against the stop bar they had welded to the trailer's rails.

They were putting the finishing touches to the tie-down when they heard the crunch of car tires on the gravel of the driveway outside. The damp, cold outside air swept in as someone opened the barn door. It was Catherine and Johnny, hurrying inside to stand next to the wood-burning stove as Bubba stoked the fire and tossed in a few more sticks of wood.

"You got a cold nose," Jodell said as he gave Catherine a hug and a quick kiss.

"But a warm heart," she smiled, returning the embrace. "Feels like snow out there."

"Hush! We need clear roads when we tow this baby over those mountains tomorrow."

Johnny Holt had already hung his coat on a nail and was rolling up his shirt sleeves to go to work. Joe pointed to the row of toolboxes lined up along the back wall of the barn. They would have to make certain they had everything they might need stowed away in one or another of them and then find a place for all of the tools to ride. They added a supply of shocks and spare suspension parts as well, everything they would need to repair the front suspension if they got into a tangle with a wall. There would no running to a junkyard or car dealer for parts.

They stacked tires in front of and behind the car on the trailer then piled on the dump can for gassing the car, the jack, water jugs, coolers, and assorted other odds and ends they might or might not need for the race but had best carry anyway. When they were done, the trailer looked as if a good-sized family of dust-bowlers might be moving west to California with all their worldly possessions piled on their jalopy.

Then they had finally gotten to the point where no one could see anything else that obviously needed to be done. Johnny Holt stretched his back and wiped his face with the sleeve of his shirt.

"I guess if that's all I can help with, I better get going. I have to be at the garage at six in the morning to put a clutch in an old '46 Buick."

"We appreciate everything you've done, John, and that you and the boys are going to do," Jodell said sincerely, then nodded toward Catherine. "You need to get your sister home, too. She's got to start packing for the bus trip and you know how women and their packing can be."

"Don't worry about me, Mr. Bob Lee. I can sleep all the way to Daytona on that old bus." She gave him a mock scowl.

Johnny ran out to crank the car and allow it to get warm inside. Jodell walked Catherine outside, each with an arm around the other's waist. The air was even colder now, biting, a frigid breeze blowing up from the west. There might have even been a grit or two of snow on their faces. He stopped, turned to her and took her into his arms, pulling her close.

"I miss you already," he said into her hair. "I know I'll see you in a few days. I'll be waiting for you at the bus station."

"You be careful driving down and when you get out on that track for the first time. That place scares me, Jodell. It going to be a lot faster than anything you have ever seen."

"I know. I will be. We can't win if we tear up the car or the driver anyway. I can't wait to see you. I love you, Catherine."

"I love you, too!" she said, squeezing him tighter. She seemed reluctant to let him go, even when Johnny honked the horn to let them know it was finally warm inside. Catherine turned her face up and kissed Jodell quickly on the lips. He thought he felt tears on her cheeks. Or maybe it really was snowing.

She finally started to pull away but Jodell pulled her back and gave her a long, hard, passionate kiss.

Johnny tooted the horn again and she moved away, walking backward.

"That dumb brother of mine is going to wake up your grandmother and most of Chandler County." She backed all the way to the car. "Do be careful out there on that big track, Jodell. Now that I've found you I don't have any intention of losing you."

"I'll be fine. I'll see you in a few days and we can win that race together."

He stood there and watched until the darkness had claimed the taillights of the car. No doubt about it. It was beginning to snow.

Back inside, he found Joe scanning the sheets of paper in his clipboard.

"Now what?" Jodell asked.

"We go through this every time we load up for a race, packing all this stuff up then unpacking it to see if we got the crescent wrench or if we remembered to bring a spare jar of cotter pins or something. We're about to wear out the hinges on these toolboxes opening and closing them checking on stuff we have done packed away. I thought I would make us a checklist so we don't miss anything."

"Good idea," Jodell said. Maybe his cousin's penchant for organization was finally going to pay off. Joe Banker had the maddening tendency to show up late for most everything they might be about, but once he did put in an appearance, he insisted that everything be in its assigned place. He already had the shop organized better than most parts stores and he was apparently working on their traveling stock as well, to bring it in line, too.

They finished up shortly after midnight and walked together back to the house through the light snowflakes that were falling. Grandma Lee had a bed turned down already for Joe and Bubba, too, so they could get an early start south in the morning.

Jodell turned out the porch light behind them as they went in the house but he lingered behind as the other two men found their beds and turned in. As he sometimes did, Jodell stood before the big rock fireplace in his grandmother's parlor. There were a few embers still visible in the grate, mostly covered over and banked to try to save for igniting some kindling first thing in the morning. He ran his hand along the smooth oak mantle his grandfather and father had hewn together from a tree that had been lightning-struck up the side of the mountain. It had fallen across the road to the still, but was too grand to simply cut and use for stove wood when they removed it from the trail. Grandpa Lee had decided to use the heart of the tree for his mantle.

His grandmother kept framed pictures of the two men on it, in frames worn almost smooth by her touch. Sometimes Jodell liked to stand before them, alone, when the house was dark and quiet. It sometimes seemed that they came close to talking to him, to telling him how proud of him they were. But even if the faded, browning photos never uttered a word, it still hardened his enthusiasm for doing this thing he was doing. He took strength in their deep, dark eyes, the arch of their brows, the strong set of their jaws. The same eyes and brows and jaw he saw in his own mirror on the dresser upstairs in his room.

Grandma Lee let them sleep in later than they had intended the next morning. She figured it was better for them to leave out a couple of hours late and be well rested for the two-day drive.

It was the perfume of frying sausage and bacon that woke Jodell. He was shocked to see that the Big Ben on his nightstand claimed it was almost eight-thirty already. He had never slept that late in his life!

He hopped up, pulled on his pants, washed up quickly and threw on a clean shirt, then headed downstairs, through the kitchen, and to the outhouse. When he got back, Bubba was already at the kitchen table, a fork in one hand and a knife in the other, making a hillock of scrambled eggs disappear.

When Bubba went to the back of the house to rouse Joe, Grandma Lee stepped to hug Jodell, consciously not wanting to embarrass him in front of the others.

"I know how set you are on this racing thing, Jodell," she said. "I can't say I understand it but I didn't exactly jump up and click my heels at the way your daddy drove around, rippin' and roarin' all through these hollers and valleys. But you know I'll be prayin' to the good Lord that He'll keep an eye on you way down yonder. And I may even say a little prayer that He'll let you win. Or at least finish up close behind whoever does. But I got a bad feeling about that place. I've heard them talking about how fast they'll go, how they don't know if a man can drive around that fast without passing out. You sure you know what you're doing?"

"Aw, Grandmaw. You know I do."

He stood and gave her a hug right back, not really caring if Bubba and Joe saw him or not. She still had a grim look on her face, though.

Outside the sun was bright already, the night's snow only a thin, frosty crust on the brown grass. The sun was warming things up nicely. Spring might be coming to the mountains after all.

Finally, it was time to get started. Jodell hopped behind the wheel of the old 'shine car, the first driving shift his. He carefully pulled the car and the tow out of the barn through the narrow doorway with Bubba's help. The race car looked even better in the bright sunlight. Mr. Williams and his advertising manager had come by two days before and had taken more pictures. They had heartily approved of the paint scheme and logos and only asked that Jodell park the car in victory lane so the Bubble Up sign would best be captured by the newsreel cameras and newspaper photographers. And he had told Jodell to come by the office for an additional hundred-dollar check.

"I want you boys thinking about putting the 'Bubble Up 34' up front, not how you're going to pay for supper," he had said.

Somehow, they had forgotten to leave space for their suitcases and had to tie them on top of the 'shine car, making them look even more like a Gypsy band that might have taken a wrong turn at Kingsport. Grandma Lee came outside to give Bubba a huge bag of fried chicken and potato salad and biscuits for the drive and he certainly had no trouble finding a place to stow that cargo.

She stepped off the porch and leaned into Jodell's window to put a hand on his arm.

"Looka here, young'un. Never mind all my worrying. You drive smart and go fast. Your Pa and your Grandpa wouldn't of never stood for second best. You boys go down there and get done what you have to do."

As he pulled away, he caught a final glimpse of her in his mirrors, standing there on the edge of the porch in the early sunlight, waving, smiling.

HIGH BANKS AND BIKINIS

Although it had only been above the horizon for a few hours, the sun already blazed brilliantly, warmly, in a partly cloudy mid-February sky. Bubba Baxter had rolled down the Ford's driver's-side window and allowed the surprisingly moderate breeze to help keep him awake. That's when he noticed a new smell, something different from the tarry aroma of the pines by the side of the highway or the exhaust smoke of whichever old jalopy he was waiting to pass on the two-lane. It reminded him of the taffy he would get at the county fair back home, a sweet yet salty fragrance, and he knew it must be the ocean out there beyond the marshes that stretched off to the east that he smelled. He had already spied some seagulls scattered around the pastures and even a stray pelican or two perched on the tops of some power poles.

He had tried to point out the birds, the salty ocean

smell, to Jodell and Joe but they slept peacefully, Jodell slumped down in the seat next to him, Joe
sprawled across the rear bench seat behind. He was
drowsy, too, and had been since he had taken the
wheel somewhere in south Georgia for the last turn
on into Daytona Beach. But he yawned, slapped himself in the face, held his head out the window and
sucked in the air, all to keep awake. Traffic was
heavy, a solid line ever since the Georgia state line
and the Florida welcome center where they had gotten free cups of orange juice and had called home to
tell everyone they had made it that far. Most of the
motorists seemed headed for either the beach or the
massive new racetrack or, more likely, to both, all to
shake off the effects of the long winter back up north.
Many of those in the cars and pickup trucks they
passed recognized that it was a race car that was
beneath the tarpaulin on the trailer behind the Ford
and they stared, trying to figure out who it might be,
or blew their horns and tossed friendly waves. Bubba
dutifully waved right back and blinked the lights at
them before he slid past them with a honk of the
horn.

Neither Joe nor Jodell stirred. The trip had been
grueling, through the mountains and down to Atlanta, then on U.S. 41 across Georgia to U.S. 82 and
on east until it picked up U.S. 1 near Waycross and
the Okefenokee. Bubba hoped he would never see
another pine tree or roadside picnic ground or filling
station or any more Rock City or Burma Shave
signs. Now the billboards advertised snake farms, al-
ligator ranches, and cheap retirement communities.
The trip had taken far longer than they had anticipated, their progress slowed by tractors with their
tillers lifted behind them and their drivers deter-

mined to not move aside for anyone trespassing on their turf, by trucks loaded with drooping pine tree carcasses bound for paper mills, and by impossibly low speed limits in all the little wide places in the highway that pretended to be real towns but made most of their income off unsuspecting tourists.

They stopped for a bit just west of Jacksonville, pulled into a roadside park, and slept for a couple of hours until Bubba had decided he was rested enough to drive and then they had continued on. He was concentrating so much on the road ahead, on keeping awake, that he hardly noticed that the pastures had given way to civilization, that the grass and swamp to his left had become sand and that the gray waters of the Atlantic Ocean stretched into the far distance beyond. He was hardly aware when he made the right-hand turn with all the other traffic at Highway 92 either. But then, before he realized it, the sudden sight of the gleaming new racetrack jarred him totally awake.

There they were. The massive sand levees straight ahead contained the track's straightaways and formed the already much-discussed high-banked curves. Bubba slowed the car down, coming to a creep there in the middle of the busy street. Several cars behind him blew their horns but he didn't even hear them.

"Boys." Joe and Jodell snored softly, ignoring him as easily as they did the impatient honkers behind that didn't understand the magnitude of this moment. "Boys!"

"Grandma, it ain't . . ." Jodell sat up slowly, confused, rubbing drool from his chin with the back of a hand, his eyes still closed against the sun's glare.

"Jodell, y'all gotta see this thing," Bubba said,

easing the Ford and its tow over to the side of the road next to a small roadside stand. Joe propped up on one elbow in the back seat, squinting.

"It better be a blonde in one of them bikinis if you woke me up for it," he growled.

But soon all three of them were staring at the incredible sight. Its size was so overwhelming it made everything else around it, the buildings and cars and palm trees, seem out of proportion, like perfectly crafted miniatures. The shimmering morning mist caused the entire place to appear magical, massive, like some kind of mystical place out of a dream. The grandstands towered above a wide gravel parking area that ran along beside the highway and they could just see a sliver of the track through a narrow opening. Meanwhile, the rest of the outside of the track seemed to stretch out forever into the distance until it was swallowed up by the morning haze or maybe by the horizon itself. Darlington had been big. This place made it look like one of those Saturday-night "bull rings."

"What can I git you boys?"

The old man at the stand took them by surprise. Bubba had not even noticed the stand was open when he pulled up next to its ramshackle front.

"Nothing, I don't reckon, thank you. We just staring at that big old thing over yonder."

"She's something else, ain't she?" the old man agreed, leaning back against the Ford's fender and admiring the track as if he had just seen it himself for the first time. "I watched them build it since the first bulldozer showed up over there. They's gonna be a passel of folks here for them races, I reckon. Real good for business. I sell lots of ice-cold soda to the folks driving by to take a look. The sody-pop truck is coming twice a day here lately."

"Did you ever see them run when they raced out on the beach?" Jodell asked.

"Sure did. Godawmighty that was fun! I don't know about this thing, though. Seems like they'll be going too fast in there. Ain't meant for no man to go that fast 'ceptin' him being in a jet airplane. Some say they hit them turns so sudden-like they'll black out, all the blood rushing out of their heads and such."

Bubba looked at Jodell, his eyes big. The old man seemed to notice the trailer for the first time.

"Y'all racing? Y'all going to drive?"

"Yep," Bubba answered.

"Who are y'all?"

Bubba pointed his thumb over his shoulder toward Jodell.

"This here's Bob Lee from Chandler Cove, Tennessee, and me and Joe there are his chief mechanics."

The old man squinted through the bug-splattered windshield at the three of them.

"Well, I ain't never heard of y'all. What can I get you?"

Bubba didn't bother to answer. He gave the guy a blank stare, eased out on the clutch and pulled back onto the street, heading back eastward now, toward the sun, the ocean, and where their motel was supposed to be. Joe and Jodell stared out the back window until they had left the track behind while Bubba sneaked a few glances in his rearview mirror.

Their motel was a squat single-story building, painted pink, and with wooden cutouts of what must supposed to have been flamingoes nailed to the walls. The old woman behind the counter inside was squat, too, and looked as if her face might have been painted pink at the same time as the motel had. She took their advance money, gave them keys, then recited a long list of don'ts. They only caught a few of them.

". . . don't use room towels at the pool, don't throw shrimp shells into the sink, don't get sand in the beds . . ." Then she looked up at them over the top of her reading glasses. "You racers?"

"Yes, ma'am," they answered proudly in unison. But somehow it seemed as if they had just admitted to being cat burglars.

"Then don't work on cars in the lot, don't wash tools or parts in the bathtub . . ." and she was off again with a totally new list, aimed directly at racers.

Soon as they had hauled their clothes into the room, Jodell collapsed onto one of the two beds. A narrow roll-away cot sat hinged up in the corner. It felt so good to stretch out, he thought he might just lie there for a while, until it was time to go to the first drivers' meeting. But Joe was standing at the back window of the room, his mouth open.

"Boys, y'all got to see this," he said.

Jodell climbed from the bed to join him at the window while Bubba put down his candy bar to stand there with them. They peered through the venetian blinds at the almost painfully white sand, the glistening green water, the bright blue sky.

"Sure ain't the mountains," Bubba said.

"Nope, not by a far sight," Jodell agreed.

"Not by a million miles," Joe said and let out a long whistle.

But he was not referring to the sand or sea or sky. He had spotted a swarm of tanned girls, spread about over a collection of brightly colored beach towels in a patch of sand near where the breakers gently washed ashore. They glistened with oily suntan lotion and wore the tiniest two-piece bathing suits any of them had ever seen in person.

Suddenly, Joe ripped off his boots and socks, danced between the beds and out the door, around the corner and down to the surf. He stopped, waited a moment, then allowed the water to wash over his feet. Jodell and Bubba followed and watched from a safe distance.

"How's the water?" Jodell called.

"Cold as any mountain stream back home," Joe answered, then bent to roll his jeans up to his knees and started to walk up the beach in the general direction of where the girls were still sunning themselves.

Jodell took in a lungful of the sea air, stretched, and yawned.

"I think I'm gonna catch an hour's nap. How about you two don't disturb me?"

But Bubba didn't answer. He had his own boots off and was walking down to wade in the cold Atlantic waters. Jodell shook his head and grinned. This might just as well have been a foreign country it was so far, so different, from the only place they knew. Racing had brought them a long way. But he knew it was an even longer way back home if they didn't show well. If they somehow didn't even make the race they had come such a distance to run.

He headed back up the beach to the room, leaving Bubba dancing comically up and down in the wet sand, trying to skitter away from the waves as they rolled in. And Joe was already talking to the girls, laughing and gesturing as if they were old friends.

Jodell knew he needed to get all the rest he could

before the track opened the next day, that time for such luxuries as sleeping would be scarce for the next little while. He stretched out again and studied the rust-colored water rings on the ceiling above his bed. As he drifted into unconsciousness, his usual dream came upon him. A dream in which he was leading all the others to the finish line in a wild, blurry-fast race. And he was on a gargantuan but familiar raceway with turns as high-banked as the Smoky Mountains and straightaways that seemed as far away as it was from Chandler Cove to Knoxville. But now he knew why the racetrack was so familiar. He had laid eyes on it himself, in real life, that very morning.

And it was called Daytona.

EVERYBODY EQUAL

Jodell couldn't believe he had slept straight through the night. That he had not heard Bubba come in early or Joe slip in and unknife the roll-away sometime just before sunrise. He supposed it had been that even as he had slept on the drive down, he still hit the gas and brake and rode the clutch the whole way, even as the other two men took their own turns at the wheel.

He allowed the other two to sleep while he walked across busy U.S. 1 to get himself a plate of eggs and biscuits at a café. All the diners around him talked of the racetrack, the upcoming race, the future of the sport. The local morning paper had devoted its entire front page to the track. He bought a copy and read as he ate, taking in the quotes from familiar folks like Lee Petty and Fireball Roberts and the track's owner, Bill France. The consensus of the drivers was that they were, to a man, excited about running on the amazing new track, but, also to a man, wary of the truly dangerous speeds that it would allow. When Jodell finished, he folded the newspaper so he could show it to Catherine when she arrived. He wanted her to know how big this trip was but he didn't want to worry her either.

Bubba was up, brushing his teeth, when Jodell got back, but Joe was still sleeping soundly. It took both of them to get him awake but soon they were headed westward once more, out Highway 92 toward the track.

The view of the track as they approached was even more awesome than yesterday. This morning the area was working and alive like a kicked-over anthill, with brightly colored cars, busy crew members, and workmen trying to get the place finished before the bulk of the spectators showed up.

They pulled off the highway and fell into line behind the other competitors, then shut off the engine to wait for the gates to open and for someone to let them inside the place.

"I see all the big teams are here already," Joe said, pointing up toward the head of the line. "They even want to be first at getting in the danged gates!"

"The Pettys, Little Joe Weatherly, Speedy Thompson. This is the big time, boys," Jodell observed. "This ain't no Friday-night dirt track feature for sure. We'll be up against the best there is."

Joe nodded in agreement and pondered the weight of that statement but Bubba gave them both a hard look.

"Yeah, that's true, but Jodell, you have a real advantage over most of these guys. They're more used to running 'round and 'round on the dirt most of the time. But here you'll be on long, fast stretches of asphalt, just like the roads you used to run 'shine back home."

"Hmmm. I don't guess I ever thought of it that way. I've been trying to learn how to drive all those short dirt tracks while a lot of these guys have been driving them since before I was born. But I've been driving on asphalt all along, and for higher stakes than a checkered flag."

"That's what I mean. Here you have a slight advantage And one other thing. Everybody is going into this thing equal. They're seeing this place for the first time just like you are."

"Bubba, you're something else!" Jodell faked giving the big man a kiss but he danced out of the way. Just then the line of cars began to move as the gates were opened a good quarter of a mile from where they waited. Joe fired up the car and they slowly began inching forward. Their excitement grew with every couple of car lengths they rolled forward toward the gate. Finally they achieved the head of the line and were waved through toward the infield.

Joe gunned the engine and they crossed through the gap in the fence and onto the track. Anticipation or not, they were not prepared for what they saw then. It was so far from where they pulled in down to the turns that they would not even have been able to see them if they had not towered high like the round-top hills back home. The back stretch was so far away that there was room for a large lake in the middle of the infield, a lake big enough to have a whole armada of motor boats floating on it.

The black stretch of asphalt appeared easily wide enough for seven or eight cars to run around the track side by side. Even so, it seemed to shrink to only a thin string as it trailed off into the big turn.

There was a long low set of grandstands running all the way along the angled front stretch, with enough seats for what surely would have been everybody in the whole state of Tennessee. Workmen in the bleachers down the way appeared tiny, dwarfed by the sheer size of the place.

They were waved into the pit area of the racetrack by a uniformed guard. They parked the tow car and climbed out, trying not to look so obviously overwhelmed.

"Man, I can't wait to get out on to the track," Jodell said. He could feel his heart pounding already. "I bet I can go wide open all the way around without hitting the brakes. I bet I can do it."

"I have no doubt about it," Joe agreed. He watched his cousin close his eyes and try to visualize it.

Even Bubba was taken in by the immensity of Daytona.

"Them turns are as tall as Chandler Mountain. You run high and I bet you that you'll run fast. I guarantee that! And this dern track is two wagon-greasings around, at least."

"Let's quit talking about it and go out there and see what we can do," Jodell said. "Let's get our passes and find out what we have to do."

As the smell of fresh paint drifted by and the sound of hammers and saws echoed off the grandstands, they parked, got their passes, and found out the schedule for drivers' meetings and practice. They noticed immediately how organized and streamlined the whole procedure was as compared to the other smaller tracks they had run. Again, this was clearly the big time.

Jodell and Bubba guided Joe as he backed the race

car down off the trailer. The car's wheels crunched
as they rolled off onto the sandy gravel, the big engine rumbling powerfully. Joe could not resist rev-
ving the motor up, just to here the results of his
handiwork over the last several weeks. The sound
of the engine was like a well-rehearsed chorus performing for a pleased choirmaster.

"She sounds sweet, don't she?" Jodell asked as he
slapped the race car's fender.

"Yeah! I can't ever get enough of that sound. You
know I spend all that time tearing these things down
and putting them back together. It's just like putting
a puzzle together. That is all there is to it."

Bubba dropped a load of tires off the trailer with
a banging and clanging as they hit the ground and
looked at them, both hands on his hips.

"Y'all gonna jabber all day or you going to help
me get all this stuff unloaded. It ain't gonna get unloaded by itself."

They pitched in and got everything off the trailer
and out of every nook and cranny of the two cars.
They only had an hour before the first drivers' meeting and they wanted to be ready to practice as
quickly as they could afterward.

The surroundings might have been foreign but Jodell and Joe spied several familiar faces when they
walked into the meeting. Little Joe Weatherly latched
onto them as soon as they entered.

"Well, looky here, fellers. It's the Whiskey Boys
from way up yonder in them old rocky-top Tennessee hills."

"Hey, Little Joe. How you doing?"

"Fine, fine. We just need to get this meeting over
with in a hurry so we can get out there on that old
track. Time is a-wastin'. And then we gonna have

ourselves a little old party tonight to celebrate this here new racetrack. Y'all are coming, ain't you?"

"Probably not because—" Jodell started but Joe cut him off.

"Absolutely. We wouldn't miss it. Where's it gonna be?"

"Me and Curtis got us a little place down on the beach. Y'all come by. We'll be going most every night. Tonight'll be good. You and your old sour-puss driver better be there! And that little bitty skinny mechanic of yours, too. Old Bubba." Little Joe turned and was gone to gladhand someone else who had just entered the room.

Then Jodell saw Richard Petty sitting next to his father so he walked over to speak to him.

"Well, howdy, Jodell Bob. What you cats doing way off down here?"

"Just trying to win a race. It is a long way from home for a bunch of mountain boys, though."

"Long way from Randleman, too. At least I've been coming down here for a while. You staying over there on the beach?"

"Yep. Down at the Sea Spray. You wrenching it this year or driving?"

Petty flashed a broad smile that answered the question before he even spoke.

"Racing," he said. "We've got two cars down here. I figure that I have as good a chance as any-body else. This track is new to everybody. These cats who grew up driving small tracks ain't got no advantage on somebody like you or me. We are all gonna be about even out yonder." He pointed over his shoulder with his thumb in the general direction of the start–finish line. "And most of 'em drove down here on the beach course but this is a whole new ball game. This thing reminds me of the roads Daddy and I drove on back home."

Jodell grinned. Richard Petty would be another one of the ones to beat.

Just then, he noticed Dash Rockford step through the door. No one spoke to the driver as he leaned against the back wall. Jodell vowed to keep his distance. The so-and-so had cost him a good finish at Darlington but he would not get in his way again. Not here. Not out there on the sparkling new track.

The group had been loud, bordering on rowdy, but suddenly the drivers and crew members went quiet as a man stepped to the lectern at the front of the room. Jodell recognized the figure from his pictures in the newspapers. He was the former filling-station owner who now owned the new track and had organized stock racing into a solid sport, far beyond the anarchy of Saturday night brawls and disorganized demolition derbies. Bill France had brought order to a basically lawless endeavor that had, up until then, been pursued mostly by former whiskey runners. And he had created a structure that was allowing stock car racing to grow rapidly and reach a burgeoning, appreciative audience that was already spreading beyond its rural Southern roots.

France recited a litany of rules and cautions, some the usual, others especially applicable to this sleek new speed palace. Jodell noticed that, unlike drivers' meetings at most tracks the competitors here listened to what France had to say and there was no foolishness going on.

"Drive a lot of laps down low on the track," he told them. "You can ease on up in the turns once you get a feel for the place, where the groove is. Slow and low while you get used to going around this place. Otherwise, we'll be scraping you off the walls or fishing you out of the lake."

He went over practice schedules, pitting and pace car procedures, and other information but in the end, he came back to his original statement. "Just ride along down there on the apron in the turns until you get used to it. Got it, fellows? We'll have ourselves a big crowd. Lots more will be following on the radio and will read about this track and our sport in the papers. Let's give 'em a show!"

With that, he sent them off to await the start of the first practice. And all of them, experienced drivers and raw, untested rookies alike, all rushed head foremost to the doorway, all ready to roll out onto that beautiful stretch of asphalt as quickly as they could get cranked up.

DAMN THE CORNERS, FULL SPEED AHEAD

Even though they had thought they had done everything possible to the race car, the three of them managed to find plenty of things to tweak and adjust and double-check before they could allow the car to have its head on the track. Joe and Bubba strung up the tarp over a couple of poles to buy them some shade in what had become a sizzling hot sun. It was hard for them to believe they had left snow only a few days before back home. Joe had even rounded up an old pith helmet somewhere and he wore it to keep the sun off his head. Jodell began calling him "Tarzan," since the only time he had seen such a hat had been in the movies at the theater back home.

Bubba went under the car and checked over the suspension and front end meticulously. At the speeds they were expecting to run, there would be no room for error in anything, and if something vital broke, it might cost them even more than a race. Joe was buried under the hood setting the jets on the carburetor and checking the timing. Jodell looked the tires over and made sure everything was ready in the driver's compartment, and especially the seat and shoulder belts. Logic told him that he had to be secured even more tightly in his seat than in previous races. Otherwise, in an accident, he might be seriously injured if he was thrown all around the cockpit. Some of the drivers, like Little Joe Weatherly, disdained the use of shoulder belts and flatly refused to use them at all.

"I don't want to be all gussied up if that thing catches on fire," Little Joe had said.

Jodell had long since decided to wear the chest belt when he raced. He had rather take his chance on fire than risk being thrown out of a car going well over a hundred miles per hour.

Finally it came time to line the cars up and get them ready to take to the track. The three of them pushed the car out onto the pit road, a stretch of asphalt that cut across the angle of the front straightaway. While the race cars lined up nose to tail, ready to take to the track, Jodell sat buckled into the seat in the Ford's cockpit, working to get his mind focused on actually running the big track.

The official who was standing stoically at the end of the pit road finally gave in and waved the green flag he held in his hand, motioning the cars out onto the track. The drivers in front of Jodell began to pull away so he shifted out of neutral up into first gear and kicked down on the accelerator while easing out on the clutch. The Ford pulled out in line at his command and began to accelerate down the pit lane, toward the banking where the front stretch hit the intersection with the pit road.

For Jodell, the mere act of getting the car in motion, of moving out onto the track, brought a sense of ease and relief. While he usually tried to act strong and confident for Joe and Bubba, the stress of the long trip had begun wearing on him like a lingering toothache. He tried to forget that so many people were depending on him . . . Joe and Bub, Catherine, the pit crew that would be coming down that day, his grandmother, old Augustus Smith, and now Homer Williams and all the folks at the Bubble Up plant. He had to do well for all of them as well as for himself. But the tension melted away as he steered the race car onto the track, the one place where he felt most confident, most in control of all that was going on around him.

The motor felt good as he rolled along the apron around the first turn. He could feel it rumbling strongly all the way up through his legs and into his gut. As he came off the second turn and hugged the apron at the bottom of the track, Jodell had to squint just to see the far end of the long back straightaway. He eased his foot into the gas, pressed harder, gained speed but it still seemed as if the third turn was getting no closer at all, like one of those dreams where the object you are trying to get to keeps growing farther and farther away.

Jodell couldn't resist. On the very first lap, he allowed the car to roll up into the low side of the steep banking as he went through the turn. It was a thrilling experience as he felt the car stick solidly to the track even though he was scooting along at better than a hundred miles an hour. Then, speed or not, it seemed like miles from the fourth turn to the finish line. He wanted to go even harder on the next lap, but he tempered himself, talked to himself like a conservative coach, and took another lap still at only around a hundred miles an hour.

The back straight stretch was thirty-six hundred feet long and it was amazing how long it took for the car to traverse that distance and come up onto the tall turns again in three and four. Again, something in his gut told him to stomp it, to work out the car, but he resisted as he drove on past the front straightaway and the grandstands. He kept this up for several more laps, using the conservative speeds to find his distances and landmarks around the track, his acceleration and, if there had been any, the braking points. He would need to have reference points to keep up with where he was on the track as the speeds built.

Finally, going low through the middle of turns three and four, he felt that he was ready to learn what this big closed course was all about. He was cruising, easily running near a hundred miles per hour when he made his decision to test the car and his own driving ability. Did he have what it took to pilot a car wide open at such gaudy speeds? He kicked downward on the gas, shoving the pedal all the way to the floor.

The motor never hesitated and actually seemed eager to finally be able to roar. The rest of the car began to dig down into the low side of the turn. The RPMs climbed as the car started to pick up speed coming off the corner. Surprisingly, there was little sensation of radical speed as the car rocketed down the front stretch. He might just as well have been driving his grandmother to church on one of the blacktops back home. Now, Jodell had a clear track since the other cars ahead were already well into the first turn. He grinned beneath the racing goggles and let out a whoop as the Ford sailed along smoothly, faster and faster.

Joe and Bubba stood nervously on the pit wall, watching the cars tentatively circling the virgin asphalt. Most were obviously taking it easy, almost fearful to see what the track was really about. But practically every lap that spun by unmasked yet another brave soul willing to toss conservatism aside, ratchet things up a few notches, and see what he and his mount could do. They watched Jodell in the Ford all the way around the track, reserving judgment on exactly how he was doing. Every lap their driver made was experimental, as he was obviously feeling out the track and its nuances.

"He'll know when to let it fly," Joe cautioned. "Jodell, he'll know."

Finally, while Jodell was still in the center of the third turn, Bubba thought he could see a subtle change in the car's trajectory. He slugged Joe on the shoulder while motioning toward Jodell.

"Here he goes!" he yelled sharply enough to be heard above the thunder of some passing cars. Joe quickly raised his stopwatch to time the lap.

From their perspective, the renewed speed of the car was evident as it came off the corner and hurtled down the front straight directly toward them. The Ford looked comfortable on the track as it flashed by them on its way into the first turn.

"Look at him go!" Bubba yelped, pumping his fist into the air. Joe watched the car, then the hand on the watch, feeling a strong pride in the knowledge that it was his engine that was propelling the race car so smartly around the world's newest, fastest track.

The car felt even better than Jodell could have hoped for as he took his first lap under full throttle. He cut through the tri-oval one lane higher up on the track than in his previous go-rounds. The car seemed perfectly willing to stick exactly where he put it. He felt for an instant that he maybe could ride along on the wall itself if he tried.

He hesitated for an instant as he tried to decide which line to take through the first corner. He settled on a middle line almost by default and then let off the gas to be safe. In an instant he knew there was no need to ease up as the car set itself perfectly and rolled through the corner as if it were locked down on a pair of rails. But then, when he stayed in the gas through turn two, he felt the car bind up a little before it came off the corner and out onto the long back stretch.

Heading into the third turn, he picked his line, the route he instinctively felt might be the best trajectory through, and he felt the car hang on and sail through the corner wide open. Although he was poised to do so if he felt the car slipping, Jodell never let up, never even considered braking. The pull of centrifugal force in the banking pushed him down in his seat and tugged his head hard to the right while he kept a tight grip on the steering wheel.

That's when he suddenly ran up on several other practicing cars and blew right on past them as if they might have been parked in some lover's lane somewhere. Already, it was clear that some of the drivers were picking up the track and its nuances and some of them weren't.

After spiraling around twenty or so laps, Jodell

eased the car off the track at the pit road and pulled
to the spot behind the wall where they had their
equipment set up. Bubba and Joe came running up
as he shut down the engine and climbed from the
car. He had to lean against the side of the Ford for
a moment. He was suddenly dizzy, out of breath, as
an intoxicating adrenaline rush swept over him.

"Wow!" Jodell was finally able to breathe as he
took an offered jar of ice water from Bubba. "That
was something else, I'll tell you!"

"This old car can really fly around this place," Joe
said, still staring at the face of the stopwatch, not sure
he could believe what it was telling him. "You were
running about as fast as anybody out there toward
the end."

"It'll fool you, boys. It feels like you're running
slow 'cause this place is so darn big. Then you try
to focus on something coming up and it's gone before you can even get your eye locked in on it."

"I kept expecting you to take off and fly like one
of them seagulls," Bubba said, his eyes wide with
excitement.

"If I put my arms out the windows, I just might!"
Jodell still wore a wide grin on his face. "It's fun out
there. Nothing like those narrow old corners at Darlington."

"What about the tires?" Joe asked. He was already
bent over, running his hand along the tread of the
left front tire, feeling for wear.

"They felt good. Not rough and no vibration that
I could feel. We sure need to check them over good
before I go out again though. Running that fast, I
don't believe I want to have one blow out on me and
cause me to bust down that brand new fence running
around this place."

"Ready for another run?" Joe asked.

"Yeah, soon as there's a few more cars out there. I want to run in a crowd and see what it feels like."

The three of them made a quick check under the hood and beneath the front end of the car, and then Jodell climbed back in through the open window and fired the car up again. He backed her out of her space, rolled out onto the pit road and headed off toward the first turn. As he brought the race car up to speed coming out of the second turn, another vehicle came up fast behind him, then slipped on past with apparently little effort. It was the number 43 convertible of his friend, Richard Petty. Jodell tucked in behind him and followed him down the back stretch, watching Petty's eyes in his mirror.

The 43 took a higher line into and through the corner than Jodell would have thought possible. Even so, he was able to pull up alongside the 43 in the center of the turn, but then he felt the motor begin to bog down from the strain of maintaining speed through the lower line. The 43, running higher on the outside, was able to keep more RPMs in his engine and that allowed Petty to pull away from Jodell a bit as they came off the fourth turn.

Even so, Jodell was able to tuck back in behind him as they raced down the front stretch. Once he had pulled back up on Richard's tail, Jodell boldly pulled down to the inside, hoping to be able to make a pass. That's when he felt something strange. His car seemed to get an extra burst of speed as he finished the pass with him applying no more pressure on the gas pedal. It was as if some giant, unseen hand was giving him a welcome extra shove.

Before he had even realized it, he had earned a dozen car-lengths' lead on the 43, but before they could clear the next corner, Richard had pulled right back up behind him, close enough to appear to be roped to his rear end. This dance went on for the next few laps as they passed each other several times, getting the feel of their cars and the track.

Jodell had begun to notice how the air affected the car as the two raced with each other lap after lap. The gap the first car was cutting through the air seemed to give the trailing car an extra burst of speed as it closed up on the one in front. Then, as the back car pulled around to pass, it seemed as if there was an extra kick, a boost that was enough to propel the car on past. It was something good to know, but Jodell was sure Petty had noticed it as well.

Richard even looked over and winked at Jodell one time when he seesawed past him. Jodell simply nodded back, crept back up on his bumper and returned the favor.

When they finally trudged back to the Sea Spray Motel that night, Jodell flopped on the bed and was soon snoring, his gas-pedal foot still twitching as if he was out there on the shiny new track yet, trying to ease past Richard Petty. Joe and Bubba had other plans besides a long, restful night in the rack, but it was hardly the plans Jodell would have predicted. They had heard of several local garages where some of the drivers and their crews liked to hang out during the Daytona races. That suited Bubba fine, but he was a little surprised that Joe wanted to hang out with a bunch of grease-monkeys instead of tracking down Little Joe Weatherly and Curtis Turner and their continuous race-week party.

"We got all week, Bub," Joe offered. "Besides, we might pick up something that'll help us out there on that big old slab of asphalt."

The days ran together as they spent every moment possible trying out the car and learning the track and figuring out the best setup to traverse it. Most nights consisted of impromptu talk sessions at this garage or that motel room with the other drivers and mechanics, all openly comparing notes as if there was no upcoming competition between them at all.

As things shook out, there were no surprises about who had found the fastest way around the loop. Lee Petty. Shorty Rollins. Little Joe Weatherly. Fireball Roberts. Each veteran driver quickly seemed to have solved the puzzle that was the new Daytona track just as they had most every other circuit they ran.

Jodell Lee seemed to fit in with the second fastest group, merely a tick slower than the first bunch, but still not quite up to their times. The motor Joe had built seemed solid, plenty fast to lead at most tracks, but it was clear that they had not found the exact tweak of the engine to make it that smidgen faster and yet still stay within the rules. And it was just as clear that some of the others had.

To win, they would have to out-drive all the others, get better pit stops, and, maybe most importantly, have a little bit of plain old luck as well. But Joe had not given up either. Every day, he operated on the Ford's motor like a neurosurgeon, trying to make the minute adjustments that might give them a tenth of a second here, a hint more power there. Of course, they all three knew that other teams were doing the same vivisection on their own cars.

Still, the more Jodell steered the car around the new track, the more his confidence grew. He knew he could take Joe's carefully honed engine and Bubba's perfectly set-up chassis and his own driving abilities and outrun everyone else out there. But even so, there were times when he pulled off the track, eased to a stop in the pit, and noticed that his hands were shaking when he finally let go his grip on the wheel.

It wasn't fear. He knew that. It was more respect for the track and the cyclone-like speeds.

And there was still no sure way to tell how the cars would behave when there were up to sixty or so of them all out there on the track at the same time, all making an insane dash for the green flag, and all of them doing it at the exact same time. Being a part of a traffic jam moving at well over one hundred miles per hour was something that would give the most ignorant or nonchalant driver pause.

And there was one other thing. No one had said it out loud yet. No one had even dared think it. But they all knew it. This track could cost a man his life and it could do it in a blink of an eye.

THE CAVALRY

After the next day's final practice session, the three of them barely had time to get back to the motel and get showered before Jodell had to leave for the bus station. Catherine, Johnny, and the boys who would make up their crew were supposed to be on the 6:20 bus from Jacksonville. Randy Weems and Clifford Stanley had agreed to come down to Florida, even if they had to pay their own way. They were that excited about being a part of the 34 pit crew and the first race on the amazing new track in Daytona. Jodell, Joe, and Bubba had agreed, though, that they would help them with their expenses, in exchange for them coming down early enough to help them get the car and pits set up.

At first, Bubba had planned to go with Jodell to the bus station, just on the off chance Joyce had met up with Catherine and the rest of the crew in Atlanta. Then, just as they were headed out the door of the

Sea Spray, he had decided that he would wait there instead, taking the extra time to shave off three days' worth of beard and get most of the grease from beneath his fingernails and work on propping up the front of his flat-top with some sticky goo he had bought at the five and dime next door to the motel. Jodell knew, though, that it was primarily because he was too shy, that he would be embarrassed if Joyce showed too much excitement at seeing him again and smothered him with hugs and kisses at such a public place as the Greyhound bus station and with his friends from back home looking on.

So Jodell waited alone in the car, parked across the street from the bus station in the shade of a bank of sweet-smelling flowering bushes, waiting for the Greyhound. He had stretched out across the seat and had slipped into a fitful doze when he heard the bus roll up with a whoosh of its air brakes. He popped up quickly and saw the bus stop in front of the station in a blue haze of diesel smoke. He checked his watch. It was forty-five minutes late and he was surprised to see that he had been asleep for the better part of an hour.

The driver hopped out and began assisting passengers as they climbed down. There were mostly elderly folk, taking their sweet time, and as Jodell watched, a mild panic started to set in when it seemed most of the bus's riders had been disgorged already and he hadn't seen Catherine yet. Maybe it was the wrong bus. Or she had missed a connection somewhere. Or maybe she had decided not to come at all.

Then, there she was. She looked wonderful in her simple, flower-print cotton dress, her hair even longer than he remembered from a few days before, blowing in the warm breeze off the Atlantic. And right behind her off the bus were her brother, Johnny, and his friends, Randy Weems and Clifford Stanley.

As he trotted across the street to meet them, Jodell couldn't help but grin. With their faded overalls, long-sleeve flannel shirts, and heavy farm work boots, the three men were obviously way out of their element. He could only hope, for the sake of the other passengers on the bus, that they had scraped the manure off their boots before they got on board.

They were busy claiming their bags from the belly of the Greyhound when Jodell trotted up.

"Y'all take a wrong turn at the pool hall?" he asked.

Catherine didn't answer. Instead, she turned and grabbed him in a powerful embrace, kissing him without shame, as if years had passed since he had driven out of the mountains headed for Florida.

"Y'all wanna quit making out right here in front of God and everybody and help us get these things off the sidewalk," Johnny fussed, but he was smiling, Catherine ignored him, leaning back just far enough to look into Jodell's eyes.

"I missed you. I've been worried about you. They've been talking on the radio about how fast everybody's going down here on that big old track."

He hugged her tighter but didn't reply. He wasn't used to somebody besides Grandma worrying about him, caring about what happened to him. Finally he pulled away and looked her over.

"You don't look any the worse for having spent all that time on a bus with these three hillbillies."

"A thousand miles is a long way to have to baby-sit. You'd think these critters had never been off the farm before."

"Heck, couple of us ain't," Randy volunteered. " 'Cept to Darlington that time, and that wadn't near as far and snaky as coming off down here." He gazed about at all the activity outside the bus station, at the traffic on Highway 1, at the palm trees that lined the thoroughfare and the sliver of white sand beach and blue water he could see in the distance. "But looky here, Jodell Bob Lee. The cavalry has done showed up to help you win this danged old race."

"The worst part," Catherine continued, "was when they all started opening their liver, cheese, and onion sandwiches about two miles outside Chandler Cove. I thought the driver was going to pull over and put them and their sack lunch right off the bus. I pretended I didn't know them. We rolled down the windows and froze until we got the smell out of that old bus."

"I wish I had one of them sandwiches right this minute," Johnny said dreamily. "You believe they don't even sell no okra or turnip greens or cornbread or butterbeans in that café at the bus station in Atlanta? Cheeseburger was about the only thing I recognized on the menu and it was three dollars. You believe that? Three dollars for a cheeseburger?"

Jodell helped them get all their bags into the Ford's trunk and crammed the three burly men into the backseat. He climbed in next to Catherine then suddenly realized he had forgotten to inquire about Joyce.

"Y'all didn't happen to see Joyce Anderson somewhere along the way did you? I left Bubba in the shower and he'll go ahead and just drown himself if she doesn't make it down here."

Catherine gave him a blank look.

"She should have gotten here a couple of hours ahead of us. Her bus left way before ours did. Was she not in the station?"

"Uh. Well. I never thought to go in and look," Jodell said sheepishly. "I thought she would leave a message at the motel if she wasn't on the same bus as y'all."

"Did you check at the desk for messages?" she asked sharply.

Jodell ducked his head farther, not wanting to look her in the eye. He climbed back out of the car and hustled across the street and into the tiny waiting room of the bus station. He scanned the dozen or so people sitting there before he spied her, sound asleep in a corner, her feet propped up on her bag and using her coat for a pillow. He breathed a sigh of relief and walked over and shook her gently.

"Joyce," he said softly. "Your taxi is here."

She opened her eyes, recognized him and smiled as she stretched awake.

"Hi, Mr. Lee. Where's Bubba?"

"Gettin' spruced up for you. You been here long? Why didn't you call the motel?"

"The bus got in early. I knew y'all were probably still at the track 'cause we could hear the cars when we came by there. Shoot, you can hear them nearly to the state line. Did Catherine and them get here yet?"

"She's out in the car with the others. Come on. Give me your bag and let's go fetch Lover Boy." He laughed and helped her to her feet.

Bubba had dragged a chair from inside the room and sat there, leaned back against the wall, waiting for them. Joyce ran from the car and leapt into his arms while he blushed deep crimson, but he ignored the whoops and gigs of all the other men and boldly returned her serious welcoming kiss. He was that happy to see her.

Johnny went down to the motel office and checked them all in while Jodell and Bubba walked down to the beach with Catherine and Joyce. The sun was dropping in the sky behind them, the water was deep green, and a healthy moon was already rising out across the Atlantic. The two men stood there, their arms around their girlfriends, gazing at the point where the water met the sky. None of them wanted to break the mood but it eventually occurred to Jodell that none of them had eaten in a while.

They finally turned, walked back through the sand, and gathered all the rest of their crew and went in search of supper. They ended up at a seafood restaurant Little Joe Weatherly had recommended, a place that featured all-you-can-eat shrimp and oysters and threatened to break their meager food budget, but Jodell figured that it would be the best way to feed the bunch of them and would get their race-day effort off on the right foot. Although leery at first of the strange fare, the Tennesseeans ultimately did their best to put the place out of business.

And over massive mounds of shrimp shells and refreshed platters of catfish and hushpuppies, they began formulating their plans for the race itself, who would do what, whose responsibility it was to keep an eye on which part of the car. They used salt and pepper shakers and sugar packs and dishes of coleslaw and scooped-out oyster shells to represent cars and toolboxes and pit paraphernalia and arranged them the way they planned to do it at the track.

Back at the motel, Joe, Johnny, Randy, and Clifford left in search of a party somewhere, anywhere. Joe had already described the pre-race festivities to the doubting farm boys and they were ready to see it all firsthand.

Meanwhile, Bubba and Joyce walked up the darkened beach in one direction while Jodell and Catherine strolled the other. Jodell had retrieved a blanket from the car and they found a deserted section of beach a half-mile down from the motel. The moon was already high and painted the ocean with shimmering light. The gentle lapping of the breakers on the sand seemed almost musical and Jodell lay there, holding Catherine close, feeling as much at peace as he could ever remember in his life.

"You know, if we took off swimming across that water, how far it would be before we got to land again?" he asked her. He could see the lights of a boat way out on the horizon and tried to imagine what the beach and its row of hotels and lights might look like to the people on it.

"All the way to Spain or England, I guess. A long way, I know. Lots farther than swimming across the Green River." She leaned closer to him and watched the lights of the boat with him until it faded out of sight. They could hear the waves but could see only the white foam that marked their progress up and down the beach.

"You ever thought about how far we are from Chandler Cove right now?" he asked her.

"Yes. In more ways than one. It scares me sometimes." She paused for a moment. He could feel her shiver slightly against him. "Do you ever get scared, Jodell?"

He thought about his answer for a while, listening to the breakers before he whispered his answer.

"I get scared if I think about what would happen to Grandma if I got hurt out there. What would happen to the farm if I wash out at racing. I worry about you, too, if something happened to me. I love you. I worry about worrying you, I guess."

She pulled him even closer and he thought he could feel her tremble again.

"And when you're racing? Do you ever get scared out there on the track?"

He knew it was a hard question for her to ask, one so personal she had never been able to frame it before. Somehow he sensed it was a mark of how deep their relationship had become that she now felt she could.

"Sometimes, just a little bit, before I first go out there. Sometimes after I get off the track and shut off the motor and think about it for a minute. But never, not even for a second, when I'm out there racing. And if I ever do feel any fear at all out there, it will be time to quit. You can't drive scared and have any hope of winning. Can you understand that, Catherine?"

"I'm trying. Believe me, I'm trying."

He kissed her then. Kissed her because he loved her. Kissed her because he knew she had told him the truth. And because she was working so hard to try to understand why he did what he did.

FORTY-LAPPER

They were at the track the next morning before the February sun had even shown up. Joyce and Catherine had taken the tow car and had done some grocery shopping so they could fix a picnic lunch for Jodell and the rest of the crew. They sat on a blanket in the infield just behind the fence that marked the pit area, spreading mayonnaise on white bread, slicing tomatoes, unwrapping luncheon meat. They were enjoying the warm Florida sun after the months of cold winter in the mountains back home and had their shirt sleeves and pedal-pusher legs rolled up to begin work on their tans.

Joe, who had shown up back at the motel long after the others had surrendered for the night, spent the morning under the hood of the race car, looking for even more power out of the motor. He wanted to try something he had picked up from another mechanic at some party.

Bubba was on his back underneath the car, checking the suspension. Johnny was checking the brakes and tires one wheel at a time. Everything needed to be right now, in race form, because this was to be the last chance at practice.

Clifford and Randy had taken a bunch of their rims down to the tire center to get some tires put on them to be held in reserve for the race. Thankfully, the new track and her high-banked turns were much easier on tires than the narrow turns of Darlington had been.

The first practice was only half an hour away and they scrambled to get the car put back together and ready to steer out on to the track while Jodell changed into his jumpsuit. By then, he was itching to get back out on the track and see what the car could do after the tweaking they had done. Finally, they got everything buttoned back up and the car pushed up to the line just before the start of the practice.

Joe found a high spot atop a platform where he could see most of the way around the track and he climbed up, armed with his clipboard and stopwatches. He knew it was now time to see what they really had in their car compared to everybody else who was just as determined to win the first Daytona race as they were.

An official in a striped referee-type shirt and red armband stood at the head of the line of cars, waiting to wave them out onto the track to start the practice. Finally receiving his cue from the flag stand, he started to vigorously wave the cars out onto the track.

Jodell tightened his safety belts and readied himself

to go out. He was now comfortable inside the car as well as out on the track, so it was time now to see how much speed they could really get out of the car. Bubba was watching all the activity going on up at the end of the pit road and he tapped on the hood and motioned for Jodell to fire up the motor.

When the motor coughed to life, Jodell carefully scanned the bank of gauges in front of him, making certain they all read what they should. He reached for the shifter and pushed it up into first gear, let out the clutch and felt the car start to roll. He allowed the car directly in front of him to pull off and get a few lengths ahead. Once he hit the track, he gunned the engine and headed off down into the first turn.

He took the car down low in the banking as he ran up through the gears. Down the long back straightaway, he continued to accelerate, finally shifting down into fourth. He set his line going into the third turn and pushed the car hard through it, but she felt good as she bit down hard and held tight through the banking. Coming off the corner, he hit full speed as he flashed for the start–finish line.

From where he stood on the platform, Joe checked his stopwatches and dutifully jotted down the times on the clipboard. Bubba stood up on the wall that lined the pits, never taking his eyes off the 34 car. Johnny Holt stood next to him, not really knowing what he was looking for but watching grim-faced, just as the big man was doing. Randy and Clifford simply stood, not knowing where to look, trying to take in all the noise and color and circling cars, more than a little bit overwhelmed.

Jodell concentrated, working hard, trying to drive as smoothly yet as fast as he could. He tried to pick the best spots as he encountered traffic, using the traffic to pull the wind off them, thus finding more speed in the process. After ten laps, he spotted the Pure Oil sign marking the entrance to the pit road, then slowed and pulled down to where Bubba stood holding the pit signboard to mark their spot behind the wall.

As soon as he had cut the engine, Bubba and Johnny scooted beneath the car to check the tires and suspension. As Jodell climbed out the open window he spotted Joe ambling up, consulting the scribbling on the clipboard. Thankfully, Joe had a broad grin on his face.

"That was a good run, Jodell! The times looked real good."

"She felt good out there. The more I drive this place the better I like it."

Joe scanned the figures on the clipboard and did some quick math in his head.

"You were within a tenth or so every lap. They were all real good, even when you were catching and passing the other cars."

"Good. It seems like I get a lift every time I come up on somebody. How are the fast guys running?"

"Pretty fast, but really not a lot better than you are. Lee Petty, Fireball, Little Joe, they're all still running about as fast as anybody but this last run of yours was about as good as any of theirs."

Little Joe Weatherly himself stopped by to rag them a bit.

"Hey, Tennessee! I seen you strugglin' to get around out there. That old buggy of yours was wheezin' worse than my grandma."

"Darn it, Little Joe," Bubba said. "Why don't you just leave us alone?"

"I was scared I was going to blow your doors off so I slowed her down every time I passed you. My car is just flying. I got this race in the bag. I'm thinking I'll just put some wings on her and fly her home after I win this thing. By the way, why haven't you or your little bitty friend here been to any of our parties? Old Joe here is the only one of your bunch that is still sociable. I'm starting to think you don't like old Little Joe and Curtis no more. We're having a party tonight so you still have time to catch up on your fun. See you there. Gotta go!"

And he was gone. Bubba stood there, grinning, shaking his head over the little man and his constant line of blarney.

They decided there was little more they could do to improve the car and pressing for more might lead to them tearing it up or wrecking it and having to start from scratch, trying to put it back together. They could learn more in the next day's forty-lap preliminary race, but finally they could allow themselves to breathe, to rest, to tear into the picnic lunch the girls had fixed.

They spent the afternoon getting the tires, tools, and equipment ready for the next day and practicing pit stops. Joe, Bubba, and Jodell also watched some of the other drivers practicing, picking out the ones to beat.

Late in the day, a car rammed hard into the outside fence, bringing out the red flag to stop the session while the track crew cleaned up the mess. The car had been ripped apart after apparently blowing a tire and skidding up into the fence as if drawn by a magnet. The race car looked as if it had been taken apart by a giant can opener, leaving shards of metal and pieces of rubber strewn all over the track.

Jodell unconsciously held his breath until he could see the driver climbing out of the wreckage, wobbly but apparently not seriously hurt. It was one of the younger drivers, a man he had spoken to a time or two at the meetings there and at Darlington. He stumbled down the steep banks to stand shakily on the flat of the track while he tried to get his helmet off. A safety worker tried to check him over but the driver waved him off disgustedly. He slammed his helmet down hard on the pavement and then gave it a sharp kick, as if booting a football. A minute ago, this driver had a car that had a chance at winning the race. Now, it was so much junk being swept up by the track crew and the driver was lucky to be able to be pitching a fit on the track's apron.

"Let's call it a day," Joe suggested. "Nothing else we can do today but sit here and worry."

They hurriedly packed their stuff up and secured the race car and left, headed for the beach. But Jodell couldn't help worrying. He wondered if their excitement at being in this strange land, at touring the brand new track, over simply being so far from home was dangerously close to taking the edge off their racing. He hoped not, but he didn't want to say anything. Catherine and Joyce were laughing, comparing the suntans they had gotten so far. Bubba was so obviously lovesick that the others had quit kidding him about it. He had not mentioned being hungry all day and was only mildly interested in where they would eat that night. The farm boys were animated, excited about spending the balance of the day lying on the sand, checking out the girls as they strolled by and then seeking out Little Joe's party after the sun had gone down.

They had all worked hard. They had earned some

fun. But Jodell couldn't help but worry.

The crowd was pouring into the track already when they got to the track the next morning. There was a solid line of traffic coming out from the beach toward the speedway and even with the sun hardly up yet, there was a festive atmosphere all around the big track as competitors and fans alike were finally ready for some serious racing. Mini-parties were breaking out everywhere, some quite clearly spill-overs from the previous night. The flags flying around the speedway snapped smartly in the warm, steady sea breeze.

The pit areas were already busy. The cars were lined up on the pit road like airplanes on an aircraft carrier waiting patiently for their pilots. People milled all about the cars, setting up the pits or making last minute alignments on the machines.

Jodell and the boys had been at the track early, waiting for the gate to the infield and pits to open. It didn't take long for the car to clear the inspections but, as usual, Jodell still held his breath until they were waved on through. The boys pushed it up to the line and left her sitting there, ready for Jodell. They would start in the middle of the field for this first race, based on a qualifying lap the day before, but at least he wasn't alone there. Only a couple of rows in front of him was the number 43 convertible of Richard Petty. They spoke briefly before the start about what they thought it would take to get to the front and win the thing. Like the growing crowd, his crew, and everyone else at the track, Jodell was get-ting more and more excited as the start time got closer. He felt something in his gut closely akin to hunger as he anticipated getting the race underway out there on the big track.

But it was still an hour before the start so the crew sat around the tow car in the infield and had a quick sandwich and a soda. Catherine went to the back of the car and retrieved her beach bag. Jodell was already dressed in his driving coveralls with the large Bubble Up patch on the back. There was a smaller patch on the front and his name was embroidered over the left breast pocket, thanks to Catherine. But she obviously had more of something in the bag.

"Mr. Williams gave these to me before we left. He wanted me to tell you how proud he is of all of you and how bad he wanted to come himself." She dug into the beach bag and pulled out five white and green Bubble Up route-driver shirts, one for each member of the crew. "He wanted everybody to be able to tell who crewed the 34 Bubble Up car when we win the race."

They all promptly stripped off their dirty, sweaty T-shirts and put on the new ones. Jodell had to admit that they looked pretty good, that they actually made them look like a team. Along with the slick paint job and logo on the back of the car, their driver's coveralls and their new shirts, they at least looked the equal of the other, more established teams. Now all they had to do was to go as fast as the others did.

Catherine and Joyce headed off for the scoring stand while the rest of the crew got the car ready to race. Bubba cleaned the windshield for at least the tenth time while Jodell and Joe sat in the shade beside the car discussing their strategies for the preliminary race.

Just then, an official worked his way down the line ordering the drivers to their cars, and the command to fire the engines finally echoed over the speedway. Jodell obediently hit the starter switch and the car

roared to life. Joe slapped him on the shoulder while
Bubba spat in his rag and took one last swipe at some
imaginary speck on the windshield before he moved
over to the pit wall. An official at the end of the pit
road waved a rolled-up green flag, emphatically urging the cars off.

For Jodell, this was the moment of truth, the instant when all the practice laps were done, when "the
hay was in the barn," as Joe put it. He followed
the cars directly in front of him but it seemed like
the lead cars were at least a half-mile ahead of him.
How in the world could he ever see and anticipate
the start when the starting line was in another
county?

As they ran through the fourth turn and on to the
short straight to take the green flag, the pace car accelerated and headed for the Pure Oil sign at the
entrance to the pit road. As he feared, Jodell never
saw the flag wave from his position so far back in
the field. He knew it was time to go when half a
dozen other cars that had been behind him went
roaring past. He stomped on the gas and took off for
the first turn.

It took him several laps to sort things out and start
to move up through the field. With five laps to go,
Jodell counted seven cars ahead of him and he was
still making his way steadily toward the front. He
had played the air off the other cars to his advantage
and that had helped him to continue to pick off spots.
He was convinced now that he could win this thing,
but then, he noticed that one of the cars ahead of
him was Richard Petty, riding in fourth position.

He shrugged his shoulders as best he could with
the grip he had on the wheel and fell into the higher
line that Petty was taking. That allowed him to keep

picking off cars. Then, with only a lap to go, Richard was in second with Jodell directly behind in third and another group of cars that they just passed tailgating right behind them. One of the veteran drivers, Shorty Rollins, led the pack but he was in Jodell's sights.

In the pits, the boys were standing on the wall, screaming, cheering wildly, as if Jodell could actually hear them above the roar of his own and all the other straining engines out there. Joe consulted his stopwatches and even he was beginning to get excited. The watch told the tale. They were actually fast enough to win if he could just get past Petty and Rollins.

Catherine and Joyce sat side by side high in the stand, scoring the cars. One advantage of a track as big as Daytona was that it took the cars so long to go around that even the scorer could watch the race between marking the times down on the laps for the car he or she was scoring. Joyce had taken to scoring much like Catherine had and was having a wonderful time while feeling as if she, too, was a key part of what was going on down there on the track. But both of them almost jumped out of the booth when Jodell passed the third car in line to take over the number three spot on the track.

Now Jodell was glued to the rear of Richard's convertible. He instinctively knew that he had to make his move when Richard made his and hope there was enough room on the track and muscle under the Ford's hood to move on past both cars when he did. As they flashed over the start–finish line to take the white flag, Jodell tightened his grip on the wheel and gritted his teeth. He ran his passing move through his mind trying to visualize what he needed to do, the way his high school football coach had always told him to do.

Shorty Rollins still held the lead as they came off the corner. That's where Richard chose to make his move, going down the back straightaway. Jodell winced. It seemed a little early to be making the move by his way of thinking. But that instant's hesitation almost let Richard get away. He quickly fell in behind the convertible, though, and they eased past Rollins, taking over first and second. As they entered the third turn, Jodell looked high, ready to blow right on past Richard and sail to the checkered flag.

But just as he did, Shorty Rollins and four of the other cars trailing behind him came flying past as if they had been shot out of a cannon, leaving Jodell and Richard to watch them take the win while they settled for sixth and seventh.

Later, Lee Petty laughed as Jodell was telling him how the other cars had simply sailed right on by. They had become the very first victims of the "Daytona slingshot move," even though they didn't really understand the science of it. As they later learned, it was based on the aerodynamics of the track and the cars running at such speeds and allowed a trailing car to get a speed boost from the air whistling around a car directly in front of it, "slingshotting" past. The proper strategy was to be in position to zip past the leaders into first place at a spot that wouldn't allow the car or cars you just passed to get themselves into a spot so they could pass you back before you could cross the finish line.

The day ended with a big barbecue on the beach behind the Sea Spray. Some of the other racers who were staying there along with a group of fans had pitched in to throw a cookout and party. For Jodell, it was the perfect way to end the day. He didn't feel like going out and yet he needed to do something to get his mind off the disappointing end to the race. Instead of taking pride in finishing so well in such a competitive race, he was left feeling empty. He had felt sure he had the race won, only to finish down the list. If the newspapers back home only mentioned the top five, as far as Mr. Williams and all the other folks were concerned, he might just as well have finished dead last.

Never mind that he outran a couple dozen others. He had finished somewhere else but first and it was eating at him.

Thank goodness for Catherine. She seemed to sense that he didn't want to talk that night. She was perfectly content to walk alongside him up and down the beach, watching the tiny pale crabs scoot and dart along in the wet sand.

Before long, they were laughing, skipping shells across the smooth surface of the ocean, playing dodge-'em with the gentle lapping surf, stopping to hold and kiss each other until the moon had climbed high in the sky and the disappointing finish in the afternoon's race was nothing more than a valuable learning experience.

RACE DAY AT DAYTONA

Race day came early to the crew at the Sea Spray. Even Joe had shown up amazingly early the night before, determined to get some sleep so he'd be fresh on race day. Jodell got up and went next door to wake Catherine and Joyce, only to find them awake and showered and ready to go racing. They splurged for a restaurant breakfast for everyone, were too worked up to eat and left most of it on their plates, and were at the track just as it opened.

The car was quickly readied and pushed through the inspection line. After running the forty-lap race, the crew knew precisely what needed to be done. But try as they might, they were all having trouble tempering their excitement. They all had to concentrate to keep focused on the race and not get lost in all the spectacle that was going on around them. That was hard to do with the huge crowd, the bands, the television film cameras, the newspaper reporters, the continual parade of wreckers and emergency vehicles with their lights flashing as they circled the track.

"I guess you heard about your good buddy, Dash Rockford," Joe asked Jodell as they paused for a moment.

"No. What?"

"He lost his ride. He won't be running today. Something about a sponsor pulling out on him."

"Too danged bad," Bubba offered from the other side of the race car.

"Yeah," Jodell said, but without Bubba Baxter's conviction. "Too danged bad."

But somehow, he felt sorry for the guy. Jodell could only imagine how it would make him feel to lose the chance to run in this inaugural race. Rockford was trouble but he would have to be hurting this morning. Maybe that was something that only someone with the blind drive of a Jodell Lee or a Dash Rockford could understand.

They pushed the car out to the starting line but not until after they had gone over every single inch of her. They checked every nut for tightness, looked at every fitting and hose, and inspected all the tires, on and off the car. Joe checked the timing and the jets on the carburetor. He and Jodell talked about precisely how they wanted the engine set for the day. They decided to be conservative with their settings to make sure the motor lasted the full distance at the tremendous RPMs it would be turning.

Catherine and Joyce headed to the scoring area early both to get set and so they wouldn't distract the men from the job at hand. Before she left, she held Jodell's hand and they silently looked into each other's eyes. Then they had kissed quickly and she had walked away. Joyce and Bubba hugged quickly, too.

"He'll be okay," Joyce told her when they settled down in the scorers' stand. She had no trouble reading the worried expression on Catherine's face.

"I know. He's good, Joyce. He knows what he is doing. But they go so fast down here. If they blow a tire or get tapped by somebody else that's not such a good driver, who knows how hard the hit will be."

"He'll be okay," Joyce said again. It was all she knew to say.

Down in the pits, Jodell was lecturing Johnny, Randy, and Clifford.

"Y'all be sure and get the pit stops done fast. We can make up a lot of ground on most of these characters if we are quick."

"Our stops will be fast," Johnny swore. "Don't you worry about that. We spent all winter out in Daddy's barn practicing."

"I know y'all will do your best but every second we can pick up here will make a big difference. Some of these other guys don't know what they're doing and we need to capitalize on it." He turned to Joe. Another thought had just occurred to him. "I'm still a little worried about the tires."

"I don't think the tires will be a problem. They were fine after the race Friday. I couldn't find anybody who had a problem that wasn't related to how the car was set up."

"I just want to make sure . . ." but he was interrupted by the call over the loudspeakers for the drivers to report to their cars and anything else he might have said would have been drowned out by the bellow of the crowd, which was now more than ready for the racing to start.

As Jodell walked along the lines of cars headed to the Bubble Up Ford he caught sight of Little Joe. He slugged the little man on the shoulder as he passed by and got an unintelligible burst of drawling words in response. He spotted Curtis Turner a couple of cars away, looking none the worse for wear from what was certainly a humdinger of a party that had been going on down the beach the last several nights.

He walked past Richard Petty's 43 car.

"Hey, Richard! Good luck, man."

"Jodell, same to you. Let's hope these cats don't put a move on us like they did the other day."

Jodell grinned. It was comforting to know the way the preliminary race had ended was still eating away at Petty, too, just as it had been him.

Jodell climbed into the car and Bubba helped him get the belts tight. Joe stood off to the side going over the notes from the drivers' meeting and making one more run through his elaborate checklist.

Jodell had to admit that the crew looked good in their Bubble Up shirts. Several newspaper photographers stopped and took photographs and a television cameraman paused to shoot film of them wiping down the race car.

Jodell was in the middle of a silent prayer for a good safe race when the command to fire the engines came so he had to stop short of "amen." He hit the starter switch and felt the usual thrill when the big, powerful engine rumbled to life. Bubba stuck his big mitt in the window and shook his hand. Joe popped the left front fender and flashed Jodell the "okay" sign and then a "V" for victory. The team moved down toward their pit while the cars sat warming up on the starting line.

Finally, they were waved off the line and out onto

the track to begin taking their warm-up laps. Jodell couldn't believe it was finally here. All the preparation, all the worry, all the planning, and they were at last on the magnificent new track, ready to take their shot at a brass ring so big and bright that they would have had trouble even dreaming of such a thing only a short while ago.

He tried to tell himself that merely being here, the sheer fact that he was behind the wheel of a competitive race car out here on this track with the likes of Lee Petty and Junior Johnson and Fireball Roberts, was victory enough. But he knew that simply wasn't so. He was here to win. To finish anywhere else but at the front would be a failure.

And as they slowly circled, he thought of his conversation with Catherine the other night on the beach. No, he wasn't afraid. He felt the weight of responsibility, though. The pressure of all those who depended on him to bring the Ford home up front. But somehow, it was a good feeling. He relished the responsibility. And he was ready to do it for everyone who was pulling for him.

The double line of fifty-nine race cars rolled down the back stretch for the last time. Almost half the field was made up of convertibles and that was an odd sight to many in the stands who were more accustomed to dirt track racing. The crowd rose as one as the cars came around, lined up two by two to take the green flag, a stray seagull or two scattering ahead of them. The accumulative thunder of all the powerful engines was almost unbearably loud but the crowd screamed anyway, adding to the din.

Jodell was ready this time for the waving of the green flag. He knew exactly where to look, and as the flag man's arm went up he was ready to kick the gas pedal to the floor. As he zoomed across the start–finish line, he pulled the Ford down to the inside and sailed past the car immediately in front of him. The start was hardly history yet and he was already charging for the front of this big freight train.

The first lap was a blur as Jodell fought for every position, as he tried to clear all the traffic he could, and as he looked to get into some clean air, free from the buffeting he was getting from all the cars running so close together at such speed. Running side by side was nerve-wracking at best and supremely dangerous at these speeds and with the inexperience of so many of the drivers in the field. Jodell followed his predetermined strategy, keeping his foot in the gas, and he tried to work his way past all the uncertain traffic and to the front of the mob. That would be the safest place to ride out the race and stay out of trouble. The closer to the front he was, the fewer cars would run over him if anything happened.

The field quickly sorted itself out into slow, faster, and fastest bunches and a furious battle for the lead. The number 49 Chevy of Bob Welborn, the 48 car of Little Joe Weatherly, and the number 59 Ford of Tom Pistone battled back and forth up there in front of Jodell as he continued to pick his way in that direction.

He was still learning as he went, getting better and better at taking advantage of the air coming off the cars in front of him, using it to be pulled along behind the cars, then practicing the "slingshot" move to get around. He vowed to look up his old high school physics teacher when he got back to Chandler Cove and talk to him about some of the forces of nature he had encountered on this track.

Catherine and Joyce watched the jockeying from

the scoring stand as they methodically marked off the laps on their scoring sheets. But their heads were spinning with the noise and the sheer number of cars out there. With this many cars on the track, it was far different from the leisurely race two days before. There were so many cars and the track was so fast that it was hard to know where to watch as the cars roared by. The good thing was that they could take a drink or stretch once the car they were scoring went by because it would be a while before it would come back around again, even though it was veritably flying out there.

For the crew in the pits, the race was a nerve-wracking experience. The only time they could actually see the cars was for the couple of seconds when they flashed by in front of them as they hit the tri-oval part of the speedway at the start–finish line. With the number of cars, along with all the convertibles, and with the sheer size of the place, it was hard to follow a particular car once it had passed directly in front. They quickly became a blur of color as they raced around the big turns and down the long backstretch.

Bubba never lost sight of the Ford, though. He maintained his perch on the wall as he followed Jodell all the way around the track. He never missed a lap.

Joe stood on the wall beside Bubba and timed the laps as their driver smoothly made his way through the field. By the twentieth lap, Jodell was knocking on the top ten. And that was when Fireball Roberts powered past the three cars that had been battling for first. Fireball held the lead for awhile, until the first series of pit stops began to scramble the field.

Jodell had moved into the tenth position by then but his pit stop was coming up, too.

Bubba held the pit board up high as the cars flashed by the pit road. He had taken the white chalk and written "PIT" in big block letters so Jodell would see it as he flashed by. They were located a couple of pits away from Lee Petty and Bubba was relieved to see that he was ready to come in for fuel as well. Jodell followed Petty's 42 into the pits. Bubba held the sign board down on the pavement, marking the spot where Jodell needed to put the nose of the Ford when he pulled to a stop.

The speed coming down the pit road was deceiving after the breakneck pace on the track. It was hard to get slowed down and Jodell was forced to jam on the brakes, locking them up and sending up a plume of smoke as he tried to keep from running over Bubba, who went dancing out of the way just in case. The boys came over the wall and went to work changing the tires and filling the car with gas. Joe handed Jodell a bottle of water and cleaned the windshield. It took just over sixty seconds to get everything done so Jodell could screech away and roar off in chase of the field.

The laps continued to reel off with Jodell continuing to run right up with the front pack of cars. The lead started to swap around again and he was right there to press his case for taking the point. His excitement level continued to rise as he moved up boldly into fourth place, then third. He rode along for several laps on the rear bumpers of the two leaders but every pass was getting harder and harder now, the cars and drivers he was trying to outrun better and faster and cagier.

Jodell held his spot directly behind the two leaders,

mostly mirroring their route around Daytona, waiting for a miscue, a bobble, or the next set of pit stops to change the dynamic enough so he could slip around them. As the field strung out more, the drivers were able to feel the effect of the wind better off the cars in front of them. Jodell used the chance to learn more about it himself. He rode for another lap or so, following precisely in their tire tracks, waiting until he finally felt the time was right to take the higher line going into the third turn. He could feel the power in Joe's motor as he swung around on the upper route, sense the power that was at his disposal, and was secure in the knowledge that the Ford would run wherever he decided she needed to go.

The two cars in front of him didn't succumb easily. They both held their own through the turn, but Jodell's motor was running much freer in the high line and he was able to swing down beneath them coming off the fourth turn. He felt the car catch the wind and he sent her roaring by the other two cars as if they were bogged down in good old Chandler County mud. He was able to put several car lengths between the Ford's rear deck and the other two cars before they fell back in line behind him.

Jodell Bob Lee was leading the first race at the new Daytona Speedway!

He caught his breath. The sight of clear track in front of him was a beautiful sight to behold. Sure, he had lead and won races on short little tracks but nothing could have ever prepared him for his first view of that stretch of speedway laid out before him, knowing fifty-eight other fire-breathing machines were chasing him.

He flashed by the start–finish line with eight car lengths' lead. With his foot to the floor, he kept the car's mill running wide open as he raced off into the wide first turn with nothing but victory in front of him.

In the pits, the crew was stunned when they saw him flash by them in front of the rest of the field. They had known that he was closing in on the leaders but to actually see him take the lead against the best there was and on the biggest and newest and fastest track in the world had them open-mouthed and wide-eyed until they suddenly erupted in wild cheers and back-slapping.

Bubba pumped his huge fist high into the air.

Joe smiled. He'd seen the lead coming in the stopwatches as Jodell's times had continued to be a tick better than the leaders from the green flag on. Now that he was out front though, it was the Ford's turn to punch a hole in the air for the cars behind him. Joe clicked his watches again to time Jodell's first lap as the leader to see what effect it would have.

Bubba hopped down from the wall and scribbled something on the signboard. He watched the cars roll all the way down the back stretch and into the wide third and fourth turns, then, as Jodell came back by their spot in the pit still leading by several car lengths, Bubba held the sign high and waved it as the group of cars growled past.

On the board was written the word "LEADER" in big bold letters. Jodell grinned as he let the message sink in. The radio commentary was running through his head as he imagined Homer Williams and Augustus Smith and everyone else back home listening.

He was the leader!

He glanced in the mirror at the cars behind him and then took the line he preferred through the center on the corner, not one dictated by a car he might be trying to pass. But then, as he glanced again in the mirror once he had cleared the second turn, he could see that the cars he'd just passed had pulled right back on his rear. They were not going to be any more satisfied to ride around out of the lead than he would have been.

Catherine had gotten so excited when Jodell made the move for the lead that she almost forgot to score his lap. Joyce had to poke her with her pencil to remind her to mark the lap. She squealed with delight as he pushed his way out to the front.

Joe quickly determined that Jodell didn't quite have the same speed once he was leading the way. He crossed his fingers and watched. Sure enough, as they were going down the backstretch, the two cars he had passed a few laps before swung out wide and sailed right back past Jodell as if he had stepped on the brakes.

Jodell didn't panic. He tucked the snout of the Ford right back in behind them and waited to make his move again.

They waltzed back and forth for the lead over the next twenty laps or so, a dance dictated by slower cars they ran up on. Several other cars joined them in the shuffle for the front. Jodell managed to pick up the point another time or two but could not seem to get out front for good. But he didn't worry about it. There were pit stops coming and that would shake up all the leaders again anyway. He did know that they would need a good stop of their own to stay with the leaders.

When they made their next stop, Jodell was proud of how well his inexperienced crew did. They got him out fast enough to keep him running with the leaders even though the field had really started to string out over the last fifty laps. Car after car had begun to go a lap or more down. Mechanical failure had taken its toll on several drivers, including Richard Petty, who had parked his convertible early and now stood and watched the show from his daddy's pits.

Jodell once more challenged for the lead as he headed down the long backstretch, a place where he felt the Ford was working especially well. He swung out wide and took the lead going into the third turn, taking the higher line that he liked, and then tried to once again hold off the cars behind him. Coming out of the corner he could feel the car seem to wiggle around on him, as if buffeted by a stiff breeze. He tightened his grip on the wheel, trying to hold the race car steady. The cars behind him once more pulled right up tight onto his rear.

Then, suddenly, without warning, he felt the car burp, hesitate, then go stone dead. The car closest behind him barely clipped him as the driver alertly jerked the wheel and steered his car down to the inside to retake the lead. Jodell wrestled with the wheel as he tried to keep the car under control and keep from getting run over by all the cars stretched out behind him. He kicked in on the clutch and gathered the car back up but the gauges told him the sad story. The engine was not turning over at all.

Once the line of cars had gone by safely, he was able to pull down to the inside of the track, out of traffic. The car rolled silently along with only the sound of the wind whistling in the open windows and the distant hum of the other cars' engines as they raced off and left him. Jodell aimed for the Pure Oil sign at the entrance to the pit road. The car was rapidly losing momentum and Jodell hoped it would have enough left to make it to the pits.

Catherine had a sinking feeling in her stomach as she saw Jodell get clipped coming out of the turn. She watched in horror as the car began to go sideways in front of a track full of traffic before Jodell was able to get it back under control. Then the other cars were gone as he crept along. That's when she realized that something was seriously wrong with the race car. She put her head in her hands in disgust. The car Joyce had been scoring had fallen out fifteen laps before and she had been watching Jodell, too. She gave her friend a consoling pat on her shoulder but she knew there was little else she could do.

Bubba saw Jodell slow off the corner and jumped down from the wall. Joe came running down from his perch on the platform.

"Let's get some tires ready," Joe yelled over the noise of the other cars. "He's coming in. He must have one going flat!"

Bubba scrambled to pick up the jack while Johnny and Clifford grabbed a pair of tires each, one under each arm. They stood poised on the wall waiting for Jodell to make it down the long pit road to them. It seemed to take the car an especially long time to get to them.

Their hopes fell as they noticed the car was silent as it coasted slowly into the slot. They quickly opened the hood. Joe signaled for Jodell to try and crank it. The motor turned over but she would not fire to life. Joe immediately went to the distributor, tearing at the cap and pulling it off. He signaled for Jodell to once again try to crank the engine. The motor turned but the rotor did not.

Joe signaled for him to stop trying and slowly, dejectedly closed the hood.

"Push it back behind the wall. We're done for," Joe said, obviously discouraged.

Jodell was already unbuckling himself as he steered the car behind the wall while the boys pushed. He could not believe his luck. One moment he was challenging for the win, jockeying for first, and the next he was being pushed behind the wall, his mount dead. He could only pound the steering wheel with his fists in frustration.

They rolled the car to a stop behind the wall and Joe quickly went under the hood. Bubba helped him take off the distributor to try to see what was wrong. Johnny brought Jodell a jar of ice water and helped him unbuckle and climb from the car. He used his rag to wipe the sweat from his forehead and only then realized how hot and tired he was.

Richard Petty had seen Jodell's car being pushed behind the wall. He watched his dad take the lead then walked over and put an arm on Jodell's shoulder.

"You had a good run going today. I figured you might be able to beat those cats the way you were running."

"Yeah, Richard. I guess you broke something, too."

"Yeah."

"I guess I'm going to have to get used to almost winning," Jodell said, not even trying to hide the disappointment in his voice. "But I'll tell you one thing. I love this track!"

"Me, too. I wish I could run her again tomorrow. I gotta go see if Daddy can hold 'em off and win this thing."

"Well, good luck."

Jodell walked over and peered under the hood where Joe and Bubba worked. Finally, Joe pulled the distributor loose and held it up so they could all intimately see the problem. All the gears on the end of the shaft were sheared off cleanly.

"Damn! I can't believe it," Joe yelped. His motors simply weren't supposed to break and this one obviously had.

Jodell knew Joe Banker was a perfectionist, that he would study the pieces until he had figured out what had gone wrong inside the distributor. He would determine what happened and do whatever he had to in order to assure it didn't throw them out of a race again.

Jodell walked over to the Petty pits to watch the rest of the race. Lee Petty was still leading but Johnny Beauchamp in the number 73 Thunderbird was beginning to put pressure on him. The two of them ran side by side, swapping back and forth for the lead. The excitement in the stands had continued to build as the action grew more feverish and the laps began to wind down. The crowd seemed to undulate like the ocean waters.

Jodell marveled at how calm everyone in the Petty pits remained while Lee raced for the lead, swapping the point with Beauchamp. Bill France and the other promoters of this massive new track had to be pleased with the show the drivers were putting on.

With two laps to go, it was still too close to call with Lee Petty dominating but Johnny Beauchamp giving him no quarter. Little Joe Weatherly had joined in the fray, running one lap down but trying to hold on to fifth place. The frenetic crowd was going berserk as the three of them roared beneath the stand to take the white flag.

Everyone in the pits had become spectators, too, standing on anything they could find to get a view of the three cars sailing around the big track for the final time. Richard, Jodell, and the others in the Petty pits strained to see the finish as the race cars came off the corner with all three of them side by side.

Joyce stood with Catherine near the end of the grandstand where they had gone to watch the finish. They jumped up and down and hugged each other as Lee Petty went for the win. Catherine was excited with the action they were watching but she couldn't help but think what it might have been like if it had been Jodell out there racing for the win with Petty and Beauchamp. If she closed her eyes, she could see it clear as day.

The three cars crossed the start–finish line in a dead heat, Beauchamp, Petty, and Weatherly lined up side by side. Little Joe was clearly a nose ahead, but that only meant that he had finished one lap down instead of two. Finally, after much debate and confusion, they collected up all the film of the finish they could find and sent it out to be developed to determine which of the two drivers had won.

In the stands, the Petty fans were certain that he had won. Others were just as sure that Beauchamp had nosed out Petty. Beauchamp celebrated in victory lane but it would be three days later before it was determined that Lee Petty had actually claimed the nineteen-thousand-dollar winner's purse.

Jodell and the crew were quiet as they began to load things up and get ready for the long ride home. A ride that would now seem much, much longer. Catherine and Joyce walked up then and Catherine gave Jodell a long hug and hushed what he was about to say with a finger on his lips.

"Honey, there will be lots more races. You can't win them all, no matter how bad you want to. Remember, there will be plenty more chances to race for glory, and the glory will come to you when it's your time. This just wasn't the time or the place. Now, let's get loaded up so you can take me back to Chandler Cove."

He smiled and held her close for a while. It was wonderful to have someone who loved him, win or lose. But even as he held her tightly against him, he was thinking of how it had felt to look out of the Ford's windshield at nothing but open track ahead of him and have all the others in his rearview mirror. Of how it would have felt to the checkered flag waving for him.

But she was right. There were already numerous other tracks they could run and rumors of even bigger ones than Daytona on the drawing boards. With a show like they had put on today, there would be plenty of interest in this sport, just as Homer Williams had predicted, and there would be more and more chances for them to win. He knew how to drive to win, and collectively, they knew how to prepare a car to finish first.

Jodell Lee knew that his dream was not dead. It had only been postponed by the shattered distributor.

And even as they dejectedly packed up and got ready to drive north, he was already planning how he would make that dream come true the next time the green flag waved.

In the race to glory, only one man
can finish first . . .

Race to Glory

Book Three in the
Rolling Thunder Stock Car Racing Series

Jodell caught up with Buck Baker and raced him
hard, trying to take sixth place away from him. It took
some maneuvering, but he finally got around the veteran driver and set himself to run down the leaders.
The car was working very well and he had just out-
dueled one of the craftiest drivers in the sport.

He inhaled the familiar perfume of blistered tire
rubber, hot exhaust fumes, and burning oil. For Jodell, that was far better than the dust of the dirt
tracks he had breathed so much of, but it still made
it tough to get a good lung full of clean, refreshing
air. He fought dizziness and tried to gulp down more
air, tainted or not. The heat coming up from the
exhaust beneath where he sat seemed to make the
car's floorboard red-hot. It felt as if his feet were on
fire through the sneakers he wore. Before they even
realized it, they were almost sixty laps into the race.
He was in fourth place on the track, with Little Joe
Weatherly, Junior Johnson, and Fireball Roberts riding up there in front of him. He had raced these men
before, knew them well from off-track encounters,
and was no longer in awe of them. But the thought
that he was racing in such heady company still struck
him hard. And so did the realization, once again, that
he belonged here with them.

Or, even better, up there ahead of them!